LIAR'S CREEK

ALSO BY MATT GOLDMAN

The Murder Show

Still Waters

A Good Family

Carolina Moonset

NILS SHAPIRO NOVELS

Gone to Dust

Broken Ice

The Shallows

Dead West

Dark Humor

LIAR'S CREEK

A Novel

MATT GOLDMAN

MINOTAUR
BOOKS
NEW YORK

This is a work of fiction. All of the names, characters, organizations, places, and events portrayed in this work are either products of the author's imagination or used fictitiously.

First published in the United States by Minotaur Books, an imprint of St. Martin's Publishing Group

EU Representative: Macmillan Publishers Ireland Ltd, 1st Floor, The Liffey Trust Centre, 117–126 Sheriff Street Upper, Dublin 1, D01 YC43

Printed in the United States of America. For information, address St. Martin's Publishing Group, 120 Broadway, New York, NY 10271.

www.minotaurbooks.com

Designed by Omar Chapa

The Library of Congress Cataloging-in-Publication Data is available upon request.

ISBN 978-1-250-40941-6 (trade paperback)
ISBN 978-1-250-40938-6 (hardcover)
ISBN 978-1-250-40942-3 (ebook)

First Edition: 2026

10 9 8 7 6 5 4 3 2 1

For Emma, Basil, Danny, Charles, Maisy, and Clara.

The best friends a writer could have.

LIAR'S CREEK

CHAPTER 1

Riverwood, Minnesota, has four stoplights, two beauty salons, nine bars, one barber shop, seven restaurants, one Center for the Arts, two hardware stores, one bakery, one police station, three auto repair shops, and one missing person.

It also has a handful of salmon—*salmon* being the nickname for residents who leave Riverwood only to return years later. One of those salmon is Clay Hawkins. Clay was gone for twenty-four years and did quite well for himself, so it's a bit odd that he moved back three months ago. But Clay has his reasons. One of them is riding shotgun in Clay's F-150 as he navigates the narrow winding roads and one-lane bridges of Fillmore County. His son, Braedon, is twelve years old and looks a little too much like his mother for Clay's comfort. Blue eyes and fair skin and black hair that glistens red when the sun hits it just right.

"Dad?" says Braedon as they turn onto Main Street. Braedon's

Irish brogue is fading fast after his short time living in the American Midwest. Clay heard that accents go away if exposed to a new language or new dialect before puberty. Braedon still has the voice of a boy. His face is as smooth as a five-year-old's. His eyes are clear and innocent.

"Yeah, bud?" says Clay, who has no Irish accent. Living in Europe for fifteen years did nothing to change how he talks. His body hasn't changed much either. He is slight in the shoulders and waist. He burned so many calories running around the soccer pitch for years that gaining weight seems impossible. His hair falls nearly to his shoulders. It was his signature look on the pitch. Now it's threaded with gray, maybe more than threaded near his temples. The length frames the lines in his face and the ache in his eyes. An ache he desperately wants to go away.

"Does Uncle Teddy disappear a lot? Like has he ever gone missing before?"

"Your uncle Teddy is a complicated man," says Clay. "Sweet as can be. But complicated."

"Why is he complicated?"

It's just after 7:00 on a Saturday morning. Downtown Riverwood is quiet. Betty-Mae's bakery is open and so is Value Foods, and of course the Kwik-Trip is open twenty-four hours a day for all your fuel, food, lottery ticket, and vehicle-washing needs. Clay checks his mirrors to see if anyone is following him. Old habit. All is clear.

He considers asking Braedon if he'd like to stop for something to eat, but he knows his son is looking forward to Grandpa Judd's pancakes.

"Some people," says Clay, "are born restless souls. Uncle

Teddy's one of them. But the man is sixty-three years old and has been married to Aunt Deb for over forty years. He's everyone's favorite member of the family. So he's doing something right."

"Then where'd he go and when will he come back?" says Braedon, lowering the window between himself and the fresh June air. "Will he be back tomorrow night for Sunday dinner?"

"I don't know," says Clay, trying not to sound concerned, which he definitely is. "Maybe Grandpa Judd has heard something. We'll ask him in a few minutes."

Braedon nods as if Clay's explanation is thorough and no follow-up questions are needed. Clay seems to have put his son's worry to rest, which is what's most important. Braedon has enough missing people in his life.

Braedon's only memory of his mother is in a photograph. Clay has only seen Braedon's mother twice. He was playing for Galway United FC in the Irish Premiership and, after a friendly against Dublin in the capital, he met Braedon's mother at a party. Her name is Eve. Clay fell for her jet-black hair, blue eyes, and wry smile. They spent the night together and, the next day, after Clay had returned to Galway with his team, he called Eve hoping that he could see her again. She did not answer his call. She did not return his voice message. Clay texted. Eve did not reply. He never heard from her again.

Until one year later when Eve stood on his front step holding a baby, her face streaked with tears. "I thought I wanted him but I don't," she said. "You're the da. He's yours if you'll have him. If not, I'll put him into care."

No *Hello*. No *How are you?* No *Sorry I didn't respond to your calls and texts*. No small talk whatsoever. Just "He's yours if you'll have him" in Eve's musical brogue.

Eve said, "His name is Braedon. Change it if you want to. I don't want anything to do with him."

Clay doubted that Eve meant what she'd said about wanting nothing to do with Braedon. Her tear-stained face told a different story, as did her pallor and the tightness of her voice.

"I'll send you pics and updates," said Clay, looking down at the bundle in his arms. He had never held a baby before. Not once. It felt foreign and familiar at the same time. He did not, in that moment, question the responsibility of raising a child. It just felt right. And Clay hoped it was a good sign that the boy slept through his mother's abandonment of him. As if Braedon somehow sensed he belonged with his father.

"You'll send me nothing," said Eve. "I want to see nothing. I changed my phone number so just let me be." Then she turned around and walked away.

"What's your full name?" said Clay.

But she didn't answer. She didn't even look back.

It was that simple. At least the handoff was. Clay had a DNA test done to confirm the baby was his and spent a fortune on lawyers to make everything legal. He hired a full-time, live-in nanny. At thirty years of age, Clay's professional soccer career was still very much alive. Between league play and tournaments, Clay had little offseason. He traveled constantly. Before Braedon attended school, Clay brought his baby boy and the nanny on his extended trips.

To this day, the only thing Braedon knows about his mother is what he can see in a snapshot that had been taken at the party where Clay met her. He keeps it in a little cedar box gifted to him by his grandpa Judd.

"Are those kids restless souls like Uncle Teddy?" says Braedon, pointing to teenagers sitting on their mountain bikes outside the Kwik-Trip, sipping on barrel-sized sodas they can barely hold with one hand.

"Why do you ask that?" says Clay.

"Because they're up so early."

"Maybe they're about to go mountain biking."

"They don't look like they're going mountain biking. They're not wearing helmets or pads."

Clay smiles.

"What?" says Braedon. "Why are you smiling? What's so funny?"

"Nothing," says Clay. "I'm just impressed by your observation and deduction skills at twelve years of age. You have a lot of your grandpa Judd in you." *And a little of me, too,* thinks Clay. But he's not ready to explain that to Braedon.

"That's good, right?"

Clay has mixed feelings about whether that's good or not, but he says, "Very good. Grandpa Judd was an excellent policeman." Clay hesitates, then says, "Do you know those boys on the bikes?"

"No," says Braedon. "But I've seen them around. I just don't get why they'd be up this early if they're not fishing or hunting or working. It seems weird."

"It might be weird," says Clay. "Maybe steer clear of those boys."

"Yeah," says Braedon. "Daniel says they're trouble."

"Daniel's lived here his whole life," says Clay. "He probably knows what he's talking about."

Braedon watches the boys pedal off down a side street and nods. Clay watches them, too. Checking out their sweatshirts to see if they're hanging unevenly, an indicator that they could be carrying something heavy in one pocket. He shakes his head. They're kids, for god's sake. He's being ridiculous.

Clay drives the F-150 through the entirety of Riverwood's eight-block-long Main Street before he turns off toward his own father's house. Three generations of Hawkins men living in one small town. Clay had never thought such a thing was possible, mostly because he never thought he'd move back. But now they're here and he has no intention of leaving anytime soon.

"Are we really going to meet Grandpa Judd's girlfriend tomorrow night?" says Braedon, whose mind, thankfully, is off Uncle Teddy's disappearance.

"That's the plan," says Clay.

Braedon shakes his head. "Grandpa Judd is in his sixties. So is Mei. She should be called his womanfriend. Or oldwomanfriend. Not girlfriend."

"That's not how it works," says Clay. "Even if Grandpa Judd and Mei were a hundred, they'd still be called boyfriend and girlfriend."

"That doesn't make any sense," says Braedon. At twelve years old he has the world figured out. Everyone else, obviously, is bonkers.

Clay catches sight of himself in the rearview mirror. He pushes his hair out of his eyes. He's due for a trim. "You sure you're okay hanging out with Grandpa today? You don't want to go fishing with me?"

"I like regular fishing," says Braedon. "Not fly-fishing. And Grandpa Judd's going to let me shoot the pistol out back. So yeah, I'm sure I'm okay hanging out with him today." He twists his lips and adds, "Sorry."

"No need to apologize," says Clay. "I'm glad you and Grandpa get along so well. And you listen to him about gun safety—you won't find a better teacher than Grandpa Judd."

Braedon watches a deer eat alfalfa in a field of green. "How old was Grandpa when his mom died?"

"He was in his fifties. You were just a little guy."

"Can he be in our Lads Without Mums club?"

"No," says Clay. "It doesn't count for people who had their moms into their fifties. I'm afraid it's just you and me. Lads Without Mums." Clay holds out his fist for Braedon to bump.

Braedon makes a fist and does just that. "Lads Without Mums."

CHAPTER 2

"Can I shoot for a while before breakfast?" says Braedon.

"Sure," says Judd. He pats his grandson on the shoulder and adds, "Go out back and set up the cans. I'll bring the gun out in a minute."

"Thanks, Grandpa." Braedon practically skips into the house and toward the sliding glass door that leads to the redwood deck out back. Clay remains on the front porch. His father didn't invite him inside, and Clay doesn't much want to go inside. He wants to get on the river.

Judd Hawkins lives on three acres backed by a limestone bluff and Liar's Creek, so named because the property once belonged to Leon Miller, who arrived in 1853 and set up shop as a cobbler. He soon married a young local woman and lobbied the county to have the creek named Miller's Creek after his new family. But when another woman showed up from Philadelphia, went straight to the local sheriff, and presented a marriage license that proved Leon Miller was her husband, the bigamist was fined three hundred dollars and sentenced to one year in jail. After that, the citizens of Fillmore County began referring to the tributary as Liar's Creek. The name became official in 1887.

This is the house Clay grew up in. One above-ground story and a half-submerged basement with a walkout to the backyard. This is the house Clay swore he'd never return to. But life has a way of teaching cocksure eighteen-year-olds what's what.

"Okay to pick him up at around three?" says Clay.

Judd nods. He is clean-shaven and wears his hair in a crew cut. Six months off the police force and Judd still keeps his hair high and tight. Clay guesses it's more out of frugality than holding on to some military-like semblance of order. Judd cuts his own hair with electric clippers. Number one guard on the sides. Number three guard on top. With some semiskilled blending between the two.

"You sure it's okay to have Braedon here? I don't want to keep you from searching for Teddy."

Judd looks at his son. Three months after Clay's return, Judd is still surprised he's here. He figured they'd never live in the same town again, let alone the same country. Judd had written Clay off as an irrecoverable loss. Clay showing up all of sudden feels like a second chance for Judd, but it's a chance he's not sure how to take.

"I've been all over the county the last twenty-four hours," says Judd. "Better I stay home for a while rather than drive around like I'm looking for a lost dog. But I'll hit the bars tonight and ask around. Somebody has to know where Teddy is."

Clay nods. He and his father are capable of communicating, but it's like they're talking through a wall. The words get through, but not much else.

"Call me if you change your mind," says Clay. "I'll check in with Deb at the property."

"And keep an eye out for Teddy on the river?" says Judd. "Deb says his fishing stuff is all at home, but you never know. He could have taken just one rod and reel and walked down without waders."

"Of course," says Clay, although he knows if he finds Teddy on the river after being missing over twenty-four hours, it'll be a grisly discovery. "Hate to ask this," adds Clay, "but—"

"No," says Judd with an edge in his voice. He doesn't intend to sound riled but the reaction is so ingrained when talking to Clay, it's hard for Judd to curb it. "Teddy didn't fall off the wagon. Earned his fifteen-year chip last month and was proud as hell about it. Posted it on Facebook and everything. He'd miss one of our funerals before he'd miss one of his meetings."

"What did Chief Jensen say?" Clay sees the cords tense in his father's neck. He's struck a nerve, though he had no intention of doing so.

"I don't need to talk to Zoey Jensen," says Judd. "Talked to Sue, Mike, and Andy. They're keeping an eye out."

Clay can feel the conversation moving into dangerous waters. Ordinarily he'd drop it, but he's concerned that Judd's closeness to Teddy is obscuring the old cop's judgment. There's no time to waste. Judd will survive another clash with his son. He may not survive the loss of Teddy. "But Chief Jensen—"

"She's not from here," says Judd. "She doesn't have the contacts.

She doesn't know the backroads. I don't need to talk to Zoey Jensen."

"Don't be stubborn," says Clay. His tone is firm but calm. "Swallow your pride and call the chief of police." Then he tries to throw a blanket on the fire by adding, "For Teddy."

"I know how this town works a lot better than you do," says Judd. "I'm not the one who left for twenty-four years."

"Whatever you're pissed off about," says Clay, maintaining his calm, "don't take it out on the new chief. She didn't push you out. She didn't even live here when the city council asked you to step down."

"Fired me," says Judd. "They fired me. Don't sugarcoat it." Judd looks at his son with cold, hard eyes. Talk about old habits. It's as if he doesn't know how to look at Clay any other way. Seeing Pam's eyes in Clay's, Judd wonders if he's fully processed his wife's death. Even all these years later. Does he blame Clay, even subconsciously, rather than the real culprit, cancer? Or if Pam's pregnancy did make the disease more difficult to detect, then maybe he should blame himself. Pam didn't get pregnant on her own.

Clay's picking up on none of this and won't back down. He appreciates Judd's relationship with Braedon, but after being gone for twenty-four years, his father needs to understand that Clay is no longer a child. It's man-to-man now, not man-to-boy. "Call Chief Jensen. You owe it to Teddy. And you owe it to Riverwood."

"Oh," says Judd. "Sure. Now you're talking about loyalty. That's rich coming from you, Clay. The army admits you to the finest military institution in the world. The government foots the bill. How do you repay them? By serving the minimum five years. First day you could, you resigned your commission and headed off to Europe to kick a ball for your adoring fans. You have no sense of duty or honor. No sense of loyalty to the country that made you who you are. Hell, I still don't know why you came back here."

Clay's about to turn and walk away when the thought comes to him. "Do you wish I hadn't come back? Do you wish Braedon and I had stayed in Europe? Because I have standing offers to coach back there if we've ruined your life by moving to Riverwood."

It's a threat Judd doesn't take lightly. He checks himself. Takes a deep breath, then another. Then he lowers his voice to just above a whisper and says, "You know how much I love that boy. Don't you dare take him away from me."

"Yeah," says Clay, "I do know how much you love *that* boy." Clay's insinuation is clear and it hits his father hard. Judd looks like he's about to counter when Clay adds, "See you at three." He turns his back on his father and walks to his F-150 without another word from Judd.

CHAPTER 3

When Clay was twelve years old, his mother went to the hospital for the last time. He was thirteen when she returned as ashes in an urn. The urn was mauve and looked like the antique pottery Clay's mother had collected. Depression pottery, she'd called it. Clay's father set the urn on the mantel and proclaimed it Pam Hawkins's eternal resting place. Clay had other ideas. When it came to Judd and his pronouncements, Clay always had other ideas. Still does.

Pam Hawkins's dream was to see Europe, the land of her favorite composers. Judd promised his wife they would make that trip. They married at nineteen and swore they wouldn't have kids until they were at least twenty-five. They had plenty of time. That was the plan, but nature wasn't listening. Judd and Pam were only twenty-one when Clay was born.

It was the lactation nurse who first discovered the lump in

Pam's breast. Pam was in and out of remission for the next twelve years. Clay had only known his mother as a sick person, sometimes home, sometimes at the hospital, hairless from chemo, burned from radiation, hopeful about the next new trial drug and disappointed when it didn't work.

Pam and Judd Hawkins never took that trip to Europe. Plenty was to blame. Clay arriving years earlier than planned. Pam's illness. And the demands of Judd's job as a police officer for the city of Riverwood, Minnesota. But Pam Hawkins talked about that trip until the day she died. As if it would be her reward for beating the big C. Pam showed Clay the books she'd collected. Books with photographs of the places she longed to see. It broke Clay's heart that his mother would die having never seen those places. Walked their cobblestone streets. Listened to their orchestras in centuries-old concert halls.

On the one-month anniversary of Pam's death, Clay took the Depression pottery urn down from the mantel and carried it into the kitchen. He lifted the lid and peeked inside to see a clear plastic bag sealed with a twist tie. As if his mother were a loaf of bread.

Clay had sat around enough campfires and their aftermaths to know the slightest movement of air could scatter ash into oblivion. He made sure the kitchen sink was clean and dry, then unfastened the twist tie and opened the bag. He used a tablespoon to carefully transfer a small heap of white ash from the urn to a Ziploc sandwich bag. He did this in the sink figuring that if he spilled, he could easily wash part of his mother down the drain. That might seem heartless, but if it happened, her going down the drain fit with Clay's plan, albeit in a less-scenic way.

He did not spill his mother. Clay zipped the sandwich bag closed, twist-tied the original bag inside the urn, and returned it to the mantel, careful to wipe away his fingerprints. Judd would notice those. He might even dust it for prints to prove Clay the culprit. And then the questions would start. Clay knew better than to invite an inquiry from Officer Judd Hawkins.

Clay pocketed the baggie that contained a bit of his mother and carried it outside to the creek behind the house. That's where he set her free. Liar's Creek merges with Camp Creek which tumbles into the Root River which feeds into the Mississippi in the town of La Crescent. The Mississippi River flows south to the Gulf of Mexico and the Atlantic Ocean where, in Clay's imagination, at least, currents would carry his mother to the shores of Europe. One heaping tablespoon of her, anyway.

He understood, even at the age of thirteen, that the gesture was symbolic. His mother wouldn't really visit Europe. Even if her ashes made it across the Atlantic they were not Pam Hawkins. Pam Hawkins, if she was anywhere, was not tied to anything physical. But the gesture of sending her ashes on their way made Clay feel the tiniest bit better. As if he could give his mother what his father had not. And she deserved that. Pam Hawkins had been Clay's steadfast champion.

His earliest memories were of his mother defending him. *He's not like you, Judd. He doesn't want to play baseball. He doesn't like sitting in a boat all day. He doesn't want to kill animals. I'm not judging you for what you like. And I am asking you to do the same toward your son. Your only child.*

Clay appreciated his mother standing up for him, although

he wasn't the sensitive artist she thought he was. Yes, he enjoyed reading more than most boys his age. And yes, he played the violin better than anyone his age, at least in southeast Minnesota. Taught by his mother, no less. And no, he did not want to sit in a boat all day or kill animals. But Clay was more like his father than he let on. He loved to fish but preferred stalking trout in small streams to sitting still in a boat. He loved athletics, but not the same sports Judd liked. And Clay felt a deep love of country and a need to protect it. But that, like everything else, manifested itself differently in Clay than it did in Judd. Differently and more quietly. Or maybe a better word is *clandestinely*.

With his mother gone, Clay turned to Judd's brother, Uncle Teddy. For advice. For a little spending money. Just to hang out. Listen to music. Fly-fish the spring creeks of Fillmore County. Teddy would have bought beer for Clay and his friends if Clay had asked. But Clay never did. He had plans on leaving Riverwood, Minnesota, and didn't want to participate in anything that might delay his departure.

Clay's friends were jealous. Uncle Teddy was the coolest uncle anyone ever had. Teddy had played rhythm guitar in a punk band up in Minneapolis. That was before Clay was born, but Teddy still had the guitar, a beat-to-shit Les Paul worn clear through the guitar's black lacquer, exposing the woodgrain of the body. Teddy had a book full of newspaper clippings, yellowed and frail, from the late seventies. Advertisements for the 7th Street Entry, the Cabooze, and the 400 Bar. All with lists of bands appearing that week. The Replacements. Hüsker Dü. The Hypstrz. And Dye the Sun Blue. That was Teddy's band.

He used to know Paul Westerberg and Tommy Stinson. Bob Mould and Prince.

In 1979, the Clash played in Minnesota for the first time. Teddy had weaseled a backstage pass from local security, and when Joe Strummer blew an amp speaker during sound check, Teddy took off for an hour and returned with the exact same amp. Joe Strummer was so grateful, he gave Teddy the small gold hoop from his right ear. Teddy removed the stud from his own ear, replaced it with Joe Strummer's hoop, and hasn't taken it out since. Coolest damn uncle ever.

Cool but far different from Clay's mother. Pam had a degree from Winona State. Teddy never graduated high school. Pam taught band and orchestra to middle-school kids before her illness forced her to stop. But even then she still made money giving private lessons on everything from piano to oboe to cello. Teddy has never held a steady job in his life. He plows driveways and mows lawns. He does some basic handyman work. Plumbing. Electrical. Carpentry. He occasionally fills in as a bartender or short-order cook. He isn't reliable or good at any of it, so the jobs don't last long. But everyone likes Teddy. Likes him so much they tend to forget what a bad employee he is so they hire him again. And the cycle repeats itself.

Teddy is Judd's fraternal twin. No one ever confused them for identical twins because they are opposites in most ways. Physically, temperamentally, and on which side of the law they've lived their lives. They were even born opposites: Judd left the womb headfirst. Teddy came out a few minutes later feetfirst. A breech birth is dangerous but the doctor thought it would be less dangerous since Judd had led the way. And it seems like ever since the day they were born, Judd has continued to lead the way, rescuing Teddy from one kind of jam or the other.

Young Clay loved his uncle Teddy, but it was Teddy's lack of reliability that led Clay to become self-reliant. Without telling Judd, he applied to Dorset-Cornwall, a private boarding school just outside of town that attracts students from all over the world for its rigorous academics, elite athletics, and world-class music education. Clay was admitted and granted a full scholarship based on test scores and an in-person violin audition. After Judd got over the shock of Clay's secretive application to, and acceptance from, Dorset-Cornwall, he agreed to let his son attend if and only if Clay commuted from home. Clay was Judd's last living connection to Pam—he wasn't about to let his son move out of the house at thirteen years of age.

During his first year at Dorset-Cornwall, Clay was introduced to soccer. He fell in love with the sport, and the sport fell in love with Clay. One year later, he made the team's starting eleven and led Dorset-Cornwall in goals and assists. By the time he was sixteen, professional clubs and colleges sent scouts to Riverwood so they could watch Clay work his magic on the pitch.

That was the same year the headmaster called Clay into his office to inform Clay that he had to make a choice. Soccer or violin. There was too much overlap in time commitment. Dorset-Cornwall was not a public high school. It was not there to serve the general well-being of its students. The school existed for one reason: to develop its students so that they could achieve at the highest level. For Clay, that meant he had to choose: violin or soccer. Clay chose soccer for the practical reason that there are about ten times more professional soccer teams in the world than there are orchestras. That meant a ten times better chance of leaving Riverwood and never coming back. Besides, Clay liked wearing shorts and a jersey more than he did black tie. And he liked the way girls responded to his scissor kicks more than the way they responded to his double stops.

Clay broke it to his dead mother while fly-fishing the Root River. That's where he did his best thinking. Where his voice was so clear and present in his head he had to wonder if he was talking aloud to himself.

"I'm sorry, Mom," he thought or said under the babble and bubble of the river.

She answered by swelling his heart and his eyes. He felt her presence and her affirmation. She *wanted* him to play soccer. Soccer would introduce him to the world.

"I'll take you with me," he whispered. "I promise."

Offers to play after Dorset-Cornwall poured in. But to everyone's surprise, especially Judd's, Clay chose to play for West Point. To this day Clay isn't quite sure why he made that choice. Maybe it was to appease Judd and alleviate his own guilt for leaving Minnesota. Maybe it was to best Judd at his own game. Tough guy. Law and order.

Five years after the day Clay sprinkled his mother's ashes in the stream behind their house, he took a second tablespoon of ash from the urn. He funneled the ash into an empty fountain pen. A fountain pen gifted to him by the governor of Minnesota as a congratulations for his acceptance to West Point. Eight years after graduating high school, after leaving the army to play professional soccer in Europe, Clay took that fountain pen to Germany, where he finally spread his mother's ashes in the land she had so longed to visit.

Today Clay Hawkins stands in the Root River, thigh deep, reading the water for where trout are holding. Uncle Teddy taught Clay everything he knows about fly-fishing. How to cast without spooking the trout and how to mend line so the fly drifts naturally in the current. How to read water, like he's doing now, so Clay knows where the fish should be even if they aren't rising or flashing their buttery flanks below the surface. The trout lie in the seams between fast and slow water. In the deep pools. In the undercut of a grassy bank. In a fast-moving riffle on a hot day where the water churns with oxygen.

Uncle Teddy taught Clay the difference between mayflies and caddisflies. About their larval stages underwater and how they morph and rise through the water column to become adult flies on the surface, drying their wings in the sun before taking flight for the first time. And about stoneflies that crawl out of the water in their larval stages and then morph into an adult fly on a rock or tree. That is if the trout don't pick them off first. Teddy taught Clay how to fish terrestrials in late summer and early fall. Mimicking grasshoppers, ants, and beetles that get blown off course and into the river, or fall from an overhanging branch.

These are technical skills. But the most valuable things Uncle Teddy taught Clay were how to find peace on the river. How to stay out of the house for hours at a time. And how to do so in places where Judd could not find him. That's how Clay survived his mother's illness and his father's ill temper. Judd was never abusive. Nor was he warm. Or supportive. Judd could not overcome his own grief to comfort Clay in his.

It's mid-June, and Clay is six weeks away from starting his new job as the director of soccer and boys U19 head coach at his alma mater, Dorset-Cornwall. The school courted him for years before he finally agreed to leave Europe and move back to where he grew up.

Clay squeezes the water out of his fly with his amadou patch and applies a fresh glob of floatant, then massages it into the feathers and fur. There's something primeval about fly-fishing, thinks Clay. Something that takes us all the way back to when the first humans walked the Earth. Kill or be killed. Eat or be eaten. The concentration of reading the river is meditative. Healing. Maybe not for the fish, but certainly for him.

When Clay was a cadet at West Point, he made a point of fishing the Hudson Valley, the birthplace of American fly-fishing. When he had a day off, he'd wade Willowemoc Creek or Croton River. After graduating, he didn't see active duty unless you count bouncing around between US Army bases in Europe, where he fished the chalk streams of England, the freestone rivers in the Bavarian Alps, and the same waters in Northern Spain that Hemingway had frequented. Learning those waters came in handy after Clay left the army to play professional soccer on the Continent. When traveling to away games, Clay carried a six-piece rod that fit into his luggage along with a fanny pack of flies, leaders, tippet, nippers, and forceps.

And now, at forty-two years old, Clay fishes the rivers and streams of his childhood. He hadn't planned on fishing today but he woke up with a want—no, a need—to be on the river. Had no idea why. But now that he's standing in the current, he wonders if it's providence. Because there is no better place to think about where Teddy might be.

CHAPTER 4

Judd keeps an eye on the backyard where Braedon shoots cans with a .22 pistol. Kid's a hell of a shot. Clay never showed any interest in guns at that age. Maybe it skips a generation, thinks Judd, like musical talent or psoriasis. Judd checks his emails and texts to see if anyone's contacted him about Teddy. Nothing.

What bothers Judd the most is that two nights ago, the Hawkins men met for dinner at the House of Bends, a bar-and-grill overlooking the Middle Branch of the Root River. Nothing felt out of the ordinary. They sat on the redwood deck watching mayflies hatch and hover over the water. Judd and Braedon discussed what they'd grill for Sunday dinner. Clay watched the Minnesota Loons game on one of the outdoor big-screen TVs. Clay has friends on the coaching staff, and Judd wonders if the real reason Clay returned home is because he wants the manager job. Coaching Major League Soccer in America isn't at the level of coaching in the Premier League, Bundesliga, Serie A, or Ligue 1, but it's a start. And Clay, at forty-two, is still considered fresh young talent when it comes to coaching at the professional level.

Teddy seemed especially interested in the Minnesota Twins game on the other big screen. He became more animated than he usually does, cursing the team that has disappointed fans in all but two years since 1961. Everything seemed normal during that dinner two nights ago. If Teddy was concerned about something, anything, Judd would have picked up on it. Judd isn't the most sensitive of men, but when it comes to his twin brother, Judd is like a seismograph. He can detect the most faint disturbance far below the surface. An apt analogy, thinks Judd, because Teddy is like a fault line. He can be quiet and boring for years and then something slips and everything shakes to hell.

Then yesterday morning, Judd woke up to a call from Deb.

"Is Teddy with you?" she said, as if Teddy were a child or a golden retriever. Before Judd could answer, he'd felt a dark vibration between him and his twin brother.

Judd steps onto the deck to watch his grandson hold the pistol at arm's length and sight the target. A Coke can sits thirty feet away on a portable tree stump, splintered and chipped by errant bullets. Braedon squeezes the trigger. Judd hears a pop from the .22, and the Coke can jumps, falls back onto the stump, and bounces off.

"That's one less bad guy in the world," says Judd.

Braedon turns to look at Judd, the sun glinting red off his dark hair. He has a big smile on his face.

"Barrel pointed down," says Judd.

"Right, sorry," says Braedon and drops his hand so the gun barrel points toward the grass.

Judd walks down the steps to the backyard. "Safety on?"

Braedon looks, realizes the safety is off, then pushes the cylinder to the other side of the trigger guard. He offers his grandfather a weak smile.

"Don't forget next time," Judd says with kindness in his voice.

"Yes, sir," says Braedon.

Sir, thinks Judd. Braedon learned that at his private school in Galway, where Clay played the last five years of his career. In a way, Braedon is the son Judd never had. The son Clay wasn't. Or could not be. Braedon likes going up north and fishing for walleye. He likes target practice. This fall, Judd plans on taking the boy hunting for ducks and maybe a trip to South Dakota for pheasant. All things Braedon is begging to do, and Clay scoffed at.

Braedon stands in the same yard his father once played in. But Clay didn't shoot Coke cans. He kicked soccer balls at a makeshift net. He bounced the ball off his feet, his knees, his head, over and over. Seeing how many consecutive times he could launch the ball back up into the air before it hit the ground. Judd didn't understand any of it.

"You just kick a ball into the air over and over again until it gets dark," said Judd. "How is that fun?"

"I like it," said a teenaged Clay. "So it's fun to me."

Judd feels grateful to have this second chance at being a father figure for Braedon. He supposes he has a second chance with Clay, too. But a few months after Clay's return, they haven't made much progress. Still, at the ages of sixty-three and forty-two, Judd and Clay are both wiser. They know some battles are worth fighting and some aren't. The rough edges seem to be worn down on both of them. *Not completely shot* are the words Judd uses when referring to his relationship with his son: "Things between me and Clay are *not completely shot*." But that's more wishful thinking than a truth put in practice. Judd knows this but has a hard time admitting it to himself. He feels his and Clay's dissonance. And feelings, in Judd's experience, are easier to ignore than deal with head-on.

"I'm ready to take a break," says Braedon.

"All right. Show me what you do when you're done shooting."

Braedon drops the clip out of the gun into his left hand, puts it in his pocket, then uses one eye to sight the barrel, making sure the chamber is empty.

"Attaboy," says Judd. "You ready for pancakes?"

"What time is it?" says Braedon with a hint of alarm in his voice.

"Eight thirty. Why?"

"I promised a friend we'd FaceTime before three o'clock Ireland time. Okay if I do that before breakfast?"

"Sure," says Judd. "Breakfast will be served at nine."

"Can we have rashers?" says Braedon.

"Never heard of 'em."

Braedon half smiles and half rolls his eyes. "Bacon."

"Oh, sure," says Judd. "We got plenty of bacon."

Braedon hands the pistol to his grandfather butt-first, just as Judd taught him. He pulls the clip from his pocket and turns that over as well. "Thank you for letting me shoot."

"Anytime, Brae. Anytime."

CHAPTER 5

"A real gun?" says Emily Riordan. She has dark hair and freckles and green eyes in her caramel-colored face.

"Yeah," says Braedon. "A twenty-two-caliber pistol that holds ten in the clip and one in the chamber. It's my grandad's. He used to be in the guards. But they're called police here."

"What's that rock behind ya?" says Emily.

They FaceTime between Riverwood, Minnesota, and Galway, Ireland. Braedon sits on the same stump he shot the Coke can off of, purposely positioning himself so the bluff is behind him and the sun shining through the river birch makes him look outdoorsy and manly.

"It's not a rock," says Braedon. "It's a bluff made of limestone. That's why it's yellowish orange. Dad says the limestone makes the rivers around here extra rich in minerals. That's why the flies like to lay their eggs in them. And that's why trout like to live in these rivers. To eat the flies."

"Flies?" says Emily. "Sounds disgusting."

"Not those kind of flies," says Braedon. "They're mayflies and caddisflies and stoneflies. They don't bother people. They don't bite or try to live on dog shit or anything. They're actually kind of pretty. I'll take a picture of one and text it to you."

When Braedon lived in Galway, Emily lived across the street. They've been friends since they were six. Now that he's twelve, he's starting to have more-than-friends feelings for Emily. And she might have them for him, too. He can't tell. Braedon's friend Daniel says if Emily does have more-than-friends feelings for Braedon, it's only because she wants Braedon to take her to Disneyland or Universal or something like that. She's just using him now because he's in America. But Braedon doesn't believe Daniel. Or maybe he does a little but he doesn't care. Daniel's just jealous he doesn't ever FaceTime with someone as pretty as Emily Riordan.

"Have you seen any cowboys or Indians?" says Emily.

"Sure," says Braedon. "Some guys around here work with horses. They wear cowboy hats and jeans with big belt buckles. But not nearly as many here as you'd see in Texas or Oklahoma. And the whole country has Indians but you're not supposed to call them that."

"What do you call them, then?"

"Indigenous people. Because they were here first."

"I don't think we have those in Ireland," says Emily. "Just Irish people."

"Yeah," says Braedon. "I think that's right."

"Like your ma."

"That's what Dad says. But I only knew her when I was a baby so I don't remember. It's like I never met her."

"I bet if she ever met you," says Emily, "she would want to be your ma." Emily offers Braedon a sad smile.

Even on his tiny phone screen, Braedon can see something nice in Emily's eyes. "I asked Dad if we can come back for a visit. He said maybe someday."

"That'd be grand," says Emily. "We could walk down to Murphy's for an ice cream. They're getting new flavors all the time."

"Perfect," says Braedon. "I'll bring my euros. They're good for nothing over here."

Emily nods. Makes sense. "You still getting along with your grandad?"

"Yeah. He's the best. But he's kind of worried now because my uncle Teddy disappeared."

"Disappeared? Where'd he go?"

"Don't know. I saw him two nights ago. But when my aunt Deb woke up yesterday, Teddy was gone. He's super nice. Everyone likes him. But Dad says Teddy used to get in trouble and sometimes still does."

"What kind of trouble?"

"I guess once he grew some marijuana plants on the land he and Deb live on. And when they got big, he dried them in the pole barn and baked it into cookies and stuff. That was before it was legal here. He had to go to jail for six months. And another time he used to buy stolen guitars and make 'em look different by refinishing them and changing the tuner knobs and stuff and then sell them on the internet. He was supposed to go to jail for that, too, but the government lawyers did something wrong so he didn't have to."

"So he's like a good outlaw?" says Emily. "Like he robs and thieves and people still like him?"

"I guess," says Braedon. "But mostly he's just nice. He's teaching me to play guitar."

"That's cool," says Emily. "Hey, do you ever go to Los Angeles?"

"No," says Braedon. "It's really far away. It would take days to drive there."

"Days to drive somewhere in the same country?" says Emily. "How's that possible?"

"The States are huge. Like as big as a whole bunch of countries over there. Kind of weird."

"If you ever go to California, maybe you'll see the Kardashians."

"I don't know. I don't know who they are."

"Really?" says Emily. "They're super famous. On the telly all the time."

Braedon shrugs.

"Oh, hey," says Emily. "Got to go. Family meeting. We're going on a trip tomorrow."

"Where to?"

"Scotland. I wanted to go to Spain but me da says it's too hot in the summer. But I'll talk to you from Scotland. And good luck. Hope your uncle shows up and he didn't do anything bad."

They end the call, and Braedon heads back up and into the house. Grandpa Judd's watching one of his World War II shows on the History Channel. He turns off the TV and sets breakfast on the kitchen table. Pancakes and bacon and glasses of orange juice. It's all kind of perfect except for the worry Braedon sees on his grandfather's face. The lines around his eyes look deeper than usual. And like they've been there for a long time. Lines that were made by Teddy because Judd always worries about Teddy. That's what Clay told Braedon. Judd has worried about Teddy since they were both babies. Because they have that special bond twins have.

"Smells sick," says Braedon, hoping to cheer up Judd.

"Sick?" says Judd, a sour look on his face.

"Delicious," says Braedon. "*Sick* means *good*. Great, even."

"Okay," says Judd. "My breakfast smells sick. Glad to hear it."

CHAPTER 6

Clay has hooked over a dozen fish but only brought seven into the net. He could catch more, he knows, if he weren't such a dry-fly snob. The dries are the flies that float on the surface. Some fish come up for them but most feed on flies in their larval stage toward the bottom of the stream. Too many dangers near the surface. Especially birds. Osprey, eagles, hawks, herons, and kingfishers. And it's especially difficult today. A thunderstorm blew over before sunrise, dumping rain, the runoff creating a stain on the water. That makes it harder for the fish to see a fly on the surface. But Clay likes the challenge of catching trout on dry flies. Loves the take on the surface of the water. The purity of it.

Dry fly-fishing takes more focus, and that's something Clay is having a hard time maintaining. His mind keeps going to Teddy and where his uncle might be. Clay struggles to sight his fly in the water's foam and to mend his line to ensure the fly dead-drifts with the current.

A branch snaps. Not a twig. Something thicker. Louder. Clay reaches for his pistol but neither it nor its holster is there. He left the gun locked in a safe box in his truck. He stands thigh deep in the middle of a river, unable to run. Unable to hide. How could he be so careless? His only possible escape is to go under, let the current take him as far as it will before he has to surface for air. He scans the riverbank. He sees no one. Nothing. Then a wild parsnip plant shakes. Clay follows the stem down toward the ground and there he sees it.

A deer staggers and stumbles into the river only twenty yards downstream. If it were hunting season, Clay would guess that it had been shot. If they were anywhere near a road, he'd guess that it had been hit by a car. But neither of those seem possible.

The doe collapses onto the far bank, and Clay wonders if she's suffering from chronic wasting disease. But the deer is hardly wasting away. She is round in the middle, and Clay realizes she's pregnant. Very pregnant. And something has gone wrong.

When asked why he fly-fishes, Clay says it's to be part of nature. Certainly the beautiful part. But he also has to admit that he becomes a player in nature's cruelty. Its brutality. Both as a witness and as a participant. Clay understands this whether he's hooking trout in the lip then letting them go or harvesting them for meat. He has hooked a trout with every intention of releasing it, but an otter saw the struggling fish and took it for itself.

And it's rare to hook a fish deep in its mouth with a fly, but it does happen. Clay cuts the line as close as he can to the fly, hoping the trout's saliva will dissolve the fly, metal hook and all. That's what is supposed to happen, but there's no way of knowing for sure if the fish will survive.

The juxtaposition of beauty and death are everywhere on the river. And now, surrounded by wildflowers and blooms of all sorts, impossible greens, the ever-changing currents of the stream, he watches the doe take its last breath. And almost as if nature's first job is to clean itself, the current dislodges the deer's body from the bank, and away she goes, floating like a fallen log.

It's all a bit too much for a founding member of Lads Without Mums, and Clay decides to call it a day. On his way back to his truck, he knocks on the front door of Deb and Teddy's doublewide. Deb answers and Clay sees the same question in her eyes that lingers in his own: *Any word from Teddy?* The answer is no.

"I'm sure he'll show up later today," says Clay, trying to sound confident and reassuring.

"I'm sure he will," says Deb. Her gray hair falls to her shoulders and her fashion sense is modern peasant. Flowing earth-tone dresses that have more layers than a foot-tall cake. She looks like she hasn't slept in twenty-four hours because she hasn't. "How did the trout treat you this morning?"

"They were somewhat cooperative."

"Good," says Deb. "I'll see you tomorrow night. I have to admit—I'm kind of nervous to meet your dad's girlfriend. Thought that would never happen."

"Me too and me too," says Clay. "And when Teddy shows up, tell him he's doing all the dishes tomorrow night for making us worry."

"Oh, I will," says Deb. "Dishes and he's making dessert, too."

"Where's my trout?!" This from a voice behind Clay.

Clay says goodbye to Deb and turns to see Ash Solbakken, Deb's first cousin and Riverwood's most eligible bachelor. According to Ash, that is. Forty-nine years old with a penchant for eighties clothing. Ralph Lauren polo style. Popped collars and wide-wale cords. Penny loafers and deck shoes. Field coats. Pea coats. Sweaters in argyle, cable-knit, and quarter zip, often tied around his shoulders. All brand-conspicuous.

Ash's and Deb's grandmother made her modest fortune selling Mary Kay cosmetics. Now she's dead and Ash is independently wealthy, at least by the standards of Riverwood, Minnesota. He owns his hundred-plus acres free and clear. Along with his 4,500-square-foot home, complete with in-ground pool, brick pizza oven, metal pole barn, stables, horses, and three llamas. "I don't really give a rat's ass about horses or llamas," Ash once told Clay with a wink. "But women? Let's just say plenty want to come up to the house to see the horses and llamas."

Clay wanted to respond that some men have personalities. They don't need horses and llamas to attract women. But he has never challenged Ash on the obnoxious things he says. One reason is because he's Deb's cousin. And the other reason is because he's Deb's neighbor. She's had her hands full being married to Teddy—Clay doesn't want to add any additional stress to her life by pissing off Ash.

It doesn't seem fair to Clay that Deb's grandmother left her five acres with no house and left Ash over a hundred. Plus a near-mansion and outbuildings. But Deb has taken it in stride.

Ash smiles his bleached-teeth smile as he leans on Clay's F-150. "I thought we had a deal. You can walk my land to get to the river, but the cost is two pan-sized trout."

"I don't remember making that deal," says Clay, matching Ash's smile.

"It's implied," says Ash. "Hey, what'd this truck run you? I'm in the market for new wheels."

"Head down to Gilley's. He has a lot full of them."

"Maybe I will," says Ash. "But I am putting solar on the barn. So maybe I'll go electric. If you get one of those Ford Lightning trucks, come over to charge anytime."

"And it'll only cost me two trout, right?" says Clay.

"That's right. I like eating trout. Just not enough to fish for 'em."

"You joining us for dinner tomorrow night?" says Clay. Deb's cousin has an open invitation to Sunday dinner, but he rarely shows up.

"No can do. Meeting a new lass down in Decorah."

"You're crossing the border into Iowa?" says Clay. "Must be a special lady."

"Prof at Luther," says Ash. "Met her on the apps. Quite the looker. She's worth the drive."

"Good luck. Hope she's the one."

Ash laughs. "No such thing."

On Clay's drive back to Judd's house to pick up Braedon, he scans the sidewalks for Teddy. No sign of his uncle. He checks every street corner for loiterers, every parked car for idle occupants, every park bench for a conversation between mismatched participants. And then, more out of compulsion than sound reasoning, he pulls into a diagonal parking spot in front of the Riverwood Police Station. The moment he steps inside he hears:

"Uh-oh. Here comes trouble." This from Sue Lodermeier. She wears her gray hair short and parted on one side. She's a civilian and prefers jeans and fishing shirts. Patagonia and Simms, mostly. Her partner, Carol, owns Nymphomaniac, the local fly shop. *Nymphs* being the common term for flies in their larval stage. *Maniac* being the joke.

Clay greets Sue with a hug. She was an important part of his childhood. Sue filled in when Clay's mother was too sick to perform parental duties. With Judd working long hours, it was Sue who made sure Clay had the clothing and school supplies he needed. Sue drove him up to Rochester for medical and dental appointments. Sue and Carol often attended Clay's soccer games at Dorset-Cornwall. And she helped Clay shop for his parents on their birthdays and holidays.

"I hear you've been keeping my better half in business," says Sue.

"I needed a new four-weight and hip pack," says Clay. "Carol took care of me."

"How'd you do this morning?" Sue can tell Clay was on the river. He is a notorious wet wader, only wearing waders during the coldest time of the year. His quick-dry pants are still damp below the knee, and she can smell the stream on him. It's a clean smell. Like moving water over smooth rocks.

"Caught a few," says Clay. "Got 'em on PMDs and caddis. Hey, is the chief in?"

Before Sue can answer, Zoey Jensen steps out of her office.

Chief Zoey Jensen wears her dark hair in one long braid that falls down the center of her back. She's half Dakota on her mother's side and that braid is Zoey's way of showing it. "Are you Clay Hawkins?" she says.

"I am."

"I heard a rumor you exist."

"The rumor is true. Buy you a cup of coffee?"

"Ooh," she says. "He wants to go straight to coffee. No *How do you do?* No presenting his calling card. Just wham, bam, cup o' joe, ma'am."

Clay has heard of Zoey's odd sense of humor. He's heard a lot of things about her, all from his father. And to Judd's credit, he's never badmouthed the police officer who replaced him as chief. Even though she's over twenty years younger than Judd. Even though she was brought in from northern Minnesota. And even though she's a she.

Zoey looks at her watch and says, "Sue, I'm going to take thirty. I'll be down at Maisy's if you need me." She looks over at Mike Wahlquist, a sixty-year-old uniform, and says, "Mind the store for me while I'm gone, Mike?"

"Yes, ma'am," says Mike, eyes on his desk. Then the officer who once served under Judd stares hard at Clay.

CHAPTER 7

Maisy's is a legit high-end, roast-their-own-beans, espresso-driven coffee shop that offers oat milk lattes and pea protein shakes and scones that would hold their own in Ireland. Maisy does not own it. Maisy does not work there. Maisy is a standard poodle, black and white, who can usually be found lying on the deck out back making sure no squirrels or rabbits come looking for handouts.

Zoey and Clay sit inside because it's June and when there's good weather in Minnesota, every sane person sits outside. The alfresco season is short and treasured in the most northern state in the continental forty-eight. Inside, the coffee shop is empty—a good place for a private conversation.

"You want a list of criminal activity in town?" says Zoey. "Why are you interested? Do criminals make good soccer players?

And how come I haven't met you before today? It's a small town. You've avoided me since you moved here."

"I haven't avoided you," says Clay. "I've just had no need to talk to the chief of police until today."

"I think you've avoided me because I replaced your dad as chief," says Zoey.

"Not true," says Clay. "I have no investment in my father being chief other than it kept him busy and out of my hair."

"You do have nice hair," says Zoey. "Do you get it cut at Hank's? I don't see Hank knowing what to do with long hair."

"I don't go anywhere near Hank's," says Clay.

Zoey sighs and nods, then puts a concerned look on her face. "Do you want to know why the city council fired him?"

"My dad?"

"Yes."

"He says it was to add diversity to the department. But knowing my dad, my guess is it's more complicated than that."

"Judd didn't do anything wrong," says Zoey. "There are no complaints registered against him. Not about harassment or getting a little rough or pulling over cars driven by Black and Brown people. No misogyny. Nothing."

"That doesn't surprise me. My dad's a lot of things. But he's not a racist. Or misogynistic. So the city council just wanted new blood?"

"Maybe a little of that," says Zoey. "They explained to me that Officers Kimmich and Wahlquist had some outdated policing practices and attitudes. Those two do have complaints against them. The council asked your dad to re-educate them, but I guess Judd was too loyal to his subordinates. And too good of a friend. After a while, the council got frustrated with Judd not straightening out Kimmich and Wahlquist and replaced him."

"Why didn't they just replace Kimmich and Wahlquist?" says Clay.

"That's a good question. Maybe someone somewhere is indebted to those two. Haven't been here long enough to know all the dynamics."

"Small-town politics," says Clay.

"Can't pretend it doesn't exist," says Zoey.

"So they bucked tradition and brought in a woman," says Clay with a gentle smile.

"A half-Native woman," says Zoey.

"And are you straightening them out?" says Clay. "Officers Kimmich and Wahlquist? Making modern men out of them? Emotionally intelligent? Racially and sexual orientation and gender sensitive?"

"I'm doing my best," says Zoey. "Of course they get to call me *chief*. A bit of a Native slur, but I am the chief. Nothing I can do about that." Zoey leans forward in her chair as if she's about to divulge a secret. "Do you mind if I ask you a personal question?"

"You can ask," says Clay.

"When you go to the men's room, do you wash your hands before or after?"

"After," says Clay.

"Why not before?" says Zoey.

"I'm not sure I understand the question," says Clay.

"Everyone washes their hands after they use the restroom.

I get it. Just in case something went amiss. But I also wash my hands before I use the restroom. Because the typical person showers in the morning, then puts on clean underwear. That way their private business is clean and remains clean inside a nice undergarment. But their hands have been out in the world since they showered. Touching all sorts of nasty things. Handrails and money and doorknobs. Other people's hands. You name it. Everything out in the world is dirty and covered in germs, so doesn't it make sense to wash your hands before pulling down your clean underwear?"

Clay looks at Zoey for a good ten seconds and then says, "The reason I'm here is—"

"I don't have OCD," says Zoey.

"It's okay if you do. There's no stigma in having OCD. Most successful people in this world have it in one form or another."

"But I don't," says Zoey. "It's just common sense to wash your hands before you go to the bathroom since there are orifices in one's nether regions. Easy access for germs. So yeah. Also, if you walk into a men's restroom and your shoelaces are untied, you should rip them out of your shoes and burn them."

Clay isn't quite sure what to make of Chief Zoey Jensen. She's smart. But she doesn't seem to be putting those smarts toward anything useful. He's about to say something when she cuts him off.

"I know why you want to talk to me. Wahlquist told me your uncle Teddy is missing."

"He is," says Clay. "Any idea where he might be?"

"Nope," says Zoey. "The entire department is looking for him. You think he's involved in something criminal?"

Clay shrugs. "Never know with Teddy. He could have gone up to the cities to see friends. He could have decided to fish Viroqua, Wisconsin. It's one of his favorite areas. And he just forgot to tell anyone. Including his wife. Which is not like Teddy. Or"—Clay throws a piece of blueberry scone into his mouth and continues—"he might be up to something he shouldn't be."

"I know he took off without his car or cell phone," says Zoey. "That's a bit odd."

"Yes," says Clay. "It is."

"Have you checked his recent calls and texts?"

"The phone's locked. Deb says she thought she knew the passcode but Teddy must have changed it. We have nothing. That's why I'm asking you about criminal activity in town. My father has spoken to the others in the department, but for some reason he's reticent about speaking to you. I don't want to leave anything to chance."

Chief Zoey Jensen thinks about that and says, "I don't know why Judd would be reticent to talk to me. He trained me for three months. We have a communicative, respectful relationship. Your dad really did put his town first. Riverwood is a better community than most around here because of him. I'm really sorry he feels reluctant to communicate with me." Zoey's posture shifts and she adds, "How come you soccer players have such good hair anyway? Why don't other athletes have hair like soccer players?"

Clay smiles. "Football players wear helmets, so why bother? Same with hockey players. Same with baseball players, only it's a cap or a helmet. And basketball players play indoors, so they get too sweaty."

"Does it hurt when you head the ball?" says Zoey.

Clay laughs. "Not if you do it right."

"You're a man of the world, Clay Hawkins. This is an interesting conversation. Not the run-of-the-mill small-town talk about weather and fishing and local gossip."

"How is talk about heading a soccer ball the start of an interesting conversation?" Clay sips his latte and awaits Zoey's answer.

"That's what we'll find out through a little back-and-forth. A tit for tat, if you will. Some talky-talk shadow boxing. A little verbal Rochambeau."

"No one's ever called you demure, have they?"

Zoey laughs. Scone shrapnel flies from her mouth and she laughs harder. "Sorry."

"It's okay," says Clay. "A little scone in the eye never hurt anyone." Clay blinks hard, then adds, "I'm asking for information that may help me and my father find Teddy."

"Hmm," says Zoey. "You're implying that I'm not looking for Teddy. But you're wrong. I am. My entire department is looking. I've also brought up Teddy with every person I've spoken to in the last twenty-four hours. So here's a question. Do you want to be friends? You and me? I'm kind of new to town. You were gone forever so it's like you're new to town. Everyone is so set in their routines. They have their friends. They're not looking for someone new. What do you think?"

Clay considers Zoey's proposition. His biggest reservation about moving back to Riverwood after being away for twenty-four years was his romantic prospects. Zoey had just said *I think we should be friends* but Clay wonders if she means *more than friends*. He does not make this assumption lightly. Or immodestly. Nor out of arrogance or obtuseness. The potential pairing of Zoey and himself seems obvious. They are both single. They are the same age. They have both lived in other places for the majority of their lives. They have both survived relationships with Judd Hawkins.

Zoey has deep brown eyes and long hair to match. Clay has heard she rowed crew in college, and she's maintained her athletic build. She stands the same height as Clay—five foot ten—and runs five miles every day, always ending with a sprint up to the top of Riverview Bluff.

"Did I ask a hard question?" says Zoey. "You seem to be having trouble answering it."

"Not hard," says Clay. "But also not exactly reassuring when it comes to my uncle. Teddy is my big concern. And you're talking about your social life."

"*Our* social life," says Zoey. "Listen, Clay. I do my job. I'm good at it. What I don't do is tell people I'm good at my job. Except just then. Because the people out there telling you they're good at their job are bad at their job or politicians or professional liars or all three."

Clay happens to agree with this. He ran into the same phenomenon as a professional athlete. Especially at the coaching level. So many incompetent coaches talk themselves into a job. That's their real skill. Buttering up the owners. But it was often the aloof coaches, the quirky thinkers and doers, who motivated their players to greatness not with a sales pitch but by instilling in them a belief that they could win. As individuals and as a team. The great coaches show their players, ownership, and fans a winning system. They don't sell them a winning a system.

"Friends?" says Clay. "I see no reason why we can't be friends."

"Well, good." Zoey extends her hand over the table. "Friends."

Clay shakes it.

"I have a question, friend," says Zoey. "Your dad's been off the job less than a year. Why don't you ask him about local criminal activity?"

"A couple of reasons," says Clay. "I don't want to look for Teddy with my dad. He doesn't exactly see things clearly when it comes to his brother. And he doesn't exactly see things clearly when it comes to me. It's a bad combination. Also, you have the most recent information. You have active cases, I assume. Or at least suspicions and hunches about what's going on out there in your jurisdiction. So I figured why not go to the best source of current information?"

Zoey's about to respond when her cell rings. She takes the call. "This is Chief Jensen."

Clay can hear Sue's garbled voice on the other end.

"Tell Wahlquist to drive out and have a look."

More garbled Sue.

"Is Kimmich out on a call . . . ? Okay, I'll head that way soon. Tell them I'll be there in twenty." Zoey ends the call.

"Busy day?" says Clay.

"The usual," says Zoey. "But it'd be less busy if that fancy boarding school of yours had its own security. We've been up there twice already this summer. Stretching my department kind of thin."

"What's going on at Dorset-Cornwall? I haven't heard anything."

"Theft. Computers out of the library. Building supplies from that new wing you're adding. A bunch of apparatus from the chem lab."

"I'll suggest we hire private security at the next staff meeting," says Clay.

"Look at that. I'm helping you, you're helping me. I love a transactional relationship. Hey, here's a question: Are you a shower or a bath guy?"

"Shower," says Clay. "Taking a bath is just sitting in your own dirt."

"Yes!" says Zoey, looking genuinely impressed. "That's exactly right! I knew I'd like you. I just knew it. What's your cell number? I'll send you my contact info."

CHAPTER 8

Clay returns to his truck to find a parking ticket on the windshield. He's not parked illegally and pulls off the ticket to see what infraction he's supposedly committed. No boxes are checked. Instead he sees handwriting in black Sharpie: *Betty-Mae's. We need to talk.* No signature. No nothing. Clay checks his watch. He has plenty of time before he has to pick up Braedon, so he shoves the ticket into his jeans pocket and walks a block and a half south on Main Street to Betty-Mae's Bakery.

The place smells of sugar and butter. Baked goods fill glass cases, and people sit at orange Formica tables in aluminum chairs. Clay spots Riverwood police officers Mike Wahlquist and Andy Kimmich with coffee and a dozen assorted donuts. Both men are about Judd's age. Clay approaches, drops the wadded-up ticket into the donut box, and says, "Heard you guys want to chat."

Mike Wahlquist carries an extra fifty pounds, mostly between his chest and former waist, and has gray eyes between heavy lids and swollen bags, a gin-blossom nose, and silver stubble atop his head. If he were standing, he'd measure six feet, three inches. He says, "Pull up a chair," in a mismatched voice for his ample size. It's weak and high-pitched, as if he'd been punched in the larynx when he was eleven and his voice didn't mature after that. "Have a donut."

"I'm good," says Clay. "Just ate a scone at Maisy's."

"A scone?" says Andy Kimmich. "Ooh-la-la. You can take the boy out of Europe . . ." Kimmich started dyeing his hair black in his thirties with a store-bought dye that might as well be called Black Hole because it sucks in everything around it. He's thin with slight shoulders and a bit of a neat freak about his appearance. His uniform is clean and pressed just so. He also has a meticulously trimmed mustache, also dyed black. It is currently flaked with specks of glaze from a just-eaten donut. "Come on, eat a donut like an American."

"No thank you," says Clay, "but I appreciate the offer."

"Used to be 'Uncle Andy'! 'Uncle Mike'! Now he won't even eat with us. Will you at least have a seat?"

Clay eyes them suspiciously. "What's going on?"

"Why you talking to the chief?" says Wahlquist.

"Because Teddy is missing. My father didn't want to talk to her. So I did."

"He spoke to us," says Kimmich. "That's good enough. You stay out of it."

"Is it good enough?" says Clay. "Because the only thing you

seem to be looking for is diabetes and a bigger belt. And I was just with your superior officer when she got a call from Sue. Sue thinks you're out on patrol. How smart of a lie is that in a town with one street?"

"What happened to you?" says Kimmich. "Your father raised you to respect your elders. I'm not feeling any respect here."

Clay says, "Why do you talk like an East Coast mobster, Andy? The farthest east you've ever been is Wisconsin."

"If you weren't the only child of my dear friend Judd," says Kimmich, "I'd take you out back and show you a thing or two."

Clay sighs. Ever since he returned three months ago, Wahlquist and Kimmich have been having a hard time accepting that he's no longer a boy. "Anything else you guys want?"

"Don't worry about your uncle," says Wahlquist. "We're leading the search for him. Got the word out in Chatfield, Preston, Lanesboro, St. Charles . . . All of Fillmore County. Let us do our jobs and we'll get your uncle back to you. No need to get Zoey involved."

Clay eyes the two men who are a few years short of retirement. He smiles.

"Come on, Clay. Don't give us that look. We know what we're talking about. Zoey's not local like we are," says Kimmich. "This is our—"

"Don't say *turf*," says Clay. "Please stop talking like that. Nobody talks like that around here."

Wahlquist pats his ample belly. "All we're saying is we don't need any interference in doing the job we've been doing for forty years. City council got a bug up their ass to hire a woman chief.

That's politics. But when it comes to actual police work, to protecting and serving the good people of Riverwood, Minnesota, Andy and I know how to get the job done."

"See," says Kimmich, brushing the crumbs out of his mustache with a tiny comb, "the city council is getting out of hand. Think they know how to run this town. They don't know how to run anything. Half of them are salmon who came back during the pandemic because they could work remote. That's why everyone around town calls the city council the *clown* council. They're a bunch of know-nothing knuckleheads. Mike here is thinking of running for mayor. Setting things straight."

"I didn't know that," says Clay. "Congratulations, Mike."

"Haven't announced it yet," says Wahlquist. "Saving it for the Fourth of July parade. And I'd appreciate your support, Clay. I was there for you when you were just a little guy. Now I'd like you to return the favor."

Clay smiles. "Happy to."

Wahlquist raises his eyebrows. "I'm getting the Ozempic," he says. "Seeing the doctor on Monday. The pounds will soon be melting off me. I'll need the energy for the campaign."

"Sounds like a good plan," says Clay.

"Clay," says a woman.

Clay turns to see Steph Becker. She is Clay's age, has long blond hair and clickety-clackety fingernails painted peach. They're long and may or may not be real. A dark line surrounds Steph's ice-blue eyes, and her lips match her peach nails. She wears tight jeans and a black T-shirt bedazzled with the word CYNIC, and holds a to-go cup of coffee and a white bag with grease stains.

"Hey, Steph. How are you?"

"I just had a cancellation. I can cut you now if you'd like. Or see you next week as scheduled."

"I'll be there in five," says Clay.

She sips her coffee, then lowers the cup, leaving a peach lip print on the cup's white plastic lid. "Great," says Steph. "See you then."

She heads out, Wahlquist and Kimmich watching her as she goes.

"Clay, you never should've let that one go," says Kimmich.

"She's over forty," says Wahlquist, "and could still win Miss Riverwood if she wasn't married."

"Guess I'll have to live with that mistake for the rest of my life," says Clay. "See you guys around. And thanks for looking for Teddy."

CHAPTER 9

"Stage one is you pop the old spent primer," says Judd. He and Braedon are down in the basement workshop, where Judd has a dedicated station for reloading shotgun shells. He demonstrates as he goes, running an empty shotgun shell through the reloader. "Next stage, you put in a new primer."

"A primer is the thing that makes the spark that lights the gunpowder?" says Braedon.

"That's right."

"And you can use the plastic shotgun shells over and over again? Like forever?"

"Maybe not forever," says Judd. "But you can use them quite a few times. That's good since they're plastic, and no sense throwing away plastic that can be reused. What's that smirk on your face?"

Braedon blushes. "I never would have guessed you're a tree hugger, Grandpa."

"Watch your tongue," says Judd, again with a smile in his eyes. "I ever hear you call me that foul name again, and you and I are done. Got that?"

"Yes, sir," says Braedon with a big grin. "What's the next stage?"

"The next stage," says Judd, "you slide over to your middle station, and that's where you dump your powder." Judd points to an inverted bottle on top of the reloading machine filled with gray-black powder.

"Is that the same kind of gun powder Bugs Bunny uses?" says Braedon. "Like when he cuts a hole in a barrel and carries it so the gunpowder falls out in a line on the ground? And then he lights it and the flame follows the line and blows up something?"

"Same stuff," says Judd. "Only let's not try that in real life. Let's leave that kind of fun to Bugs."

Braedon nods.

"Next stage is your shot." Judd points to another inverted bottle atop the reloader, this one filled with tiny BBs. He pulls a lever and some fall into the shell. "Then you put your wad in. And then you finish it off with an eight-point crimp." He finishes his demonstration, then hands the reloaded shell to Braedon.

"Whoa," says Braedon. "It's heavy."

"Because it's full of metal shot."

"Is the shot made out of lead?"

"Steel," says Judd. "Used to be lead. But . . ." Judd laughs.

"You're trying to bait me into tree-hugger talk again, aren't you, boy?"

Braedon laughs. "Maybe."

Judd shakes his finger at Braedon and says, "I warned you." Then he tousles the boy's black hair and says, "Now you try."

Braedon takes an empty shotgun shell and runs it through the first stages on the reloading machine, popping out the spent primer. "Grandpa?"

"Yeah?"

"Are we going to use these shells to hunt pheasant?"

"Pheasant. Or ducks. Or grouse."

"I'd like to shoot a pheasant," says Braedon, shifting over to the reloader's second stage. He takes a new primer from the pack and levers it into the rim.

"Why a pheasant?"

"Dad uses the feathers to tie flies. He says pheasant is important on a lot of nymphs. The flies that sink underwater."

"I remember," says Judd. "Your dad always wanted pheasant tail feathers. He started tying when he was about your age."

"Because Uncle Teddy taught him," says Braedon.

"That's right."

Judd's cell phone rings. He doesn't recognize the caller ID but it's a 507 area code so it's local. "I'd better take this," he says. "You keep going." Judd stands and crosses over to the other side of the workshop where he can watch Braedon run the shell through the remaining stages of the reloader. "Hello?" he says into his phone.

"Chief Hawkins?" says a voice on the other end.

"Yep," says Judd. "But I'm not the chief anymore. Just Judd Hawkins."

"Right." The voice is male. "Sorry. Forgot. This is Pete Lindelof down at the Kwik-Trip. I heard you're looking for information about your brother, Teddy."

Judd lowers his voice and presses his back against the cinder-block wall, as if that gives him more distance from Braedon. "That's right." He leaves it at that. He doesn't want to color what Pete says next. A tried-and-true interrogation technique. No need to stop using it now.

"Well," says Pete, "Teddy came into the Kwik-Trip at about three in the morning a couple days ago."

"Do you remember which day?" says Judd.

"It was early Friday morning. I was working a midnight to eight, then I drove up to the cities to see my girlfriend, Cass. She goes to Hamline. And I just got back and heard that the cops--I mean the police—are asking around about Teddy. You know, if anyone's seen him. And they left your number, not the police station's. Anyway, so that's why I'm calling."

"I appreciate that, Pete. Is it okay if I ask you a couple questions?"

"Sure."

Clay watches Braedon shift the shell over to the reloader's third station where he pulls the lever and drops a measure of gunpowder into the shell. "Was Teddy alone when you saw him early Friday morning?"

"Yeah," says Pete. "He came into the store by himself."

"Do you remember what he bought?"

"Yeah," says Pete. "A breakfast sandwich and a cup of coffee. He heated up the sandwich in the microwave. Oh, and also, he bought a pair of work gloves."

"Work gloves?" says Judd.

"Yeah. Leather ones, I think."

"And do you by chance remember how he paid for that stuff?" says Judd. "Credit card? Cash?"

"It was cash," says Pete, "if you can call it that."

"What do you mean?"

"Well, it was a few crumpled-up ones and the rest was change. You know, like how kids come into the store to buy a can of pop or a candy bar or something. That's why I remember it. Change is a pain in the you-know-what. It took a minute for him to count it out. It was to the penny."

"That's good to know, Pete. Thank you. One last question. You said he was alone. But do you know if he walked there? Or did he get a ride? Was anyone waiting for him in the parking lot?"

"You know what?" says Pete. "Yeah. There was. I forgot about that. There was a car or truck in the parking lot. I remember the headlights."

"Do you remember anything else about the vehicle?" says Judd. "High up or lower to the ground? Round headlights or rectangular? Could you hear the engine from inside the store or was it quiet?"

"Uh . . . let me think . . ." says Pete. "No. I don't remember any details. I was putting donuts in the pastry case when Teddy walked in and I was kind of focused on that. Sorry, Chief—I mean, Mr. Hawkins."

"No need to apologize," says Judd. "Appreciate you calling. You've been very helpful. And if you remember anything else about the vehicle in the parking lot, give me another ring. Sound good?"

"Yeah. If I remember anything, I'll let you know."

Judd ends the call. *Work gloves,* he thinks. Why would Teddy buy new work gloves? He and Deb probably have a dozen pairs out in the pole barn. Judd walks back toward Braedon, who's putting the final crimp on his reloaded shotgun shell. "Looks a little short, Brae. Did you remember all the stages?"

"Ugh," says Braedon. "Forgot the wadding."

"That's okay. Happens to the best of us. We'll pry that baby open and start again."

CHAPTER 10

C3 (for Cut, Color, and Chat) is a full-service salon with four stylists and one nail specialist. It caters to women and men, technically. Clay has never seen another man in the place when he's been there. He doesn't ask if he's the only man the salon cuts because he doesn't want Steph to feel self-conscious about the pink walls, abundance of orchids, and magazines that mostly cater to women. *Cosmopolitan, Vogue, Elle,* and that sort. He wishes he could get his hair cut at the barber shop, but Hank doesn't do well with longer hair. And he doesn't seem all that willing to learn. Even Teddy won't go to Hank. Deb cuts his hair.

Deb has offered to cut Clay's, too. But Steph does a good job, and Clay enjoys seeing her every couple of months. Clay also likes that it drives Judd nuts, Clay getting his hair cut at a beauty salon. Take your pleasures where you can find them.

Steph shampoos Clay's hair in the sink. He feels her long nails on his scalp as he breathes in the scent of tea tree oil and lavender. Steph and Clay dated in high school, although they didn't attend the same school. Steph was the hottest townie. That was according to the other boys at Dorset-Cornwall. They objectified the local girls. And even before Clay could fully understand the dynamic, he felt the Dorset-Cornwall boys' sense of entitlement over the townies. Like they were there for the taking, the using and abusing. To bow to the boarding schoolboys' whims in the hopes of being lifted out of obscurity. None of this was said aloud, of course. But it was implied. These guys were Clay's friends, but he didn't like it. Nor did he participate in their locker-room talk.

Rather than lecture his classmates, Clay dated Steph and treated her as if she were a Dorset-Cornwall girl. He took her to parties. He made no off-color remarks about her. He didn't cheat on her.

"You finally ready to get rid of your gray?" says Steph, wrapping Clay's head in a towel.

"No thanks," says Clay. "That's an unwinnable battle I'd rather not fight."

"Just trying to make you look less distinguished. You got enough going your way."

Clay responds with a half-smile, gets up from the shampoo chair, and follows Steph toward her station.

Their high school romance seemed perfect on the surface and, in many ways, it was. Clay and Steph lived down the block from each other. They were both occupied with school and extracurricular activities. Steph kept busy with her after-school and weekend job. Clay's soccer obligations made it seem like he had a full-time job in addition to his academically rigorous coursework. They found time for each other on weekend evenings.

But the relationship struggled for light in the shadow of Clay's inevitable departure. He was honest and up-front with Steph from the beginning. He had no intention of staying in Riverwood after graduating. And no intention of returning. There seemed to be no solution. Steph wasn't headed to a four-year college, and Clay was headed to a top-tier school, or maybe even straight into professional soccer. She wouldn't go with him. Their romance had an expiration date.

"I'm sorry about Teddy," says Steph, pulling a comb through Clay's hair and judging the unevenness of its ends.

"Thanks," says Clay. "You know Teddy. He's the best. Until he isn't."

"I do know Teddy," says Steph, and Clay knows she's referencing the high school years when they dated. He would bring her to Teddy and Deb's place for dinner rather than home to his father. Those were the worst years between Clay and Judd, when Clay was morphing into a man and making decisions that might cleave him from his father forever.

Clay catches the subtext of her reference to their past and decides to stay on topic. "I'm pretty worried about him," says Clay. "Do you know if he might have got mixed up in something he shouldn't have? Any good gossip coming through the shop about criminally active boyfriends or husbands?"

Steph grabs a section of Clay's hair between her index and

middle fingers and uses them as a guide to snip off the ends. "I do know about one thing," says Steph. "And it's not really gossip. It's a fact. Last year, I'd just about had it with Wags's antics so I gave him an ultimatum. One more ruse or pyramid scheme or get-rich-quick idea and I'd leave him. He knew I meant business so he straightened up. Focused on his job at the garage. Didn't stay out all hours. Then . . ." Steph grabs another section of Clay's hair on the opposite side of his head and compares it to the section she'd just trimmed. "He starts getting up at three, four in the morning. Told me they were falling behind with all the brake jobs and tune-ups, so he was getting a jump on his days until they got caught up. Sounded reasonable to me. Every morning. Up well before the sun and out he goes. Home for dinner as usual and early to bed. Mr. Busy Bee, right?"

Clay doesn't answer.

"Well, one Sunday, this was just last month, Wags was back at the garage getting caught up some more, and I was thinking, Riverwood, Minnesota, is a small town. We don't have a big enough population to back up an auto shop that bad, especially since we have a few garages in town. I started to get suspicious. You know what I mean? Like I didn't outright think, *Oh, Wags is up to something again*, but I was getting that sick feeling. Like something's wrong.

"And you know me, Clay. When something feels off, I don't sulk. I don't drink. I like to be as industrious as possible, you know, like I'm a counterweight to whatever bad is going on. So I thought I'd gather up all the old paint cans we have lying around and take them to the toxic-waste place over in Preston. Hell, half of those paint cans came with the house when we bought it. They're just taking up space. So I start sifting through the storage shed and I find this huge box of metal things. Kind of looked like oval-shaped metal cans but with pipes coming out of each end. I didn't know what the hell I'd stumbled on. I took a picture of one and did a reverse-image search and do you know what they were?"

Clay shakes his head.

"Catalytic converters," says Steph. "And believe you me, Clay, I'd heard plenty about those. They're getting stolen left and right around here. Half my clients have complained to me about it. It's gotten so bad you can't park your car outside overnight. Apparently, there's some kind of valuable metal in them. Palladium, I think it's called. They sell it to scrap dealers."

"And Wags is the one stealing them?" says Clay.

"Well, I confronted him, and he tried to deny it. Said he was taking bad ones home from the garage and he was going to weld them into some kind of sculpture. Total bullshit if I've ever heard it. He's doesn't have an artistic bone in his body. Wags got real nasty about it. Like threatening. So I told him I'd made myself clear. No more chances. No more warnings. I kicked his ass to the curb. And then I told everyone that if anything happened to me or the kids, it would be Wags who did it. I've told your dad he's threatened me. And I've told Chief Jensen. And I hired a lawyer and we are into it. Wagner Becker and I are done. Forever this time."

Clay separates the two pieces of information Steph has just given him. One is that catalytic converters are being stolen and, her implication is, Teddy could be involved by working with Steph's soon-to-be ex-husband, Wags. It makes sense—it's the kind of thing Teddy has done in the past. Once he stole a combine from a farmer who'd left it running in the middle of a field. Teddy tried to sell it for parts and, if not for Judd cutting a deal with the farmer not to press charges, Teddy would have served time. Clay's uncle is also friends with Wags Becker, so that increases the chances of Teddy's involvement in the catalytic converter thefts.

The other big piece of information Steph just laid on him is that she and Wags are done. Her marriage has always felt like a safety net for Clay. It's been okay for Steph to cut his hair. It's been okay for them to feel like friends. But anything beyond that has been squashed by the simple fact that Steph is married. News of that marriage's demise has the potential to shift the dynamic.

Clay plans on being cautious when it comes to dating in a small town. He'll only date when Braedon is on a trip with Judd. Hunting or fishing in northern Minnesota. He'll steer clear of Riverwood. Instead he'll use the apps to meet women who live in Rochester or even all the way up in the Twin Cities. His romantic life will be discreet. Clean. Uncomplicated.

He makes no assumptions about Steph's interest in dating again. If she puts herself back out there, he'll make no assumptions she's interested in him. The idea of rekindling their old romance jumbles his gut. Clay and Steph have a history together. And history with a person, especially someone you knew growing up, seems to carry more weight the older you get.

Clay says, "Sorry to hear you're going through that. Must be brutal."

Steph sighs. "Wags is begging me to take him back. Apologizing all over the place. Says it'll never happen again. But hey, I've heard that before. And now there's a nasty threat in his voice, like the words are nice, but he sounds anything but nice. So sorry, mister. You're on your own."

"How are the kids doing with it?" says Clay.

"They get it. It's not easy for kids having a dad be just another kid in the house. Especially for Thomas. He's fifteen. He needs a strong male role model. In a way, it's kind of more normal now that Wags is out of the house. But still. A family splintering. The whole thing is just sad. Regardless of the why. The kids will have their hard times, but they'll be okay. I'll make sure of it."

Clay understands this. He makes sure Braedon's okay. Doesn't mean it's easy for either of them. But he does whatever he can for Braedon. And Clay hasn't regretted a minute or a dollar spent to ensure Braedon's well-being.

This conversation is making him feel closer to Steph. And his respect for her grows that much more. It's uncomfortable as she leans her chest over his face to cut his hair. Uncomfortable but not unpleasant.

Clay says, "Do you think Teddy might have been working with Wags to steal those catalytic converters? Or to sell them? Maybe drive them to some scrap metal dealer out of the county?"

"It's possible. Teddy and Wags hang out. They like to play pool at Knut's. I wouldn't be surprised if Wags started shooting off his mouth and one thing led to another."

"Are you comfortable with me talking to Wags?"

"Oh hell," says Steph, "sure. I don't care. But just a heads-up. In one of our more heated arguments, the one that led to me carrying his stuff out and tossing it in the bed of his pickup, he accused me of ending our marriage because you're back in town. He said that was the real reason I gave him an ultimatum. That I want to get back together with you."

Clay is so tempted to ask, *Well, do you?* But there are a number of reasons that question is a bad idea. Mostly, he doesn't know if he's interested in Steph. Sure, he's intrigued. The old attraction still feels present. She's built a nice business for herself. She's a good mother and has taken the courageous step to stand up for herself by demanding good behavior from her husband. Soon to be her ex-husband. Of all the women in town, he finds her the most attractive in all sorts of ways.

Or at least he did until this morning. Chief of Police Zoey Jensen is quirky as hell but she's interesting. Clay thinks she's beautiful. Smart and accomplished and, yes, a bit strange, but strange is interesting. And how weird is it that Clay kept his romantic distance in this town for a few months, then two women-of-interest swirl into his orbit on the same day? But that's life, he figures. Ebbs and flows. The natural order of things is chaotic. Human beings want to make sense of it all, but that's a fool's folly.

"Well," says Clay, "I'll just level with Wags and tell him I see you on a regular basis. Once every six weeks. And he's just going to have to deal with that. No matter how much it hurts him. Best to be honest."

Steph laughs her sweet little laugh. That hasn't changed in the last twenty-four years. "This is on me today. Your money is no good here."

"No," says Clay. "This is your job. This is how you support your kids. Wags sure as hell can't contribute much."

"That is true." Steph lifts pieces of Clay's hair to check them for length against each other. "But you're not paying today. And there's nothing you can say or do to change my mind."

CHAPTER 11

Frank's Tire & Auto is a mile up the road. It's an old building made of brick painted white. The brick and grout have been covered in so many coats that the imperfections have been filled and smoothed to almost nothing. The building's exterior is beginning to look more like white vinyl than paint. The garage has three bays, and Clay sees Wags standing in one of them, reaching up to work on the undercarriage of a car that's on the hydraulic lift. Wags stands about just under six feet and has a wiry frame and a six-months-pregnant beer belly. His black hair lies straggly and unwashed under a gray cap that matches his overalls.

Clay knew Wags when they were kids and back then didn't have a problem with him. Nice enough guy. Not blessed with brains or a work ethic, but he wasn't a bad kid. But kids have hopes and dreams and when those aspirations turn to shit, kids can grow into unpleasant adults. Clay doesn't think Wags is violent, but he also doesn't think it's a good idea to connect Steph to the upcoming conversation. He pulls his hat down tight on his head, hoping its years of use without a wash will not only hide his professionally groomed hair, but also the scent of shampoo and conditioner.

"Hey, Wags," says Clay when he's a few feet outside the garage.

It takes a moment to recognize who's walking toward him. "Oh, hey, Clay." He doesn't sound thrilled.

"Got a minute?" says Clay. "Want to ask you about something."

"A minute," says Wags. "Got to get this done by four."

"I seem to have misplaced my uncle. Wondering if you've seen him recently."

Wags wipes his hands on a greasy rag. "Teddy?"

"Only uncle I got," says Clay.

"Why you asking me?" says Wags.

"Because I'm asking everyone. And you fit into the category of everyone."

Wags thinks for a moment, then says, "I saw him last week at Knut's. Beat him three out of five in nine-ball. Cost him a six-pack of Schell's."

"Sounds like Teddy. Did he pay up?" says Clay.

"Yep. That very night. Ran to the liquor store and returned with a brown paper bag. Teddy always pays his debts. You can count on him for that."

"Can you count on him for anything else?" says Clay.

"What do you mean by that?" says Wags.

"Did you two have any extracurricular projects together? Any side businesses? For fun or profit?"

"What are you getting at, Clay?"

Clay has to be careful here. He doesn't want to involve Steph in this. "I was talking to Mike Wahlquist and Andy Kimmich this morning at Betty-Mae's. They told me to make sure I park my truck in the garage at night. Said someone's been stealing catalytic converters. I asked if they know who it is, and they said they had a pretty good idea it was you. But no one has stepped forward to press charges yet, so unless they catch you in the act, there's not a whole lot they can do."

"That's bullshit," says Wags.

"I don't know," says Clay. "They seemed pretty confident that it's you. You're welcome for the heads-up, by the way. And Teddy has got mixed up in his share of mischief over the years, so I thought maybe he got himself involved with you. Tough for Teddy to say no to making a quick buck."

Wags just shakes his head. "I got nothing to do with any stolen catalytic converters. The only time I touch one is to install it on a car that had one stolen. Or if someone's went bad, but that doesn't happen all that often. And if I was stealing catalytic converters and needed help, I wouldn't go to Teddy Hawkins."

"Why not?" says Clay.

"Because he's too old. You'd need someone young and spry who can wriggle under a parked car. If Teddy tried that, it'd take him ten minutes to get back onto his feet and another ten minutes until his head stopped spinning."

"Sounds like you have some experience with catalytic converter theft."

Wags tosses the greasy rag onto a rolling tool cabinet. "I'm an auto mechanic. I know how to install and remove parts. What's the real reason you're here, Clay?"

Clay knows he has the upper hand. He believes that Steph told the truth. She found a box of catalytic converters in the back of her toolshed. Steph doesn't need to pin a crime on Wags to make her divorce go easier. She's the breadwinner. Her kids are in high school—Wags can't take them away from her. It's Wags who's doing all the lying.

"Teddy's missing," says Clay. "I'm trying to find out where he might be. That means finding out if he's caught up in something he shouldn't be. I heard you're caught up in something you shouldn't be. I know you and Teddy spend time together. I'm just doing the math and checking my results."

"I had nothing to do with Teddy disappearing," says Wags. "I think the real reason you're here is to pin something on me so I'm not in your way anymore. So you have a clean shot at Steph with me out of the picture. She's your first love, right? That never goes away."

Clay's had enough of Wags. He honestly can't read much into the denials. Just because Wags is lying about stealing catalytic converters doesn't mean he's lying about Teddy's involvement. Clay says, "Last I heard Steph is a married woman. Not my style." Then Clay walks out of the bay and gets in his truck.

Clay decides to make one more stop. Hensel Metals is a ten-minute drive north toward Rochester. Clay parks at the far end of the lot, trying to minimize the chance of his tires eating a nail or a sharp-edged piece of scrap metal. He walks the designated path of safety toward the office, passing mounds of twisted metal. The scrapyard has three giant machines: One a crane with jaws to grab the scrap metal and move it from one pile to another.

The other a shredder that cuts up appliances and coins and pipes. The third a crusher to smash cars and trucks and other large metal objects. Clay can't think of a more fun place to hang out—that is, if you're eight years old and like breaking stuff.

He isn't looking forward to seeing Bobby Hensel. When Clay was growing up, Bobby was a bully and a thief who had a fondness for harassing Clay. The torment only increased after Clay left public school for Dorset-Cornwall. Not in frequency, because Clay was at that elite private institution on the hill, but in intensity. It was almost enough to make Clay want to live in a dorm at school so he'd never have to run into Bobby.

As Clay grew bigger and stronger and more athletic, he was tempted to pay back Bobby for all the anguish he'd caused him, but Clay never wanted to risk his ticket out of Riverwood. He didn't want to get hurt, and he didn't want to get arrested. One thing about being the son of the police chief in a small community—Judd couldn't show Clay any favoritism or the entire community would cry foul.

The office is built out of a few old shipping containers welded together with cutouts for doors and windows and HVAC and plumbing. Clay hesitates outside the entrance. He hasn't spoken to Bobby since returning to Riverwood. He's seen him a few times but neither Clay nor his old nemesis has ventured a *hello*. Clay isn't much looking forward to it now, but this is about Teddy, not him. Besides, he's grown up now. He's faced far scarier characters than Bobby Hensel on and off the pitch.

Clay enters and scans the building for alternative exits. A service door on the south side of the building. A lift-up garage door on the north side. He approaches the counter where a young man sits reading a book. He has voluminous curly black hair and round wire-rim glasses and wears a button-down shirt of blue oxford. His face is stubbly save for a full mustache and an accompanying jazz dot in the center of his chin.

The young man looks up from his book and says, "May I help you?"

"Yeah," says Clay, "is Bobby Hensel around?"

"He's out back at the moment. Should be in here pretty soon. Anything I can do for you in the meantime?"

"Are you related to Bobby?" says Clay.

"Yeah," he says, not particularly proud of that fact. "I'm Eli, his son."

"Nice to meet you, Eli." He shakes the man's hand, feeling it odd that a former classmate has a son Eli's age, even though Judd was only twenty-one when Clay was born. "Clay Hawkins. I knew your dad in the olden days. What are you reading?"

"*Anna Karenina,*" says Eli, holding up the book. "I'm obsessed. People always go on and on about *War and Peace,* but it's not in the same league as this book."

"I agree," says Clay.

"You've read them?" says Eli, sounding both surprised and delighted.

"Both," says Clay. He smiles. "You don't seem like the typical scrapyard worker."

Eli shakes his head. "Just trying to save up enough money to move to England. My dad won't help. He wants me to stay and work here."

"Where in England?" says Clay.

"London," says Eli. "I just graduated from the University of

Minnesota with a degree in English lit. I'm ready to write my first novel. A retelling of *Oliver Twist* in modern times. I want the book to be faithfully accurate to today's London the way Dickens's was to the London of his time."

"I played a lot of matches in London."

"Oh, wait. Are you the soccer player?"

"The one and only."

"I've heard about you. Do you mind if we grab a drink sometime so I can pick your brain about the move?"

"Happy to," says Clay.

"I figure it'll take me a year to save up enough money. And that's living bare bones. I had to put myself through college by working at a scrapyard in the cities, but I couldn't save a dime. I signed up for one year of servitude, then I'm out of here. Can. Not. Wait."

"I know the feeling. Hey, Eli, I do have a question for you. Does anyone come in here trying to sell catalytic converters? You know, more than one?"

Bobby Hensel emerges from a door behind the counter. He wears grease-stained coveralls complete with an embroidered patch on his right pec that reads ROBERT. He has a few days' growth on his face, salt-and-pepper stubble, and dull, brown, bloodshot eyes.

He takes one look at Clay and says, "Fuckin' A. I heard you were back in town."

"How are you, Bobby?" says Clay. "Been a while."

Bobby points to his name patch. "It's Robert now. Bobby was a child."

Clay hates when people start going by their full given name

after decades of going by the less-formal version. John becomes Jonathan. Becky becomes Rebecca. Gus becomes August. Lizzy becomes Elizabeth. It's a last-ditch effort at respectability, thinks Clay. One that requires no work or merit. He sure as hell isn't going to insist people call him Clayton.

"Nice to see you again, Robert."

"He wants to know if we buy catalytic converters," says Eli.

"You trying to unload some?" says Robert, FKA Bobby. He may have changed his name, but he has the same mean smile. "You finally hit on hard times, Clay?"

Clay puts a pleasant smile on his face. He can think of a few satisfying comebacks to Robert's question but doesn't want to play that game, especially in front of Eli, whom Clay likes and feels sorry for. Instead he just says, "My uncle Teddy is missing."

"Yeah," says Robert. "Heard about that."

"Teddy's had his troubles in the past, and I'm wondering if maybe he's out there stealing catalytic converters to raise a little cash. This is the closest scrapyard to Riverwood, so I thought I'd stop in and ask if Teddy's been in here."

"Nope," says Robert. "Besides, I won't touch a catalytic converter anymore. They're all stolen. It would have to be stamped with a vehicle identification number and the person bringing it in would have to show me a pink slip with that same number on it for me to even consider taking it. I run a respectable business here, Clay. I don't need any trouble with the law."

"Of course not," says Clay. "Neither of you have happened to see Teddy around, have you?"

"I'm sorry," says Eli. "I don't know him."

"Midsixties," says Clay. "Long hair. Kind of looks like Neil Young."

"Oh, that guy," says Eli. "Yeah. No. Haven't seen him for a while, and never up here."

"Same," says Robert. "Sorry. Wish we could be of some help."

"I appreciate your time," says Clay. "Nice meeting you, Eli. And good to see you again, Robert."

Robert laughs. "Is it?"

"We were kids, Robert. We were just kids."

CHAPTER 12

"Grandpa said he's going to buy me a shotgun when I turn fifteen," says Braedon.

"I have to check the law of the land," says Clay, "but I think I have some say in the matter."

"Oh, come on, Dad. It's my own shotgun!"

They're in the kitchen of Clay's shoebox. That's what he and Braedon call the modern rectangular house perched on three acres a few miles out of town. It was designed by a professor of architecture who taught at Carleton College up in Northfield. It's been featured in several magazines, although it always looks better in the magazines than it does in person. The shoebox is sided in copper and limestone cut from local bluffs. It has an open floor plan with big windows that flood the place with light. It's not a gigantic home, square-footage-wise. Three bedrooms and two and a half baths. A walkout basement that's half finished and half unfinished. The unfinished side is where Clay ties flies, not unlike the space where Judd reloads shotgun shells. Having a place like that where they can make things they could otherwise buy is one of Clay and Judd's similarities.

Clay hasn't touched the place since moving in except for having an alarm system installed and every dead bolt replaced with a Medeco 4. Is that too much security for Riverwood? Probably. But *probably* isn't *definitely*. And Clay doesn't take unnecessary chances.

"We'll see how you've matured when you're fifteen," says Clay. "No sense getting worked up about a shotgun now."

Clay butterflies a whole chicken, using kitchen shears to cut down the bird's spine.

"What does that mean?" says Braedon. "How I've matured?"

"It means we'll see how you're doing in school. We'll see if you're keeping yourself out of trouble. And we'll see how you do shooting clay pigeons." He flattens the bird on a cutting board and takes a pinch of kosher salt from the salt pig.

"Why do they make pigeons out of clay and why do people want to shoot them?"

"They're not really pigeons," says Clay. "That's the name for clay disks that get launched in the air like Frisbees. It's how you practice shooting a flying target. Grandpa didn't tell you about shooting clay pigeons?"

"No," says Braedon. "He said something about skeet and trap shooting. But I'm not sure what that is."

"Skeet and trap mean shooting clay pigeons."

"Then why don't they just call it shooting clay disks?"

"I don't know, Brae. Someone named it that long before I was born. And long before Grandpa Judd was born. Could you please grind some pepper onto the chicken so I don't have to wash my hands before I flip the bird?"

"Ha," says Braedon with exaggerated flatness. "Never heard that one before."

"It's a classic."

"According to you." Braedon grabs the pepper mill and grinds away.

"What else did you and Grandpa talk about today?" says Clay.

"Well," says Braedon, "Grandpa Judd asked if I was going to play soccer at Dorset-Cornwall like you did."

"And what'd you say?"

"I told him I didn't know. I'm not as good at soccer as you are. I told him I might play American football instead. He said that would be great and I should also try hockey."

Clay flips the butterflied chicken and indicates that Braedon should hit it with the pepper grinder again. "Do you want to try hockey?"

Braedon shakes his head. "Everyone who grew up here learned to skate when they were two. I could never catch up."

"Did you say that to Grandpa?"

"Yeah," says Braedon, grinding a new layer of pepper. "But he said I could learn if I went to a hockey camp. And he said it would be good for me because hockey players never complain about injuries. Sometimes they have broken bones and don't even tell their coaches so they can keep playing. And . . ." Braedon makes eye contact with Clay, then hesitates.

"And what?" says Clay.

"Nothing . . ."

"It's okay. You can tell me."

"Well," says Braedon, "Grandpa said soccer players are the opposite. They're total babies. That they fake getting hurt all the time so the referee will call a foul. They scream and roll around on the ground and they're not even hurt. He said it's embarrassing. And he'd never want me to do anything like that."

"Grandpa Judd is right."

"Really?"

"Partly," says Clay. He washes his hands in the sink. "Soccer players do fake getting hurt sometimes so the other team gets a foul. And it is kind of embarrassing. The refs are starting to crack down on it. On the other hand, unlike American football players or hockey players, soccer players wear no pads or helmets. They collide into each other going full speed and jump to head the ball when another player is jumping to head the ball. You have to be really tough to play soccer. Tough and brave."

Braedon nods. This he understands. "I still can't get used to calling football soccer, and American football regular football. Because American football shouldn't even be called football. The ball hardly ever gets kicked. It should be called tackleball or something like that."

Clay salts the flipped-up side of the chicken. "That's a good idea, Brae. How about you and me just start calling it tackleball. See if we can get it to catch on. We'll say tackleball and clay disks. See if we can make some changes around here."

Braedon nods. "Yeah. Let's do it."

The doorbell rings, and Braedon goes to answer it. Clay actually hopes it's someone selling magazine subscriptions or asking them to make a political donation instead of someone they know. He doesn't want the interruption. Clay cherishes his one-on-one time with Braedon. He can't imagine life without his son. How empty it would be. But every time he feels the overwhelming gratitude and love for Braedon, he can't ignore the dark juxtaposition to his relationship with his own father.

Judd had the same opportunity Clay has now. To be the sole parent. To be a guide and a friend. A disciplinarian and playmate. To be present for his child's new discoveries, thoughts, and feelings. But Judd seemed unwilling to be that parent. Or maybe he was simply incapable. Or maybe he does blame Clay for Pam's illness and death. Not that pregnancy can cause breast cancer, but it can, in rare instances, make it more difficult to detect. Clay knows. He's looked it up a hundred times to see if there's any new research shedding light on how he may have contributed to his mother's death.

Clay knows it's not his fault. He didn't ask to be brought into this world. He had nothing to do with it. But still. It's an unsettling feeling knowing that both he and cancer grew inside Pam at the same time.

"Hey, Dad," says Braedon, walking into the kitchen and jolting Clay from his thoughts. "Can Daniel stay for dinner?"

Clay looks over to see Daniel standing next to Braedon. Daniel is one of those twelve-year-olds who hasn't had even the faintest growth spurt. Braedon, who isn't particularly tall for his age, stands a full head higher than Daniel. The kid looks more like he's nine or ten. Maybe to make up for his literal shortcoming, Daniel exudes a cockiness. He's not a bad kid, thinks Clay. He's just trying to find his place in the hierarchy of Riverwood's twelve-year-old boys. Besides, Daniel is a neighbor kid who goes to the local middle school. Braedon will meet plenty of other kids and influences at Dorset-Cornwall when school starts, but it's nice that Braedon has a friend until then.

"Of course," says Clay. He supposes getting to know Daniel a bit better has its own value. "We have plenty of food. Daniel, do you like chicken and french fries and salad?"

"I like chicken and french fries," says Daniel.

"That's good enough," says Clay. "Make sure to let your parents know, okay?"

"Already did," says Daniel.

Clay laughs.

"Dad, is it okay if we ride Daniel's new mountain bike out back?"

"Sure," says Clay. "Just wear a helmet. When did you get a new mountain bike, Daniel?"

"Today," says Daniel. "Some guys gave it to me."

"Some guys?" says Clay. He sees worry in Braedon's eyes. And fidgety hands.

"Some older boys," says Daniel. "They seem nice. Just walked up to me pushing the bike and said I could have it and that maybe I could ride with them sometime."

"What else did they say?" says Clay.

"I don't know . . ." says Daniel, his confidence waning. "They said something like now I owe them."

"Owe them money?"

"No. I asked if I owe them money. They said maybe a favor sometime. They didn't say when."

"Is it okay if I see your new bike?"

The mountain bike is on the front porch, leaning against the limestone facade. It's flat black, painted recently, and Clay spots a few drips from the shoddy spray job. "Nice bike," says Clay.

"Thanks," says Daniel.

Clay lifts the bike. "Light."

"Yeah," says Daniel. "I think it's a good one."

"Cool if I flip it over?"

"I guess," says Daniel.

Braedon watches his father flip the bike in his hands so the handlebars and seat are near the ground. "Why are you doing that?"

Clay doesn't answer. He's reading the serial number on the underside of the bottom bracket. When he's pretty sure he's committed it to memory, he says, "Do you mind, Daniel, if I rub a fingernail on this bottom part?"

Daniel shrugs. "I guess it's fine."

Clay draws his fingernail along the bottom bracket. After a few passes, a line of lime green emerges. He flips the bike right side up and presents it to Daniel. "You guys have fun. Dinner will be ready in about forty-five minutes."

"Hey, new friend," says Clay into his phone. The chicken is in the oven, a sheet of frozen french fries getting unfrozen on the rack below it. The kitchen smells like heaven. That is if you like chicken and french fries.

"Why, hello, new friend," says Chief of Police Zoey Jensen. "I didn't expect to hear from you so soon. Aren't you supposed to play it cool? Not contact me for a few days? Maybe a week? You're coming off as kind of desperate."

Clay laughs. He doesn't want to laugh, but he can't help it. "Have any bikes been reported stolen recently?"

CHAPTER 13

"Is Daniel going to get in trouble?" says Braedon.

It's the next day, late Sunday afternoon. Clay has just explained to Braedon that the bike given to Daniel by the older boys is stolen. Most likely by those boys. Clay and Braedon are in the truck, headed to Judd's for Sunday dinner. Only this one will be different because Teddy won't be there unless he shows up from wherever he's been, and Mei, Judd's girlfriend, will be. They're going to meet her for the first time, something no one is comfortable with.

"No," says Clay. "Daniel won't get in trouble. I told the police what happened. That the boys gave it to him, and Daniel had nothing to do with where it came from. But Daniel will have to turn in the bike. I just want to figure out a way he can do it without those boys thinking that Daniel ratted them out."

"Yeah," says Braedon. "That would be bad."

"Really? What else do you know about those boys?"

"Nothing," says Braedon. "I don't know anything about them. I don't know any kids other than Daniel."

"Don't worry. You'll meet plenty of kids when you start school in the fall. And you'll meet more local kids, too, I bet. It's good to have different friends in different groups of people. It helps you understand people better."

Braedon lets that sink in but he's not sure he agrees. He spent the first eleven years of his life in Europe and the last few months here in the United States. It seems to him that people are people. Same everywhere. But maybe that's his dad's point. Knowing that one group of people isn't better because of where they were born. Or what school they go to. Or a whole bunch of stuff. Still, he knows if those boys stole a bike and painted over it, they must be trouble. And he's worried about his friend Daniel being on the wrong side of them.

"Dad, how can Daniel give the bike to the police without those guys knowing he ratted them out?"

"We'll have to work something out. Like Daniel rides it and parks it somewhere and the police find it that way. And I think Chief Jensen will do us a favor. Get the bike back to its rightful owner but not arrest the boys. She'll just keep an eye on them so if they steal another bike, she can arrest them for that one. Daniel will have nothing to do with it."

"Why would the chief do that?" says Braedon. "Are you guys friends?"

"I don't know," says Clay. "I just met her yesterday when I talked to her about Teddy. She's a nice person. I think she'll help us out."

They drive in silence for two minutes, then Braedon says, "Do you like her?"

"What do you mean?"

"I mean, do you like-like Chief Jensen? Are you going to go on a date with her?"

Clay doesn't answer right away. He doesn't answer because he doesn't know. Finally, he says, "How would you feel if I did go on a date with her?"

"Fine," says Braedon without hesitation. "You have to go on a date with somebody sometime, otherwise you'll end up like Grandpa Judd and not have a girlfriend-woman-friend whatever you call it until you're sixty-three. What's the point in that?"

"Cut your grandpa some slack. He loved Grandma Pam very much. It's not easy to start dating when you're in love with someone else. Even if that person isn't with us anymore."

"Is that why Grandma Pam still lives in a jar on Grandpa's fireplace?"

"It's called an urn. And yes, I think so, Brae."

Braedon considers this for a moment, then says, "Well, you shouldn't wait until you're sixty-three to get a girlfriend because I'll be long gone by then."

"You will?" says Clay through a laugh. "Where're you going?"

"I don't know," says Braedon. "Maybe I'll go to West Point like you did. Or I'll go back to Ireland to live with my friends."

"Maybe I'll go with you," says Clay.

"That's fine," says Braedon. "You can do whatever you want."

"Appreciate that." Clay turns onto the road toward Judd's house. The corn in the fields is about shin high. It's supposed to be knee high by the Fourth of July. That's the saying, anyway. Looks like the farmers are off to a good start.

"Have those boys given bikes to anyone else you know?" says Clay.

Braedon shakes his head. "I don't think so."

"Let me know if you ever hear of anything like that."

"I am so pleased to meet you, Clay," says Dr. Mei Hsiao. She is sixty-four years old, one year older than Judd. But if Clay didn't know that, he'd guess she was closer to fifty. Straight dark hair just past her shoulders. Round wire-rim glasses in green. Her build is slight. She wears a button-front jumper of indigo cotton over a white T-shirt and green shoes that match the rims of her eyeglasses. It's something a child might wear, but it suits her.

Clay finds Mei engaging and interesting and attractive. He understands why his father decided to end his long streak of being single. Judd had the occasional date over the years. At least that Clay knows about. He assumes there's plenty about his father's love life that he doesn't know and doesn't want to know. But one thing Clay is sure of is that since Pam died, Judd has not had a long-term relationship. Not once in the last thirty years. If he had, Teddy and Deb would have known about it. Hell, it's Riverwood. Everyone would know about it.

"Very nice to meet you, Mei," says Clay. He wants to say he's heard a lot about her but that's not true. Judd has been tight-lipped about Mei. All Clay knows is that she's a cardiologist up at Mayo. "Thanks for driving down to Riverwood. We're thrilled to have you here."

Clay notices a proactive warmth between them. He assumes Judd told Mei of their fractured father-son relationship and that it goes back to well before Pam died. He guesses there's some sense on both their parts that she could help heal that fractured relationship. If they both get along with Mei, maybe they can find a way to get along with each other.

They're sitting in the living room of Teddy and Deb's doublewide. When Judd was chief of police, he confiscated the doublewide in a meth bust. After its occupants were convicted, the home went to auction. Judd couldn't just take it for himself. But he did exaggerate its drugginess by mentioning in the auctioneer's listing that the doublewide had been used for the manufacturing and storage of methamphetamine, its ingredients, and processing equipment. That was true except that the bust happened before the actual manufacturing took place. Police found cases of pseudoephedrine, boiling flasks, Bunsen burners, rubber tubing, baking dishes, and other chemicals and accoutrements all neatly stored in their original packaging. Still, Judd added to the auctioneer's listing: "May not be safe for human habitation."

It was plenty safe. That's how he bought it through a proxy for eight thousand dollars. He paid another two grand to have it towed onto the five-acre parcel of land Deb had inherited from her grandmother. That was fifteen years ago, and it was the only way Deb and Teddy could afford to actually live on that five-acre parcel.

From their seats, Clay and Mei can see into the kitchen where Deb cuts a watermelon into cubes and out to the deck through a sliding glass door, where Judd teaches Braedon the art of grilling. Burgers on one side of the grill. Brats on the other. Buns on a rack eight inches above the grill, splayed open, toasting face down. A plate of sliced cheese sits off to the side waiting to be put into the game.

Mei offered five times to help Deb in the kitchen, and Deb refused every one. It seems the whole family thinks or at least hopes Mei can help bring peace between Judd and Clay. Even Clay thinks it's possible, especially after Braedon said he'd be okay if Clay dated Zoey Jensen. It forced him to reconcile with his own long-buried wish for a family of origin. A real family. Not just him and Judd. If anything, it was Deb and Teddy and Sue Lodermeier who gave Clay the feeling of family. Now he's wondering if that's how Braedon feels. That Clay isn't enough. There's no critical mass to make a family with just two of them. Clay gets a sick feeling in his gut.

"You've led a very interesting life," says Mei. "Your father told me how you applied to Dorset-Cornwall without even telling him. And West Point. And about playing professional soccer in Europe. I hope this isn't too personal of a question, or insulting, but why did you come back?"

Clay offers Mei a warm smile. "Not too personal or insulting at all," he says in a tone that can only be interpreted as earnest. "I just felt it was time to come home. And by home I mean the States. I had applied for a number of coaching positions. Some universities and in Major League Soccer. Dorset-Cornwall had been courting me for a while. They made a nice offer. My dad and Teddy and Deb aren't getting any younger. I figured it wouldn't be a bad idea to reacclimate to life in the States in a place I know.

And to have Braedon get to know his family better. What about you?" says Clay. "Where are you from?"

"I'm from Monterey Park outside of Los Angeles," says Mei. "It's like a suburban Chinatown. But I went to university in upstate New York and to medical school in Connecticut. I worked at Johns Hopkins for twenty years, then I moved to Rochester. I'm very happy at the Mayo Clinic."

"Do you ever miss Calif—"

"Clay," says Judd.

Clay looks over and sees his father stepping inside the open sliding glass door. "Yeah?"

"A word, please."

Clay hasn't heard that tone from his father since he was a teenager. It triggers a fight-or-flight response, but he has the skills to cloak that from Mei. "Sure," he says casually and without concern. "Excuse me, Mei."

Judd offers Mei a smile and says, "This will just take a minute." He grasps her hand, gives it a squeeze, then heads for the front door, leaving Braedon to man the grill solo. Clay follows Judd outside.

CHAPTER 14

"What are you doing talking to Chief Jensen behind my back?" says Judd in just above a whisper. It's a seventy-degree day, and all the windows in the doublewide are cranked open.

"I didn't go behind your back," says Clay. "I just went. And the only reason I did is because you chose not to. You think Mike and Andy can handle it. But Mike and Andy seem preoccupied with being Mike and Andy."

"That is not true," says Judd. "They're good police. They've got the word out all over the county. They're talking to their sources. They're talking to everyone who knows Teddy. They're doing their job."

"Are they? When I spoke to them yesterday, they gave me the same talking-to about going to Zoey. What's their problem with her? What's your problem with her?"

"Zoey Jensen doesn't know Teddy. She doesn't know his history. She doesn't know the way this town works. Hell, how could she? She's only been on the job six months. I have no problem with Zoey. It's just that this is a family issue. You and me, we're family. Mike and Andy and Sue, they're family. Zoey Jensen isn't family. We don't need her sticking her nose into this."

Clay feels his sixteen-year-old self begin to boil. "What are you talking about? We have no idea what Teddy's been mixed up in. And do you know why we don't? Because we're *family*. Because we love Teddy. Because we only want to think the best of him. Because we don't want to think the unthinkable. We're too close, Dad. We're too goddamn close to Teddy. Zoey Jensen is exactly who needs to be investigating his disappearance. Asking questions. Finding out who Teddy's been seen with lately. What he's been up to. Because we can't see clearly when it comes to Teddy. And you especially can't. You've been bailing him out of trouble since you were kids. I love him to death but the man can't hold a job and can't keep his hands clean. And you've enabled it. Why should he straighten out his life when you keep cleaning up his messes?"

Judd curls his lower lip into his mouth to let his anger cool to a simmer. He checks the open kitchen window to make sure Deb isn't lurking near the screen. "Just stay out of this," says Judd in a low growl. "I don't need some soccer player out there stirring up an already murky situation."

"*Some soccer player*?" says Clay. "That's who I am to you? Not your son? Not Teddy's nephew? But *some soccer player*?"

"Dammit, Clay, I don't care if you're a soccer player or an accountant or a ballet dancer. The point is you don't understand or appreciate the delicacy of this situation. You spook the wrong people, they'll clam up. And that will make finding Teddy ten times harder. Just leave it to me and Mike and Andy. We'll find Teddy. That's what we do."

Clay turns away from Judd and stares out at the gravel driveway leading from the road. His truck is pulled off to one side. He wants to get in it and drive away. He did something like that twenty-four years ago and things turned out pretty well. Maybe he and Judd just aren't meant to be. Would it have made a difference if Pam had lived? Might she have found a way to bring father and son together without combustion? Clay has no idea but the answer doesn't much matter now, does it?

He turns toward his father and says, "I'll do whatever the hell I want. Don't take out your guilt on me."

"I have no guilt. What do you think I'd feel guilty about?"

"Oh, man. So many things. Not helping Teddy turn it around. Not treating this disappearance seriously."

"What do you mean—"

"I mean you refused to take this to the chief of police. You and Mike and Andy are just nosing around. No one's done any real investigative work."

"I—"

"What have you done?" says Clay. He hears his voice rise to a volume that can be heard inside the house. He takes a breath, steps toward his father, and almost whispers, "By now you and your good buddies Mike and Andy should have Teddy's cell phone records. You should know who he's been calling and texting. You should know which cell towers he's been pinging over the last few weeks to see if there's any location patterns that might give some insight into where he's been and what he's been up to lately. Every criminal complaint, questioning, and arrest in town should be referenced and cross-referenced for known friends and associates of Teddy. And they should run every Facebook, Instagram, and X account of every friend Teddy has or has had through Sprout Social to analyze every picture and post in search for a connection. And get back to basics. Why hasn't a K-9 unit tried to track his scent? It hasn't rained since early Friday morning but it could any time."

Judd looks at Clay with a hint of a smile in his eyes. Looks but doesn't say a word.

"What?" says Clay. "Why are you looking at me like that?"

Judd scratches his head, then shakes it. He shrugs.

Clay turns and walks back into the house, where he manages a smile for Deb and Mei, then heads out to the deck to see how Braedon's doing on the grill.

The rest of the evening is pleasant enough. Judd and Clay are so used to conflict that they put it behind them rather easily. They don't get over it. They bank it. But banked conflict is better than boiling-over conflict—at least they can function. And it helps that Mei is a talker. They learn she was married once in her twenties to a man her parents pushed on her. He turned out to be bad at business and bad at monogamy. When she divorced him, her family practically divorced her.

"They have some very old-world ways of thinking," says Mei. "Even now, almost thirty years later, they say I should have never left him. That's why I've been content to build my life here in Minnesota."

Mei looks at Judd, and the two share a smile. Despite Teddy's disappearance, Judd has reasons to be happy. He's introduced Mei to his family. They all seem to be getting along well. More importantly, they all seem like they want to be getting along. Mei has questioned Braedon about his science studies, and she's been impressed with what the boy knows at twelve years of age. Deb is being especially welcoming to Mei. Clay is treating her as if she's already a member of the family. And Judd won't shut up about Braedon's prowess on the grill. It almost feels like a happy occasion.

Then there's a knock on the front door.

CHAPTER 15

Judd almost jumps out of his seat. He opens the front door and slumps with disappointment.

"Picked a bad day to leave my windows open," says Ash Solbakken, Deb's first cousin and neighbor. He wears Nantucket red shorts, Top-Siders with no socks, and a butter-yellow cable-knit sweater over a kelly-green polo shirt buttoned up to his neck. "Your grilling smells too good to pass up. I think I'll join you for dinner after all."

He has come empty-handed. Judd leads Ash to the dining room table, introduces him to Mei, and finds another chair.

Judd wants Mei's counsel. He wants to share everything with her, good and bad. He wants to show her his weaknesses. His mistakes. He wants to be vulnerable and turn himself inside out, and Mei can accept or reject the real him. He's only been dating her for four months, but hell, he knows her well enough to understand that he doesn't need to know her better to feel the way he does. Judd hasn't felt this way about anyone other than Pam.

They've just made love. Judd and Mei stare up at the modest rambler's popcorn ceiling, the room lit by a small lamp. The kind that holds a single candelabra bulb in a tiny linen shade. The lamp has been there so long that Judd can't remember where it came from. His guess is Pam found it at a garage sale. Maybe even before they were married. She loved a good garage sale. Mei is the first woman he's allowed into the room where Pam once convalesced and slept. It's not the same mattress—Pam died thirty years ago—but it's the same bed made of antique maple that matches the dresser and two nightstands. The furniture had belonged to Judd's grandparents.

Now Judd's a grandparent. So much of his life is behind him. He never had a problem getting older. Not when he turned forty. Not when he turned fifty. But when he turned sixty, the finiteness of life hit him hard. You can't call yourself "middle-aged" when you're sixty. No one lives to 120. Sixty felt like smelling salts under his nose. Sixty woke up Judd. He downloaded the dating apps. He met Mei.

And then Clay and Braedon moved to Riverwood. The boy took to him right away, as if Judd and Braedon had both been waiting for each other. There was no getting-to-know-you warm-up period. No dance. No nothing other than instant chemistry, enthusiasm, and affection for one another. Braedon was and is more than Judd dared to hope for. The only downside to his grandson is that he's a living measuring stick for Judd and Clay's relationship.

Just as inexplicable as Judd and Braedon getting on the way they do is Judd and Clay not getting on at all. Their enmity feels preordained to Judd. Even when Clay was a baby, he'd cry whenever Judd picked him up. What alchemy is at play? And to make matters more strange, why is it that Judd and Pam loved each other, Clay and Pam loved each other, but Judd and Clay can't seem to agree on the color of the sky?

Judd wonders if this is life's way of balancing things out. He has been blessed with Braedon and Mei but haunted by his disconnect with Clay and getting sacked by the city council for no good reason. All is even.

And just as unexplainable as Judd's relationship with Braedon is his relationship with Mei. They're an odd couple, he and Mei. She's Ivy League educated. He has an associate's degree from the University of Minnesota's General College. Mei is a medical doctor. Judd's a retired cop. She grew up in the suburbs of Los Angeles. He's lived in the same small Minnesota town his entire life.

But he and Pam were also opposites. That relationship would have lasted—Judd's sure of it. He hears a truck rumble past on his quiet small-town street. He feels Mei squeeze his hand. And then, without thinking, like it's an involuntary muscle twitch, Judd says, "I love you."

Judd hopes to feel another squeeze from Mei's hand but it doesn't come. He expects to be washed away by embarrassment and shame, but those feelings don't come. What he does experience is a wave of relief. *Is that weird?* thinks Judd. Why does he feel relief? It might have something to do with communicating his truth. It might—

"I love you, too," says Mei.

Judd lets go of her hand and rolls onto his side to face her. He can feel his stupid smile. "You don't have to say that just because I did."

"I didn't," says Mei. "I said it because I feel it. It's actually kind of embarrassing. I think I knew I loved you after our third date. So thank you for saying it first. I was too scared."

"Are we crazy?" said Judd. "Are we being foolish? After only four months?"

"We're in our midsixties," says Mei. "We know who we are. We know what we want. Both of us have been single for a long time . . . I think we know what we're doing." She grabs both of Judd's hands in hers and adds, "But . . . are you sure you're not feeling this way because Teddy's missing? Is it possible I'm some kind of substitute for your feelings?"

Judd smiles. "I'm one hundred percent sure. Because I wanted to tell you last week up in Rochester but I chickened out. And Teddy wasn't missing then."

"Good answer, Judd. Very good answer." She kisses him.

Judd can't believe this is happening at sixty-three years old. The love. The sex. That he looks at Mei the same way he looked at Pam forty years ago. He thought that part of him would have ended up on the shelf long ago, and in a way it did. But now it's off the shelf, shiny and new as ever.

He's about to cup her cheek in his palm when Judd hears the crash of broken glass.

CHAPTER 16

Judd throws on his T-shirt, underwear, and jeans. He then opens the drawer of his nightstand, removes a pistol, and gets out of bed. He calls out through the open bedroom door, "I'm armed. If you're in this house I advise you to get out. Now."

"Judd," says Mei. "What's happening?"

Judd doesn't seem to hear her. He peeks out the bedroom and into the hallway. He stops to listen and hears nothing. Two hands on the pistol, he crouches into the hallway and starts toward the living room. Three steps, then he stops to listen again. The house is dead quiet. Two more steps and then he sees it.

The front door's sidelight window is shattered. Broken glass litters the small foyer, along with a softball-sized rock that has an envelope taped to it. Judd returns to the bedroom.

"Is everything okay?" says Mei.

"Someone threw a rock through a window. I don't think

there's anyone in the house, but I'm going to make sure." He grabs a pair of running shoes from the closet, sits on the bed, and puts them on. "Stay here until I give you the all clear."

It takes five minutes for Judd to make sure no intruders are in the house, then he calls for Mei to come out with shoes on and lights off. The next thing Judd does is retrieve some cardboard from the garage, which he cuts to size and tapes over the frame of the former window using only the light from the front porch lamp. Turning on an interior light would attract flying insects into the house. When he's done sealing the window, he gets a broom and dustpan and sweeps up the broken glass. Then he gets a pair of rubber gloves from under the kitchen sink, picks up the rock, and carries it to the kitchen table.

"We might be able to pull fingerprints off the envelope or the tape used to secure it to the rock," says Judd.

Mei boils water for tea. "Will you be able to read what's inside?"

"I think so," says Judd. "Just want to be careful removing the envelope."

Judd pulls a paring knife from the knife block and uses it to wedge the tape off the rock. He then flips over the envelope, exposing the tape's sticky side and sticks Post-its to it so the envelope doesn't stick to anything else. The envelope is also sealed by tape. Judd removes it, careful not to tear it, and sticks that piece onto another Post-it. He then lifts the envelope and peers inside.

"What's wrong?" says Mei. "Why are you making that face?"

Clay's cell phone rings on his nightstand. It's an old habit, leaving his ringer on at night. He started doing so while on the road with his team when Braedon was home with the nanny. He looks at the screen. It's 11:57 PM, and the caller ID says JUDD HAWKINS. In Braedon's phone, Clay is listed as Dad. Clay picks up his phone.

"Hey," he says.

"Can you come over?"

"Anything new with Teddy?"

"Just please get over here. I'll explain then."

"Be there in fifteen," says Clay.

Clay gets dressed, brushes his teeth, and softly knocks on Braedon's bedroom door. When he gets no response, he cracks the door open, peers inside, and sees nothing but dark. "Brae," whispers Clay. "Brae, sorry to wake you up."

"Huh . . ." says Braedon.

Clay opens the door and a wedge of light from the hall shines across Braedon's bedroom floor and wall. "Grandpa just called. He wants me to come over. I don't know why yet, but I'm guessing it has something to do with Uncle Teddy. You want to come with me or stay here?"

"Stay here," says Braedon, his voice dry and raspy.

"Okay. I'm going to lock up behind me. You need anything, just call."

When Clay gets there, Mei has already left. She has to be at work at the Mayo Clinic at seven AM and didn't feel she could get back to sleep anytime soon. Better to use the next half hour for travel time. Clay finds his father sitting at the kitchen table with a rock, an envelope, and a letter. He's wearing rubber gloves.

"This arrived through my window about forty-five minutes

ago," says Judd. He lifts the letter from the table and then looks at what is underneath it.

Clay's eyes follow Judd's. "Is that Teddy's earring?"

"Yep. And read this. But put on these gloves first." Judd hands Clay an extra set of nitrile gloves.

Clay takes the gloves from his father and snaps them on like he's done it a hundred times before. He then takes the letter. It appears to have been printed on an inkjet printer.

IF YOU EVER WANT TO SEE TEDDY HAWKINS ALIVE AGAIN, PUT $45,000 IN A BEAR CANISTER AND SEAL IT TIGHT. DROP IT IN THE ROOT RIVER AT MOEN'S BRIDGE AT 12:01 A.M. TUESDAY MORNING. DO NOT NOTIFY THE POLICE. DO NOT GO DOWNSTREAM FROM MOEN'S BRIDGE OR STATION ANYONE DOWNSTREAM. IF YOU DO EITHER, TEDDY WILL DIE. ONCE THE MONEY IS RECEIVED, YOU WILL GET FURTHER INSTRUCTIONS ON YOUR MOBILE PHONE.

Clay sighs and returns the letter to Judd.

"What do you make of it?" says Judd.

"First of all," says Clay, "are we sure that's Teddy's earring? A small gold ring is not exactly one of a kind."

"Pretty sure," says Judd. He pushes the earring toward Clay with a gloved hand. "See the backing thing that goes behind the ear? Teddy lost his in 1980. He took it off to clean the earring and misplaced that clasp thing. Your mother had an extra one laying around, but it didn't match. The earring is gold. The back thing she had was pink. Teddy said he didn't care—no one would see it anyway. So he took it and has used it ever since. Maybe someone else out there knows that, but I doubt it. Teddy hardly ever took off that earring, and as far as I know, never did so in public."

Clay folds his arms over his chest. "So whoever threw this rock through your window plans on camping out somewhere downstream of Moen's Bridge with a fishing net or something like that to haul it in. Water's still high from spring runoff. One of those bear canisters could make it all the way to the Mississippi River. That's over fifty miles of stream we'd have to cover. Impossible."

"Or I could just pay it," says Judd.

"You can't just pay it," says Clay. "We're not even sure Teddy's alive. We need some kind of proof."

"We have the earring."

"The earring, if it is Teddy's, does not prove he's alive. We need to talk to him on the phone or see a video of him or something."

Judd shakes his head. "You've been watching too many cop shows. Old cop shows. You can't make a phone call or send a video without leaving yourself vulnerable to being traced. Only an idiot wouldn't know that."

"Thank you," says Clay. "Thanks very much. I know how modern technology works. But there are still camcorders and memory cards and VPNs and . . ." Clay wonders why Judd asked him to come over if he's just going to belittle all of Clay's ideas. Same old Judd, he guesses. "I'm just saying forty-five thousand dollars is a lot of money to toss into a river if you're not sure Teddy's alive."

"I've been saving my pennies for decades," says Judd. "You got a full scholarship to Dorset-Cornwall. No tuition at West Point. House was paid off a long time ago. I can risk losing forty-five grand. I'll be just fine without it."

Clay shakes his head, almost to himself.

"What?" says Judd.

"Forty-five thousand is an odd number. Why not fifty?"

"Maybe whoever has Teddy thinks I don't have fifty. Maybe Teddy told them I might only be good for forty-five."

"Does Teddy know your finances?" says Clay.

Judd shakes his head. "We don't discuss things like that in Riverwood."

"You don't discuss money? With your own brother? With your *twin* brother?"

"Nope," says Judd. "Decent people don't."

Clay pulls up a chair and sits across the table from his father. The table and chairs are of the same vintage as Judd's bedroom furniture. All inherited from Clay's great-grandparents on the Hawkins side.

"Listen," says Judd, "unless the kidnapper or kidnappers contact me again, I have no way of asking for proof of Teddy's life. And if there's one thing I know from forty years of law enforcement, it's that criminals are generally stupid. Scared criminals are even more stupid. They do stupid things. They've given me a simple set of instructions. My gut says follow them and that'll give me the best chance of seeing my brother again. Otherwise, I'm just putting Teddy's life in more danger."

Clay wants to say *if Teddy even has a life anymore* but the resulting argument would be pointless. If Judd's socked away half a million dollars over the years and he wants to blow forty-five thousand of it on a Hail Mary to save Teddy, that's his business. He decides to try another tactic. "Can we at least bring the police in on this?"

"Why?" says Judd.

"Maybe the kidnapper has tried something like this before. Maybe they've seen a similar ransom note. Maybe—"

"No," says Judd. "I'm leaving Mike and Andy and Zoey out of this. Their involvement could lead to the Minnesota Bureau of Criminal Apprehension sticking their nose in. Or worse, the FBI. I say let's just get Teddy back. If we're going to catch whoever took him, we can work on that after he's safe at home. Teddy must know something that can help us. Something about the kidnapper. The sound of his voice. A scent. Maybe even a location. I'm fine risking the forty-five grand. Teddy's safety is my main concern."

"Okay," says Clay. "If your mind is made up. Think you can get forty-five thousand in cash tomorrow?"

"Technically, it is tomorrow. And I don't see why not," says Judd. "Every penny I have is at F&M Community Bank."

"Your retirement savings aren't with a brokerage service?" says Clay.

"Hell no. Janice down at F&M takes care of all that. Sends me statements every month. Some money is in mutual funds. Some is in bonds. But the bulk of it is in cash in case an emergency comes up. And I'd call this an emergency."

"But banks don't have that much cash on hand."

"I know that," says Judd, "but I'll call Janice first thing. Before the armored truck comes. Plus there are half a dozen other branches in our corner of the state. Janice can pull the cash together by the end of the day for a lifelong customer like me."

Clay looks into his father's eyes and sees there's no room for negotiation. He gets up, goes to the kitchen, and fills a glass with water from the tap. He returns to the table and says, "Criminals might be stupid, but whoever wrote that note isn't an idiot. They were very careful not to give any hints about their identity. They spelled *received* correctly. They used the word *further* correctly. And the plan is smart. It's pretty easy to station a lookout on a fixed location, but over fifty miles of river? Almost impossible to cover that without being detected."

"Yep," says Judd. "That's why I want to keep this between us. I don't even want to tell Deb. She'll get her hopes up. And you never know what could happen in a situation like this. We don't know what kind of conditions Teddy's being held in. We don't know how he's handling the stress. He and I are not young men. The physical demands could take a toll on him. I don't want to say anything to Deb except, *Here's your husband.*"

Clay sips his water, sets down the glass, and says, "Are you at least going to get this to the crime lab? See if they can find any prints on the rock, tape, or paper? Maybe ID the printer ink used?"

"What do you like better, *CSI* or *Law & Order*?"

"Am. I. Wrong?"

"Listen," says Judd. "Mike and Andy are my guys. They're good cops. But I can't take the chance that they'll talk. Even if it's just in their sleep. I don't want anyone else knowing about dropping that money into the river. I don't want anyone trying to be a hero. Or a thief. Besides, the forensic lab for Fillmore County is up in Rochester. They're always backed up. Wouldn't get any results before midnight anyway."

Clay leans back in his chair and says, "Why did you call me over here in the middle of the night if you were just going to shoot down all my ideas?"

"No one else I can trust," says Judd.

"Out of all the people in town, you trust *some soccer player*? How is that possible?"

"Yep. Some soccer player who's blood. Some soccer player who loves Teddy as much as I do."

Clay can't argue with that. "All right," he says. "Do you want my opinion on this?"

"I bet I already know what it is," says Judd. "You think Teddy faked his own kidnapping to milk me for forty-five grand."

Clay half laughs. He can't believe his father guessed correctly. He shakes his head and says, "Maybe Teddy got himself in a jam. I'm not saying it's a strong possibility. But you should dust the rock, the earring, and the note for prints and compare what we find to Teddy's fingerprints, which are all over his and Deb's place. If we find Teddy's prints on this stuff, we'll have to face the likelihood that Teddy's behind this. If we find someone else's prints, even if we can't identify them, we'll know odds are that this is legit."

Judd just stares at Clay and doesn't say a word.

"Why are you looking at me like that?" says Clay.

"That's a good idea," says Judd.

"Is it hard to believe I have a good idea?"

"Not if it's about kicking a ball into a net. But I didn't expect a good idea about investigating a crime."

"Well," says Clay. "I do watch TV."

Judd almost smiles. He stands, walks to a kitchen cabinet, and pulls down a bottle of Canadian Club. He brings that and two small glasses to the table and eyeball-pours two ounces for Clay and two for himself.

Judd lifts his glass. Clay hesitates, but does the same. Judd reaches across the table and clinks Clay's glass. "I don't want to consider the possibility that Teddy's behind his own kidnapping, but you're right. I'll dust for prints in the morning. Compare them to Teddy's. Now drink up. We need something to quiet our brains so we can get some sleep. Big day ahead."

Clay sips his whiskey. *What the hell is happening here?* he thinks. *What in the bloody hell?*

CHAPTER 17

Braedon wakes to his cell phone playing the Cranberries' "When You're Gone." It's Emily's favorite song, so he made it her ringtone. It's a FaceTime voice call, so he doesn't have to flick on the light. He tests his voice, hoping it doesn't sound like he just woke up, then takes the call.

"Hi, Emily. Aren't you in Scotland?"

"Yeah," says Emily. "Up early. What time is it there?"

Braedon looks at the clock on his phone. "Just after midnight."

"Oh, no. Sorry. I get the earlier/later thing mixed up all the time. I thought it was afternoon there. You should go back to sleep."

"I wasn't sleeping," lies Braedon, adjusting his pillow against his headboard so he can sit up. "Dad just had to go see my grandpa about something."

"What?" says Emily.

"Don't know. Probably something with my uncle Teddy. He still hasn't come home."

"I'm sorry. Is your grandad freaking out?"

"Not too bad. At least in front of me. But I can tell he's worried."

"Yeah," says Emily. "He must be. I wonder if what happened to your uncle will ever be on one of those true crime podcasts. It sounds like a good story. I mean, it's not good what happened, but it's the kind of story they would do."

"Yeah," says Braedon. "Maybe. Hey, how's Scotland?"

"Windy," says Emily. "And kind of cold for summer. And kind of like Ireland except we have to use different money here. We're in St. Andrews. There's loads of golfers everywhere. Like St. Andrews was the patron saint of golfing. My da wants to get on some famous golf course, but my ma said no way. She didn't go on a family vacation so he could take off and play all day by himself. They got in a big row about it and then my da went to have a pint by himself. My ma was going to switch flats while he was gone and not tell him where we went. You know, to teach him a lesson. But instead we had a late dinner and didn't tell him where we went for that. I heard him come back to the flat at around four in the morning. My ma's in sleeping with my sister, so I don't know what's going to happen when everyone wakes up."

"Sounds like no one's getting any sleep," says Braedon. "Right after Dad left, I got a bunch of texts from my friend, Daniel. He's got himself in a mess with some older boys."

"What kind of mess?"

"They gave him a real nice mountain bike."

"For free?" says Emily.

"Yeah," says Braedon. "Well, kind of. Because they expect something in return. Like a favor. But they didn't say what when they gave it to him. Then they saw him tonight watching a Little League game."

"What's that?"

"Baseball."

"Oh."

"Yeah," says Braedon. "And they told Daniel they want their favor now. Which is to nick a bunch of frozen pizzas from a truck when it's making a delivery to Value Foods."

"What's that?" says Emily.

"A supermarket."

"Oh. Makes sense."

"Yeah. And there's a bluff right behind the supermarket so he can throw the pizzas in a backpack and ride up a trail so he won't get caught."

"Is that why the boys gave Daniel the bike?"

"I guess. Except turns out they stole the bike and painted it a different color so people wouldn't know. But Dad figured it out. Daniel's going to turn it in to the police but the police aren't going to tell anyone it was him who did it so he doesn't get in trouble with those boys."

"Is Daniel going to do it? Is he going to nick the pizzas for them?" says Emily.

"He doesn't know. He's scared. He wants to just give the bike back and tell them he's not nicking anything, but he can't give it back because it has to be returned to its owner. Daniel sounds really worried, which he never is. So it's weird."

"What if," says Emily, "Daniel gave the bike back to the boys, then a couple days later, the police arrested them for having the stolen bike? Then Daniel wouldn't get in trouble with anyone, and the owner of the bike would get it back, and maybe the boys would go to jail or something, and not bother Daniel anymore."

"Whoa, Emily! That's a really good idea. I'll tell Dad in the morning. See what he says."

Braedon can practically hear Emily smiling on the other end of the phone. Neither says anything for a few seconds, then Emily says, "When are you coming to Galway to visit?"

"Don't know," says Braedon. "I want to come this summer but Dad says he has to get ready for his new coaching job. And with Teddy disappearing . . . Maybe Christmas." He hesitates, then adds, "I sure hope so. It'd be fun to see you."

"It would be fun," says Emily. "I wonder who's taller now."

"We'll have to measure," says Braedon. "Wait. Hold on. I hear someone coming through the front door." Braedon puts the phone down to dedicate both ears to listening. He recognizes his father's familiar gait, then picks up the phone. "It's Dad. Maybe he knows something about Teddy."

"Let me know, okay?"

"Sure."

"Hey," says Emily, "before you get off the phone. Think maybe you'll bring some euros?"

"Definitely," says Braedon.

"How much, do you think?"

"I don't know. I have about a hundred and fifty now. Maybe I'll have more by the time I visit."

"Whoa. How'd you get so much?"

"When we moved to America, we found a bunch of euros unpacking. Like a mess were in pockets in Dad's clothes. He said I could keep them for when we visited."

"I have fifty-seven euros. Want to take a train ride to Dublin and walk around there and eat lunch and maybe go to a play or something?"

Braedon thinks that going to Dublin with Emily—just the two of them without any adults—sounds like the most amazing adventure ever. "Whoa, Emily. You're full of good ideas. I definitely want to if Dad lets me. Oh! He's coming. I'll get back to you tomorrow. I mean today, your time."

"Okay, bye."

"Bye."

CHAPTER 18

Judd gave Braedon a fingerprint kit for his birthday, and after playing with it for a few days, Braedon stuck it on the upper shelf of his closet under boxes of board games. The next morning before breakfast, Clay asks if he and Grandpa can borrow it.

Braedon says, "Did someone break into Grandpa's house and you're trying to find out who did it?"

"No," says Clay. He doesn't want to tell Braedon about the earring and ransom note, so he just says, "We're going to dust some of Uncle Teddy's things so we can give his fingerprints to the police. That way they'll have them just in case."

Braedon buys Clay's excuse, even though, if he thought it through, he'd realize the police already have Teddy's fingerprints from his multiple stumbles onto the other side of the law. But most twelve-year-old boys don't stop to think things through. Instead of questioning the logic of his father's plan, Braedon pitches Emily's idea of Daniel giving the bike back to the boys and then, after a few days, the police arresting the boys and giving the bike back to its rightful owner.

Clay thinks about it as they're getting into the truck. "Are those boys giving Daniel a hard time?"

Braedon doesn't want to tell his father the whole story, but he's talked himself into a corner and doesn't see a way out. "Yeah," he says. "They want him to rob something for them."

"Steal," says Clay.

"What?"

"We say *steal* in America. They say *rob* back in Ireland."

"Oh. Well. Yeah, then. They want Daniel to steal something for them. They say he has to because they gave him the bike."

"And when did you discuss this with Emily?"

"Last night while you were at Grandpa's. She called me because she got the time difference wrong. But I was mostly up because I just got done texting with Daniel. That's how I know about them wanting him to r—steal something."

"Let me think about Emily's idea," said Clay. "Maybe I'll run it by the chief of police. I'll be sure to give Emily credit." Clay glances over at Braedon in the passenger seat for a reaction, but Braedon thinks Clay's being serious about giving Emily credit. "In the meantime, you should text Daniel and tell him not to steal something or do anything else for those boys until he hears back from you."

Braedon nods. Makes sense.

They stop first at Deb and Teddy's doublewide to pick up some of Teddy's things. This tracks with the excuse Clay gave Braedon about dusting them for Teddy's prints, which is the truth. Clay only lied by omission about also dusting the rock, ransom note, and Teddy's earring. Braedon's waiting in the car when Deb opens the door.

She leans against the doorjamb and manages a smile. "Come on in, Clay. I have some of Teddy's things all ready to go."

In the kitchen, Clay looks over what Deb has gathered for him and Judd. Teddy's toothbrush and hairbrush, a few tortoiseshell guitar picks, his fly-tying vise, and several puzzle pieces from one end of a puzzle that Teddy and Deb were working on together before Teddy disappeared.

"Thanks for putting all this together. We should find plenty of prints."

"Don't the police have Teddy's prints?" says Deb. She is smarter than a twelve-year-old boy.

"They should," says Clay, "but with all the digitizing of records and storing them in a central server, we don't want to take any chances." The excuse is completely fabricated, but it sounds good enough for Deb to stop asking questions. "How are you holding up?"

Deb cuts three pieces from a carrot cake she made last night. "Baking takes my mind off things," she says. She seals them in cling wrap and adds, "But to answer your question, I feel tired. And strangely calm. You know how it is when you spend so much time and energy worrying that something bad will happen, but when it actually does happen, it somehow isn't as bad as the worrying?"

"Like when you're a kid," says Clay, "worrying about getting a shot at the doctor is ten times worse than actually getting the shot."

"Kind of," says Deb. "It's more about control, I think. When Teddy wasn't in any trouble, when he was home safe and sound,

I was constantly thinking about what I could do to keep it that way. I cooked dinners he loved. We watched a lot of TV together. I even found a way to love watching sports the way he does. I thought he might watch less sports as he aged. That his interest would wane. But just the opposite happened. Especially lately. I've had to find a way to share that with him. I figured out if I read about the players to learn their personal stories, what they've overcome and things like that, then I have something to cheer for. I watch so much with him. And he loves it."

Deb puts the three wrapped pieces of cake on a paper plate and secures them all together with a second layer of cling wrap. She hands it to Clay and says, "For you, Braedon, and Judd."

"Thank you."

Deb carries the knife over to the sink and, with her back to Clay, says, "You know, I had this constant hum of anxiety about doing everything I could to keep Teddy out of trouble. Even in my sleep I felt it. But now there's nothing I can do. I guess it's more like when you're a caregiver to a terminally ill person. When they finally die, it's terrible. But it's also a relief because your responsibility to them is gone forever. There's some guilt that comes along with it. And a whole lot of sadness. But whatever has happened or is happening with Teddy, it's out of my hands. I feel both relieved and so damn guilty. So guilty about the relief." She turns around to face Clay. "God, I hope he's okay. But that's all I can do. Hope."

Braedon's down in Judd's basement playing *FIFA* on the PS5 Judd bought for his grandson's visits. Judd and Clay are upstairs and have just discovered that there are no fingerprints on the envelope, letter, tape, or earring. No fingerprints at all. Which means someone took the time to wipe them off.

"That's inconclusive," says Judd. "Best to assume the note is legit. The bank's going to call when the cash is ready. I used to have a bear canister around here somewhere but I think I got rid of it. My boundary waters days are over."

"I'll run up to Rochester and get one."

"Appreciate it," says Judd. "This morning I woke up dreaming about Teddy. He just walked up to me looking like he wanted to apologize, and I gave him a big hug. It felt so damn real, you know? One of those kind of dreams you're sorry to wake up from."

Clay looks at his father. It's the most introspective thing he has ever heard come out of Judd's mouth. And it wasn't all that introspective. But it gives him a glimpse into a man he doesn't know. Judd's not a hugger in real life, but apparently he is in his dreams. "Are you glad you had that dream?" says Clay. "Or did it feel like the rug getting yanked out from under you?"

"No," says Judd. "I'm glad I had the dream. Better to see Teddy in my sleep than not at all."

Both men feel something strange. An unfamiliar air. It's cooperation. The change is not touchy-feely. It's not like two old friends hit a bump and now they're back to being best pals. In fact, the feeling is so unfamiliar between father and son, they hardly recognize what's happening. It is, in reality and at least for the moment, a thaw. But all they know is that something feels different. And different doesn't necessarily mean better. What they feel is an absence. An absence of animosity. An animosity that's been between them from Clay's earliest memories. And for Judd, an animosity that came home from the hospital with Clay bundled in his rear-facing car seat as Pam sat in back with him. Taking home her baby for the first time. Along with her cancer diagnosis.

"Forty-five thousand dollars is a lot of money," says Clay. "You sure you want to do this?"

"You got any other ideas?" says Judd. His tone is earnest, not challenging.

"A couple," says Clay. "One is we don't put money in the canister. We booby-trap it. The kidnapper will either open it on the spot to check the contents or take it to another location to open it. Either way, when they do open it, it will trigger a stun grenade or noxious gas or even pepper spray. Something that disables the kidnapper long enough for us to get there and take them into custody."

"You know how to do something like that?"

Clay hesitates. "No. Of course not. Maybe we should bring Zoey into it. Neither of us has the authority to pepper bomb or zip-tie or—"

"You think the police do?" says Judd. "They'd get in a hell of a lot more trouble than we would. Plus a good criminal defense attorney would have a field day with a booby-trapped canister. What if a kid fishes it out of there? Or just an innocent bystander who happens to be on the river? Could lead to lawsuits against you and me. And if we involve Zoey, lawsuits against the Riverwood Police Department and maybe even the city. And worst of all, whoever took Teddy will likely walk free."

"You think we'd get sued?"

"This is America," says Judd. "We'd definitely get sued. Even if we catch the right person. Clay, I like your thinking on this, but I'd rather stick with my plan. The question we have to ask ourselves is: Why would someone kidnap Teddy?"

"I agree," says Clay. "Why Teddy?"

"The answer that keeps popping into my head is the kidnapper has a grudge against me. Someone who's blaming me for their problems. That happens to cops. Maybe the kidnapper is a person I arrested or the kid of a person I sent to prison. Someone who missed out on a chunk of their life or grew up without their daddy because mean old Judd Hawkins did his job. This feels like payback to me. And Teddy's not exactly difficult prey. Good-natured and trusting and tries to get along with everyone. It'd be easy to lure him into a trap.

"My guess is the kidnapper is trying to even things out, and forty-five grand of my retirement savings will do the trick. Legal tender for my beloved brother. That's why I want to play this one straight up. Cash for Teddy. If we catch 'em after, great. If we don't, we'll still have Teddy."

Clay pauses to check in with himself. Does he agree with Judd or is he just not wanting to rock the boat during their unofficial ceasefire? He decides Judd's reasoning is solid. This isn't a military mission. Some lowlife nabbed Teddy and is trying to profit from it. Disabling or injuring that person might lead to all sorts of problems. One of them Judd didn't even mention. The kidnapper could be fatally injured by a booby-trapped canister, especially if they open it on the bank of the river. The chance of drowning is real. If that happened, they may never find Teddy.

"Meet you back here at ten o'clock tonight?" says Clay. "That'll give us plenty of time to pack the money into the canister and get to the bridge."

"Sorry, Clay. I'm flying solo tonight."

"You think that's a good idea?" says Clay.

"I do," says Judd. "That's why I said it."

Clay nods. "Okay," he says. "I'll drop off the bear canister then leave you to it."

CHAPTER 19

Clay has no intention of leaving Judd to it. But he does leave Braedon with Judd then makes the half-hour drive up to Rochester. He buys the bear canister at a sporting goods store, then goes to a pet store and buys a GPS dog collar. It isn't cheap, but it has an excellent battery life, is waterproof, and provides live GPS tracking so even if the kidnappers miss the canister, Clay can track it all the way to the Mississippi River and down to New Orleans if need be to retrieve Judd's forty-five thousand dollars.

The bear canister is translucent blue like a five-gallon water bottle, with a big black lid that screws onto one end. Clay fashions a false inner end cap for the lid out of black sheet plastic. He removes the GPS component from the dog collar, tapes it inside the lid, then covers it with the sheet plastic.

He runs a few more errands up in Rochester, then returns to Riverwood and takes Braedon out for pizza.

"You sure you want to sleep at Daniel's tonight?" says Clay, sprinkling his slice with red pepper flakes. "Sue and Carol are happy to have you."

"Dad," says Braedon, unable to stifle an eye roll. "Why would I want to stay with two old ladies when I can stay at Daniel's? He has an Xbox. We're going to play *Halo* all night. They don't make *Halo* for PlayStation. It's going to be epic."

"Just checking. And you have to promise me you'll stay in tonight. No matter what. I don't want you getting mixed up with those boys who stole the bike. They're trouble. And Daniel needs to give the bike back to them during the day in a public place. Or he can just lock it to a bike rack, and the police can find it that way. The boys' less-than-professional paint job on that thing is more than a little suspicious."

"Yeah . . ." says Braedon. "But did you ask the police about Emily's plan?"

"I did." Clay can see that this is important to Braedon. Maybe more than important. The boy's childhood friendship with Emily might be morphing into something more adolescent. "The police like Emily's idea. So that's also a possibility. Daniel could give the bike back to them, and a few days later, the police will bust them for it. But not tonight."

"Awesome," says Braedon. "Emily's going to be psyched. And Daniel and I won't go out. I promise."

"If you promise," says Clay, "then that's good enough for me."

Clay drops Braedon at Daniel's. His parents are both software engineers and work up in Rochester. You can buy a hell of a house in Riverwood on the salary of two software engineers, and they did. He leaves the boys as they play *Halo* on an eighty-inch screen in a family room big enough for several families.

He drops the canister off at Judd's and makes no mention of the tracker. Clay guesses his father didn't suggest using a tracker because he wants to keep the plan as clean as possible. And that's why Clay doesn't tell Judd what he's done. Play it straight. Keep it simple.

Clay has some time to kill, so he heads over to Knut's Sports Bar and finds a table in back near the jukebox and pool table. It's busy for a Monday night, thanks to a meat raffle being held to raise money for the local parks and rec department. He watches a bar employee walking around with a roll of tickets and a wad of cash, making sales and giving change.

Clay scans the place to see if there's anyone who looks like they're dressed for night fishing but has stopped by the bar first for some liquid courage. No such luck. Clay does, however, see people he knows. Wags Becker, Steph's estranged husband, the auto mechanic and denier of stealing catalytic converters, stands at the bar with a few friends. One is Robert Hensel, owner of the scrapyard, bully of young Clay. They're speaking in loud bar voices. Clay can't make out the words, but he can isolate Wags and Robert in the din. They don't look like they're planning on wading into a river in a few hours, but that doesn't mean they won't be. If Teddy was stealing catalytic converters for either or both of them, they had plenty of opportunity to nab Teddy.

Wags has a motive. He's losing Steph's income and the lifestyle it provided him. Forty-five thousand dollars would go a long way toward giving Wags a comfortable transition into the single life. Forty-five thousand dollars that won't show up in his bank account or on his payroll statements. Forty-five thousand dollars that would be free and clear of a divorce agreement or court-ordered settlement.

Clay also spots Steph gathered with her employees up toward the front window, looking red and blue in the light of a Hamm's Beer neon sign. She wears a sleeveless blouse and old jeans and from this distance, Clay can see the girl he dated in high school. He watches Steph to see if she's stealing glimpses of Wags. Divorce in a small town. Not a lot of space for the combatants to get away from each other. But Steph doesn't look over at her soon-to-be ex-husband. She does, however, make eye contact with another familiar face sitting on the opposite side of the bar.

Eli Hensel, whom Clay met at the scrapyard, sits with a few other twentysomethings. The want-to-be re-teller of *Oliver Twist* throws a wry smile in Steph's direction. Clay is pretty sure he's the only one in Knut's who's noticed the cross-bar connection. Steph and Eli. She's forty-two. He's twenty-two. *Good for her,* thinks Clay. Eli's not a bad stepping stone out of her marriage. Smart. Interesting. Ambitious. And good for Eli. He's not going to let twenty years get in the way of him and a beautiful, accomplished woman.

And then, as if sensing Clay's observation, Steph looks over and offers Clay a slight smile and wave. He returns both. But Steph doesn't walk over to say hello.

Deb's cousin, Ash, chats up a woman who looks half his age. He wears a cherry-red polo shirt, collar popped, and paper-white pants. He's drinking a cocktail of some sort, and the woman, or maybe she's a girl, drinks what looks like a Long Island iced tea in a big snifter. Ash is probably asking if she wants to come up to the house to see the horses and llamas. Maybe he'd better wait until she finishes her fishbowl of alcohol.

Everything else happening in Knut's looks normal. The drink of choice by most is beer. Clay sees a handful of people downing shots, most likely Jägermeister or Fireball. The Minnesota Twins are on all the TVs except for one that shows a Stanley Cup finals game. The Minnesota Wild are not in it, and few people seem to be paying attention. Some patrons are eating pizzas that were frozen a few minutes ago. That and bags of chips are all Knut's has to offer food-wise.

Clay's about to get up and go to the bar to order a beer when a server approaches with a pink drink.

"Hello," says the server. "This is for you." She sets the glass down on his table.

"What is it?" says Clay.

"A Shirley Temple," says the server. "Your secret admirer has sent you one."

"May I please have a Grain Belt to go along with it?"

"You certainly may. Be right back." The server heads toward the bar.

Clay feels like an idiot sitting in Knut's with a Shirley Temple. He doesn't like the attention it might draw. He considers carrying it into the men's room to dump it, but if Steph sent it, he doesn't want to hurt her feelings. He looks over to see if she's watching him for a reaction, but she appears to be deep in conversation with her colleagues.

"If you use the straw, you won't get a pink mustache."

He looks to his right. Zoey Jensen stands near the jukebox.

Out of uniform and wearing a baby-blue Minnesota Twins T-shirt and jeans. Her dark hair, freed from its braid, falls down well past her shoulders. She smiles. There must be a fluorescent light somewhere because her teeth glow white.

"I'm not afraid of getting a pink mustache," says Clay. "But thank you. And have a seat."

Zoey pulls up a chair and sits opposite Clay, blocking his view of Steph. "The Shirley Temple is a symbol of my wholesome intentions for our friendship. We are still friends, right?"

"Of course," says Clay. "Some might say besties."

"Let's not get carried away," says Zoey. "So let me ask you, friend. What's a guy like you doing at a meat raffle like this? Out all on your lonesome on a Monday night?"

"Braedon's at a sleepover. So why not?"

"Because you're not a sit-in-a-bar kind of guy," says Zoey.

"Yes, I am. I've sat in lots of bars."

"People who sit in lots of bars usually sit at *the* bar. They don't find the most out-of-the-way table and press their back against a wall to observe the shenanigans. If I didn't know better, I'd say you're staking out the place."

"If I am," says Clay, "I'm not doing a very good job. I didn't see you coming."

"That's true. You're not doing a very good job because I'm also staking out the place. Thought maybe I'd pick up on something that might lead to your uncle's whereabouts."

The front door opens, and in walk Officers Mike Wahlquist and Andy Kimmich, in uniform, guns in holsters, smiles on faces.

"Uh-oh. The entire Riverwood police force is here. Is this

some kind of three-cop operation? Mike and Andy draw the attention, you observe reactions from the clientele?"

Zoey turns around to see what Clay sees. When she turns back toward him, Clay can see on Zoey's face that this is not a three-cop operation.

Zoey says, "Mind if I sit next to you, friend?"

Without waiting for Clay's response, Zoey scooches her chair around the table so she's sitting next to him. Like a couple might do. She keeps her eyes on her underlings and says, "I sent a K-9 team out to Teddy and Deb's this afternoon. They didn't detect any scents that walked off the property."

"Do you think Teddy was picked up in a vehicle?"

"Maybe," says Zoey. "Or maybe he walked down to the river through Deb's cousin's property. What's his name?"

"Ash. Ash Solbakken."

"Right. He's hit on me a few times. Interesting sense of fashion." Zoey helps herself to a sip of Clay's Shirley Temple, then adds, "The dogs tracked Teddy's scent down to the river on Ash's property, but they lost it at the river. Of course there were several scent trails leading down there. He's walked down there a million times. But if Teddy's intent was to disappear, that would be a good way to do it."

With Zoey sitting next to him, practically touching her shoulder to his, Clay catches Steph looking their way. This time she's not smiling. Wags has also spotted them. He's far from smiling, seeing Clay sit next to the chief of police the day after Clay accused Wags of stealing catalytic converters. But the real show is watching Andy and Mike buy a wad of meat raffle tickets, maybe a few hundred dollars' worth, and handing them out to bar-goers and making a big deal of it like they're a couple of Santa Clauses.

"Are they on duty or did they just get off?" says Clay.

"They're on duty until midnight," says Zoey. "Which begs the question: What the hell are they doing? It's nine o'clock." She sighs. "It's hard to find good help these days."

The bartender hands Officers Wahlquist and Kimmich bottles of Coke. Wahlquist slaps a bill on the counter. The bartender thanks him with praying hands and a slight bow.

"I have a guess," says Clay. "Wahlquist told me he's running for mayor this fall. Said he's had it with the city council and they need to be put in their place."

"So he's buying votes with meat raffle tickets?"

"Welcome to Riverwood," says Clay. "He hasn't announced or filed his candidacy yet. Says he's going to make the big reveal at the Fourth of July parade. So I suppose what he's doing isn't illegal. Just a good old boy trying to help his fellow citizens win some meat."

"He shouldn't be doing that while he's on duty," says Zoey. "I don't mind him and Mike dropping in for a Coke. It's solid community police work. But he shouldn't be campaigning or bribing the good citizens of Riverwood for their votes."

"You want to slip out of here before they realize you're watching them?"

"Aren't you supposed to buy me a drink first? Brag about your playing days in Europe? Try to impress me? Come on. I want to be wooed. Swept off my feet."

"Oh," says Clay. "Sorry, I didn't mean slip out together. I have plans." Clay has to be careful with Zoey. Her bullshit detector is cranked up to ten. "My dad and I are going to hit a few other bars in the county to see if we can learn anything new about Teddy."

"Hmm," says Zoey. "Judd probably wouldn't want me to tag along." She sighs. "On the other hand, we're going to have to break it to him sooner or later. Our friendship, that is. Maybe the three of us could talk it out while we're on the road between here and St. Charles. Lot of miles to cover. And tonight's as good a time as any. I can't live with our friendship in the closet anymore."

Clay sees a playful smile in Zoey's eyes. He doesn't want to admit to himself how attractive he finds her but he can't help it. Lucky for Clay, he's trained in being wary of attractive women. Especially one who comes on strong. Not being wary is how professional athletes can get in big trouble.

"Let me break it to my dad when it's just him and me," says Clay. He almost wonders why he's playing along, but he knows why. He likes Zoey Jensen. And that's okay. Especially now that he's pretty sure Steph has plucked herself a boyfriend from the just-old-enough-to-drink pile. What wouldn't be okay is if Clay rushed into something with Zoey. Small town. Big stakes. He has to take things slowly.

"All right," says Zoey. "Tell Judd yourself. But until then, let's sit here and wait for these two idiots to realize their boss is watching them."

CHAPTER 20

Clay sits in his F-150 on the road outside his father's house. He looks through a pair of binoculars and into the kitchen window. The bear canister sits on the kitchen table. Judd feeds bundled bills into its open mouth. He does not inspect the inside of the lid. His mind is on Teddy. Nothing but Teddy. That's why Clay is going to follow him to the drop spot to ensure that Judd, in his single-mindedness, doesn't do anything stupid.

Judd looks at his watch. Clay lowers the binoculars and checks the time on his dash. He starts his truck and throws it in reverse. Judd is a seasoned cop—Clay will have to tail him from some distance. Shouldn't be a problem since Clay knows exactly where his father is headed.

"This is the greatest movie in the history of movies," says Daniel. The Xbox is off and now the eighty-inch TV screen shows *Talladega Nights*. It's the part where Will Ferrell thinks he's on fire but he's not and runs around the racetrack stripping off his clothes.

"It is the greatest movie ever," says Braedon. "I am going to memorize every line. '*Chip, I'm gonna come at you like a spider monkey.*'"

Daniel laughs. "'*I'm just a big hairy American winning machine. If you ain't first, you're last.*'"

They've eaten a whole bag of chips, are halfway through a two-liter bottle of A&W Root Beer, and a quarter way through a package of Oreo Double Stuf cookies. Sleeping bags are spread on opposite sides of a humongous sectional, and the room smells like twelve-year-old boy.

"Think you could memorize the whole thing, bro?" says Daniel.

"Pretty sure," says Braedon. "But I'll have to do it during the summer, otherwise my head will be filled with movie lines and I'll fail all my classes."

"Bet you five bucks you can't do it before school starts," says Daniel.

"You're on."

Daniel's phone lights up. He looks down at the screen and says, "Shit, bro."

"What?"

"Graham Collins is calling."

"Who's Graham Collins?"

"He's one of the guys who gave me the stolen bike. Shit, shit, shit."

"Don't answer it."

"I have to," says Daniel. "They told me if I didn't, they'd come to the house." The air seems to deflate out of him as he takes the call and puts it on speaker. "Hi, Graham."

"Little man," says Graham. "We need your services tonight."

"I'm in bed," says Daniel. "I'm not allowed to go out after nine o'clock."

"Yeah, that's your problem," says Graham. "We need you to start a fire for us."

"What?" says Daniel. He looks over at Braedon, who shakes his head so hard it might pop off his neck.

"There's some guys from Chatfield who are pissed and out looking for us. They're driving a beat-to-shit Dodge Ram, and we need you to bring us some fire."

"What? How am I supposed to bring fire? Like in a torch or something?"

"Not with a torch, you idiot. That would draw too much attention. Put some gas in a bottle, find an old rag, and matches or a lighter."

"Like gas that goes in a car?" says Daniel.

Braedon watches his friend's eyes dart back and forth in a pale, damp face.

"No, we want you to fart in a bottle. Yes, the kind of gas that goes in a car! Now quit screwing around. We'll meet you in the parking lot behind the community center."

Now Braedon is on his feet, standing on the sectional, shaking his head and waving his arms and mouthing *No way.*

Daniel says, "I'm giving the bike back. I don't want it. I can't help you guys. I'm only twelve."

"Dude," says Graham. "You already took the bike. No give-backs. So bring us what we asked for, or we're lighting your house on fire."

The call ends, and Daniel looks up at the ceiling. "What am I going to do?"

"You have to call the police," says Braedon. "Or at least tell your parents."

"No," says Daniel. "They'll kill me."

"Who will kill you?"

"Everyone. Graham and those guys. My parents. And the police."

"No they won't," says Braedon. "The police already know about the stolen bike. They won't be mad."

"If the police get into this, Graham will know it was me. And you don't have to do anything. Just stay here. I can ride my bike down there, give them the stuff, and be back in half an hour. We have gas in the garage. And a bunch of empty bottles in the recycling bin. I'll do this one thing for them and then I'll be done."

Braedon shakes his head. "It's called a Molotov cocktail."

"What is?"

"The stuff they want you to bring. It's called a Molotov cocktail. You fill the bottle with gas, shove the rag in the top, then light the rag on fire. When you throw it, the glass breaks when the bottle lands and gas goes everywhere and catches on fire. I've heard people talk about them in Ireland. Not in the part I lived in, but in Northern Ireland, people burned stuff all the time with Molotov cocktails during the Troubles."

"I don't know what you're talking about," says Daniel. "But I have to go."

"Don't," says Braedon. "If you get caught with a bottle and gas, you're the one who will get in trouble. Graham and those guys won't."

Daniel pulls on his sweatshirt and slips into his shoes. "If my parents come downstairs, tell them I'm in the bathroom. And tell them I have diarrhea or something so they don't expect me to come out soon."

"Dude," says Braedon. "You can't leave me here alone."

"Why not?"

"It's weird," says Braedon. "And kind of creepy."

"Then come with me," says Daniel. He pushes his hair out of his eyes and hitches up his jeans. "You can ride my brother's bike. I'm going upstairs to get one of those reusable shopping bags. Then we can sneak out the back door down here."

Moen's Bridge is a canoe landing on the Root River between the towns of Chatfield and Lanesboro. Judd parks his Tahoe on County Road 21 on a pull-out just before the bridge. It's dead quiet and dead dark at 11:55 PM.

Clay parks three hundred yards behind Judd. He checks the clock on his dash. Six more minutes. He checks his phone. The signal from the tracking device comes through clearly. Clay rolls down his window. The frogs and crickets are making a racket. Clay knows his father. He'll do this by the book. By the book and to the minute. He waits a little longer and then raises the binoculars to his eyes.

It's not long before Judd exits the Tahoe carrying the bear canister loaded with forty-five thousand dollars. He walks to the edge of the bridge and looks down at the Root River. Clay observes his father checking his watch one more time. Then he sees a shadow approaching Judd from behind.

CHAPTER 21

"Where are they?" says Daniel.

"Must be busy with something else," says Braedon. "Let's get out of here."

They stand still, straddling their bikes, a block away from Riverwood's community center. Braedon convinced Daniel to take his old bike, not the stolen one given to him by Graham and the other two boys. Taking that bike would just cement Daniel's indebtedness. And if they get in any kind of official trouble, riding a stolen bike won't help matters. Braedon straddles Daniel's little brother's bike. It's too small for him and, if there's some kind of bike sprint to get away from who-knows-what, he'll be the slowest wildebeest in the pack.

Braedon feels the odd sensation of dread juxtaposed with excitement. He promised his father he wouldn't go out tonight. Even if he hadn't, he has enough common sense to know this is a terrible idea, accompanying Daniel to deliver the ingredients of a Molotov cocktail. If they get caught, Braedon could get kicked out of Dorset-Cornwall. And then there's the possibility of juvenile detention, which Braedon knows about from hearing Grandpa Judd talk about it. How he hated arresting kids who might get sent there because, even though Grandpa Judd is a law-and-order kind of guy, sending a criminal kid to live with a bunch of other criminal kids just gives them the connections to become criminal adults.

But Braedon also feels the thrill of being out at midnight. When every other kid his age is probably asleep or watching TV in the safety and comfort of home, he's getting a whiff of independence and its risk/reward possibilities. He's not being told what life is in a classroom or around the dinner table. He's experiencing it firsthand. And at twelve years old, the difference between the two is gargantuan.

"Shit," says Daniel, looking down at his phone. "They want us to torch a truck."

"What?" says Braedon.

"A red pickup truck in the lot. They want me to do what you said. Make that cocktail thing, light it on fire, and toss it into a red pickup truck. Shit. I'm cooked."

"Forget it, Daniel. We're not doing it. Let's just get the hell back to your house."

"No," says Daniel. "I have to get this over with. You stay here. I'll pedal up, light the thing and toss it in, and we ride for our lives."

Braedon considers offering to go with Daniel, but he's proved his friendship enough just by biking into town with him. Instead he says, "Be careful. Don't light yourself on fire."

"I won't." Daniel holds out his fist, and Braedon bumps it.

Daniel reaches down to the bike's water bottle holder. The plastic water bottle is gone, replaced by an empty Dad's Root Beer bottle made of dark brown glass. It's filled with gas from the red plastic gas can in Daniel's garage, the original cap twisted back on. Daniel lifts the bottle, unscrews the cap, then removes a rag from his front pocket. That, too, came from the garage, where his father keeps a box of old rags under the workbench. He stuffs one end of the rag into the bottle, removes a barbecue grill lighter from his back pocket, and says, "Here goes."

"Won't be necessary," says a voice. It's Graham, on his bike, the other two boys behind him.

Braedon wants to take off but knows he can't outrun them. Even if he wasn't on a too-small bike, Graham and the other guys are three years older and a whole lot bigger. They look like adults with kid faces. This is the first time Braedon has seen them up close. They're not as scary as he thought they'd be. They appear awkward and maybe a bit confused. Nervous. Braedon supposes a person can only be so intimidating on a bicycle. Graham and his buddies aren't even old enough to have driver's licenses yet.

"Okay," says Daniel. "That's cool."

"It was a test," says Graham. "A loyalty test. And you passed. Although you shouldn't have brought him with you." Graham points his chin at Braedon.

"He's sleeping over at my house," says Daniel. "I had to."

"Who are you?" says Graham.

"Daniel's friend," says Braedon.

"I know that," says Graham. "But who are you? How come I don't know who you are?"

"Oh," says Braedon. "I just moved here a few months ago."

Graham doesn't respond. They hear a dog bark in the distance, and the low rumble of a truck on Main Street. The other two boys remain behind Graham, their faces in and out of shadows made by a street light and recently leafed-out oak trees.

"You can have this if you want it," says Daniel, holding the Molotov cocktail out toward Graham. The scent of gas has permeated the rag, an olfactory reminder of the little firebomb's potential.

Graham shakes his head. "Hold on to it. You guys are coming with us."

"Uhh . . ." Braedon hears himself say. "I can't. I'm already in huge trouble."

"You don't know what huge trouble is," says Graham. "But you're going to find out if you don't do what we tell you."

"My parents are going to know we're gone," says Daniel. "And they'll call the police."

"This won't take long," says Graham. "We just need your help hiding something."

"What?"

"None of your business."

"Why do you need us?" says Braedon. "Why can't you hide it yourself?"

"We don't need you," says Graham. "Just him," he adds, eying Daniel. "He's the only one small enough to fit through the pipe. And quit asking questions. It's not like you have a choice."

"No," says Braedon. "We do have a choice." He hears his voice quiver and hopes they don't notice. "And we choose not to go with you."

Graham laughs. "You are so dead, kid."

Braedon reaches over with both hands and grabs the Molotov cocktail and lighter out of Daniel's hands. He pulls the trigger on the long lighter, and a flame emerges on the other end. "I'm going to light this and throw it. And pretty soon a whole bunch of people will come over to check it out. You can either stick around and I'll throw it at you, or you can get the hell out of here."

Graham reaches behind his back. When his hand returns, it's holding a pistol. "What did you say you were going to do?"

Braedon catches the light reflect off the gun's short barrel. Then hears a click, and a bright flash blinds him.

CHAPTER 22

"Dad?" Clay places a hand on Judd's shoulder. "Dad, are you awake?"

Judd opens his eyes and sees a star-filled sky. A single mayfly hovers a few feet above his face, and he feels a throbbing pain on the back of his head. The crickets and frogs are in a shouting match, but Judd can hear trout taking bugs off the river's surface. He takes an inventory of his body, wiggling his fingers and toes, slightly bending his knees and elbows. Other than his hurting head, Judd seems to be all right.

"What happened?" says Judd.

"Give yourself a minute," says Clay. "See if you can sit up."

Judd takes a couple of deep breaths, then lifts his body into a sitting position. His head hurts like hell. He touches the back of it but feels no blood. He looks around to confirm that he's still on Moen's Bridge.

"What the hell?" says Judd. "Where's the canister?"

"How's your vision?" says Clay.

"I can see the canister is gone. Did I drop it in the river? And why are you here?"

Clay sits on the ground. "I followed you."

"Why?"

"I didn't want you coming out here alone."

"I don't need a babysitter," says Judd.

"Apparently, you do."

Judd turns his head to the left and then the right to test his neck's range of motion. "Fair enough."

"I was three hundred yards back, watching you through binoculars. You were about to drop the canister into the river, when someone snuck up behind you and bopped you on the head. I gunned it to the bridge, but the person took off in a sprint. I jumped out of my truck and ran to you."

"When was this?"

"About forty-five minutes ago. I didn't want to leave you and no one's driven by yet. I kept checking your pulse. Maybe you just needed a nap."

Judd looks around. "Then where the hell is your truck?"

Clay sighs. "There was another guy I didn't know about. He jumped into my truck and peeled out of here. I left my keys in the cupholder."

Judd looks down at the ground and then up at the sky. "Have you called for help?"

"My phone was in the other cupholder."

Judd reaches into his pocket.

"Don't bother," says Clay. "They took your phone. And your keys."

"Well," says Judd, "we'd better start moving."

"Town's closest," says Clay.

"I don't want anyone asking questions. I know it's a hike, but let's head to my place."

They've been walking the shoulder of County Road 21 for almost an hour and have thirty minutes more to go.

"I, uh . . ." starts Judd. "I screwed up. I should have considered the possibility I was being set up. Of being ambushed. I mean, what kind of idiot hangs out in a river waiting for forty-five thousand dollars to float by? I didn't think that through very well." The gravel crunches under their feet. Judd feels the back of his head and says, "You were right. I'm too close to this. I can't think straight when it comes to Teddy. Hopefully, the kidnappers were just sewing up loose ends by knocking me on the head. They have their forty-five grand. Now they can return Teddy to us."

"I put a tracker in the canister," says Clay.

Judd stops. Clay takes another step, then also stops. He turns around and looks at his father. "Are you okay? Do you need to rest?"

"You put a tracker in the canister?" says Judd. "It was clear plastic. How come I didn't see it?"

"I hid it in the lid behind some sheet plastic. The tracker

has a triaxial accelerometer, GPS, Bt5, LTE-M, and a ten-day battery. We'll find it."

Judd stares at Clay and doesn't say a word.

"If you didn't see it, I bet the kidnappers won't see it either," says Clay. "I can't track it without my phone, but we can download the app onto another device. We'll be able to locate it and—Why are you looking at me like that?"

"I had the strangest feeling earlier today," says Judd. "You know, when you came over after the ransom note was delivered through my window. You asked a lot of questions and made a few suggestions."

"Yeah . . ." says Clay. "What about it?"

"You seem quite current on your investigative techniques."

"Are you talking about the dog-collar tracker? It's obvious. Anyone would have thought of that."

"It's not just the tracker," says Judd. He looks at Clay for a good ten seconds before he adds, "Listen, you and I have our differences. Always have. But I've known you since you entered this world. I know your expressions. What each little eye movement and facial tic means. I know your tells."

"Are you okay, Dad? Maybe that hit on the head—"

"My head's just fine," says Judd. "Earlier today you talked about running the ransom note through the Message Switch System using Sprout Social on Teddy's friends."

"So?" says Clay. The stars and moon emit enough light for Clay and Judd to see each other's faces. Clay catches a glint in his father's eye. "What's going on here?"

"My God," says Judd. He stares at Clay dumfounded. Lips

parted. Brows hanging heavy over his eyes. "Why didn't you tell me?"

"Tell you how to investigate a missing person? I didn't think I had to. You're supposed to—"

"You know," says Judd, "one thing has never made sense to me. Why would West Point recruit a player good enough to play European soccer? They must have known you'd leave the army as soon as you served your five years. Why make that investment in you if you were going to just take off?"

"They recruited me because they wanted a good soccer team."

Judd shakes his head. "No, Clay. They didn't. Tell me the truth. Were you double-timing it over there?"

"Double-timing it?"

"Soccer player by day. CIA by night?"

Clay hesitates, then says, "Dad, let's get you to the hospital."

"You're CIA," says Judd. He looks calm. Almost happy. Almost thrilled, even. "Or you're working for one of the other intelligence agencies. You didn't walk away from your country. Professional soccer was your cover." Judd smiles. Smiles at his son in a way Clay hasn't seen since he told Judd he was headed to West Point. "What were you really doing over in Europe? Eyes-and-ears kind of stuff? Recruiting informants?"

Clay wants to deny it. Knows he should deny it. But denying it would only make the search for Teddy worse. More difficult. Less focused. And for all of Judd's faults, Clay knows his father can be trusted. He is, despite their fractured relationship, a man of honor and a patriot. A man who tries to do the right thing.

He makes eye contact with Judd, and calm blankets the two of them. "I was in Warsaw playing a friendly," says Clay. "Galway against Legia. And my cover was blown. That's why I had to rush back home. And it's why I'm not coaching in Europe or MLS or at a university. Riverwood, Minnesota, and Dorset-Cornwall is as far from the spotlight as I can get."

"I'll be," says Judd. "I was right."

"And you have to keep this to yourself," says Clay. "It's a matter of national security."

Judd looks like he's going to cry. Cry tears of happiness. "I'm so proud of you, Clay. Just so damn proud." Judd sticks out his hand to shake Clay's.

Clay steps back.

"What's the matter?" says Judd. "Can't a father congratulate his son?"

"You have judged me on what I do, not who I am, ever since I was a little kid. You didn't like me because I played soccer. You gave me no credit for working my ass off to be an elite player. Same with violin and same with academics. I didn't want to hunt so I wasn't a real boy. I didn't want to sit in a boat so I wasn't a real fisherman. I read Dostoyevsky instead of *Sports Illustrated* so I wasn't a son worth paying attention to. I went to West Point and all of a sudden, I was the golden boy. I told you I quit the army to play professional soccer and I was back to persona non grata. Now you find out I never stopped serving my country and I'm the greatest son a father could ever ask for."

Clay looks hard at his father and adds, "Let me know when you decide to care about me as a person instead of only caring about what I do or don't do. And not one word about this to anyone, including Braedon. He has no idea." Clay turns and walks away.

Judd walks after him. He feels proud of his son and ashamed of himself because he knows Clay has spoken the truth. Both about continuing to work for his country while in Europe, and about Judd judging Clay for what he does, not who he is. He swallows. Swallows the hard truth that he's been in the wrong for decades. He can't just apologize for forty-two years of bad fatherhood and make everything okay. Regaining Clay's trust will take some time. Maybe a lot of time. He'll have to earn it step by step.

"Hey," says Judd, "I was thinking about something you suggested earlier, and you're right. We should bring Zoey Jensen in on the kidnapping."

Clay keeps walking but says, "You want to bring in Zoey? That's a big change."

"I trained her for three months," says Judd. "She's a bit of an odd duck, but she's good police. She's not as close to the case as you and I are."

"You don't have to sell me," says Clay. "I'm all for bringing Zoey in."

A pair of headlights crests a swell in the road. Judd stands on the yellow dotted line and waves down the vehicle. It appears to be a sedan, but Judd and Clay can see two headlights and not much else. The car stops twenty feet short of them, and they hear a window roll down.

"Judd?" says a voice.

"Mike?" says Judd. "Is that you?"

Mike Wahlquist leaves the engine running and gets out of the car. He approaches Clay and Judd still wearing his Riverwood police uniform. "What the hell are you two doing out here?"

"We'll tell you in the car," says Judd. "That is, if you can give us a ride to my place."

"Of course I can," says Mike. "Come on. Let's get you boys home."

Judd rides shotgun, and Clay sits in back. Judd tells Mike the entire story. The rock through the window with the ransom note. Judd's decision to give the kidnapper the money without involving the police. And his own shortsightedness in not anticipating an ambush before dropping the canister of cash in the river. And how fortunate he is that Clay followed him.

"I mean, Moen's Bridge isn't near anything or anyone," says Judd. "I should have known better than to go alone."

"You want to stop at the hospital?" says Mike. "Make sure you don't got a concussion?"

Clay looks at the clock on Mike's dash. It's 2:02 AM. He doesn't remember the last time he was out and about at 2:02 AM. The last thing he wants to do is sit in an emergency room under glaring fluorescents next to a cougher and sneezer. Plus Judd's brain seems to be just fine—he just deduced Clay's biggest secret. "I can check him at the house," says Clay. "I've been through enough concussion protocols to know the drill. If he fails, we'll go to the hospital."

"Whose house?" says Mike.

"My dad's," says Clay. "It's closer."

The cornfields look black in the passing windows. Clay sees a ghost of himself in the window. He can't help but wonder who that guy is now. He went from playing professional soccer in

Europe where he was also a US intelligence agent. Both were fairly routine jobs, one serving the other, where Clay lurked below the surface. That wasn't his first choice when it came to soccer. He'd much rather have played for top-tier teams like Liverpool or Real Madrid than Galway United FC.

But in espionage, lurking below the surface served him well. Unseen. Unheard. No one suspected a damn thing until the game blew up in his face. The diplomatic explosion that sent him running back to Riverwood, Minnesota. And yet, here he is once again. Not as an agent, but as a participant in a clandestine mission. So much for the quiet life.

Mike pulls into Judd's driveway. It's two hundred yards of winding gravel through river birch and maples. They come around the last bend and Judd says, "I don't remember leaving all those lights on."

"No," says Clay. "You didn't." He spots Zoey Jensen's squad car parked where Judd's Tahoe usually is. "And I don't remember the chief of police being parked outside the house when you left."

"What the hell is she doing here?" says Mike.

Clay feels something gnaw at his gut. He opens the rear door before the car comes to a complete stop.

CHAPTER 23

When Clay was thirteen years old, he thought he was old enough to stay home by himself. Either that or sit vigil with his father at the hospital. He was almost a teenager. But instead he had to spend the night at Uncle Teddy and Aunt Deb's. This was before Judd had acquired the doublewide for them. Back then they lived in a regular trailer. They had a bedroom with four walls in the rear of the trailer, but Clay had to sleep on a bunk that folded down and hovered over the dining table. The only things between Clay and the back bedroom were a tiny bathroom, a tiny kitchen, and a couch-like storage thing.

Judd usually gave Clay a choice between staying with Teddy and Deb or staying with Sue and Carol. Sue and Carol had a real house with a guest bedroom. He had his own bathroom there. And Carol was an excellent cook. She was also a nurse in case

Clay happened to be not feeling well—this was before she retired from nursing and opened her Nymphomaniac fly shop.

But not that night. That night Judd insisted Clay stay at Teddy and Deb's. Clay understood why. She could die tonight. She being his mother, Pam. She could die, and Judd, as much as he loved Sue and Carol, wanted Clay to be with blood relatives even if the quarters were cramped.

The partition between the bedroom and the rest of the trailer opened, and Uncle Teddy emerged, slid the partition shut, and disappeared into the bathroom. When he emerged, Clay watched Teddy reach for the partition handle to return to the bedroom. But Teddy must have felt Clay's eyes on him. He stopped, turned around, and took a few steps toward Clay.

"You up, little man?" whispered Teddy.

"Yeah," said Clay. "Can't sleep."

"Me either," said Teddy. "But Deb can, so let's keep our voices real low so we don't wake her up."

"Okay," whispered Clay. He looked at his uncle's shadowed face, the gold ring in his right ear reflecting a whisper of light.

"Can I get you something to eat? Bowl of cereal or a Pop-Tart?"

"Sure," said Clay. "I'd eat a Pop-Tart."

"That sounds good to me, too." Teddy turned on an under-cabinet light, opened a cupboard near his head, and pulled down a box of Pop-Tarts. "We got brown sugar cinnamon. That work?"

"Yeah," said Clay.

"Toasted?" said Teddy.

"No thank you."

Clay heard the tearing and crumpling of Mylar. He watched

Teddy put two Pop-Tarts on a paper towel, then another two on a second paper towel. He handed one paper towel to Clay up in his bunk, took the other for himself, and sat on the couch. They ate without talking for a minute and then Clay said, "Is she ever going to come home?"

Teddy swallowed and said, "I don't know, little man. I'm not going to sit here and tell you everything will be fine because it won't be. If not this time, then some other time. I'm sorry about that. It's not fair."

"How come they won't let me sleep at the hospital with her? Dad gets to."

"Because you're only thirteen," said Teddy. "And even if you were older, I think only one person can stay there. No matter if they're family or not."

Clay swallowed. The brown sugar melted down his throat. "I bet if she wasn't asleep for three days, she would have chose me. Not him."

"That's probably true," said Teddy.

"Dad knows that," said Clay. "So he should let me stay there instead of him."

Teddy didn't respond right away. He ate another half of a Pop-Tart and said: "Want to hear a story about your dad when he was your age?"

"All right."

"It was 1976. And it was the bicentennial. Know what that is?"

"No."

"It was the country's two hundredth birthday. The revolution started in 1776, so 1976 was two hundred years. The whole summer was like the Fourth of July. Red, white, and blue all over the place. Everyone wearing bicentennial hats and T-shirts every day. And then on the actual Fourth of July, the whole day was like times ten."

"Was it fun?" said Clay.

"We thought it was," said Teddy. "We were fourteen. Of course the coolest part about it, to me anyway, was the fireworks. And sometimes firecrackers. They were illegal in Minnesota, but you could buy them in Wisconsin. Only an hour away. So one day your grandpa Karl, he tells me and your dad we're going fishing over in Wisconsin. And we did go fishing. He was a plunker like your dad."

"What's a plunker?" said Clay.

"Anglers who throw big lures. Or live bait. Things that make a *kerplunk* sound when they hit the water. But not fly fishermen. We're quiet. We fished this small lake over there. Caught some nice ones. Grandpa Karl and your dad always kept their keepers. We had a cooler to put 'em in, but we didn't have any ice for the drive back. We stopped to get some at a gas station, and there was a fireworks store right next to it."

"Did you get some?" said Clay.

"Well," said Teddy, "there was some begging involved. More by me than Judd. Even at fourteen years old, he was kind of a rule follower. Fireworks were legal in Wisconsin, but we didn't live in Wisconsin. We lived right here in Minnesota where fireworks are not legal, and he had mixed feelings about breaking the law."

"Sounds like him."

"But I kept pushing and eventually Grandpa Karl agreed to let us get a few things. Mostly sparklers and snakes and things that didn't go boom. But he did let us get some ladyfingers, which are basically skinny firecrackers. They do the same thing but seem less dangerous. Anyway, when we were in there and Grandpa Karl was paying, I did something I shouldn't have done. I stole a whole brick of firecrackers."

"How'd you do that?"

"Overalls. Slipped the firecrackers in 'em and walked out. Then when we got home, I opened up a bunch of firecrackers from the brick I stole and emptied out the black powder. Now you got to promise me, Clay, I mean swear on your mother's soul, that you'll never try what I'm about to tell you."

"I promise," said Clay.

"You swear on your mother's soul? Because if you don't, I can't tell you the rest of the story."

"I swear on my mother's soul," said Clay.

"All right, then," said Teddy. "You ever hear of a big firecracker called an M-80?"

"I've heard about 'em," said Clay. "They're really powerful. Can blow stuff up and everything."

"They sure can," said Teddy. "That's why they're illegal. Plenty of people out there who can only count to seven on both hands because they were messing around with M-80s."

"Man," said Clay.

"*Man* is an understatement. And I'm not proud of what I'm about to tell you. Because I had my mind set on making an M-80. I'd seen one before. They look like a big fat firecracker in a cardboard tube, and the fuse comes out of the side, not the top. I don't know why it comes out the side, but it does. So I found a narrow cardboard tube, filled it with the black powder I took from the firecrackers, plugged the ends, and drilled a little hole in the side for the fuse."

"Did you light it?"

"I sure did. Thought it would be fun to blow up one of my toy trucks. I put the M-80 in it and set the truck on the dirt in your grandma Lila's garden. Then I lit the fuse and ran like hell. And it's a good thing I did. Because my homemade M-80 blew that truck to smithereens."

"Wow."

"Yeah, wow. It also blew the hell out of a ceramic fountain, took out all her flowers and vegetables, knocked down a section of white picket fence, and left a crater two feet deep."

"You're lucky you didn't get hurt."

"Sure am. But I knew I was in big trouble. Huge trouble. And it wasn't the first time. I'd had a bad year. Got kicked out of school. Got caught letting the air out of the tires on a garbage truck. Got busted for painting a mustache and pirate eye patch on a real estate billboard. So when I saw the damage I'd done, I took off."

"Where'd you go?" said Clay.

"To a buddy's house. Hung out there for a few hours. Every time the phone rang, I expected it would be my mom or dad looking for me, but it never was. After a while I felt like I was wearing out my welcome, so I left and started walking home. Real slow. I was in no hurry to get what was coming to me. I was cutting through the park and saw Judd's baseball team practicing on the far diamond. Thought I'd go over and watch the rest of his practice, then walk home with Judd. Figured it'd be easier to face Grandpa Karl and Grandma Lila with my brother by my side."

Clay nodded. That made sense.

"But guess what. Judd wasn't at practice with his team. I was standing behind the backstop, searching for him, and the kid playing catcher asked me if I was looking for my brother. I said I was. And he said why. Didn't I know Judd was grounded and wouldn't be at practice for a whole week? How could I not know that when the entire baseball team knew it?"

Clay thought he understood why, but he looked for confirmation in his uncle's eyes.

"And then I understood," said Teddy. "Judd took the blame for what I did. He'd never been in trouble a day in his life. He knew, even as a kid, that the punishment handed out for his first offense would be far less severe than the punishment handed out for my tenth."

"But why? He couldn't play baseball for a week," said Clay.

"Not only that," said Teddy. "He missed the big bicentennial celebration. Grandpa Karl and Grandma Lila did not make exceptions. Judd spent the Fourth of July in our bedroom. But to answer the *why* of it, your dad did that because he's a protector. He feels the need to keep people safe. That's why he's a cop. I don't know if he was just born that way or maybe I made him that way because I always needed someone looking out for me. Hell, Clay. To be honest, I still do. I can't get out of my own way. Bad wiring or something."

Teddy stood and walked over to the tiny kitchen, held his wristwatch under the light, and looked at the time. Then he glanced up at his nephew and said, "I know you and your dad don't get along all the time. He's been in a bad place since your mom got sick. I know he wants to protect her. To save her. But he can't do it. It's tearing him up inside. And you . . . Well, Clay. Hope you take this as a compliment—you don't need protecting. You got a strength in you like your dad's. Maybe even more so. You're good at stuff. Everything you try. I know seeing your mom sick hurts. And it's all you've ever known since the day you were born. But no matter what happens, you're going to be okay. Not because of me and Aunt Deb. Not because of Sue and Carol. Not because of your dad. But because of you."

A sadness spread throughout Clay's entire body. It was like Uncle Teddy was saying that Clay's troubles didn't matter. They didn't matter because they couldn't hurt him the way they hurt other people. But that didn't feel true. He did hurt. Just because he was good at violin and fly-fishing and school didn't mean he didn't hurt.

"You ready to go back to sleep?"

Clay shook his head. "Still not tired."

"Me either," said Teddy. "So listen up. Official sunrise is in one hour. That means we can legally be on the river in thirty minutes. Those big browns will still be hunting until the sky lightens up. I say we go down to the river, tie on a couple of deer-hair mouse patterns, and see if one of us can hook a monster."

"Yeah," said Clay, "can we?"

"Shh. Glad you're excited. I am, too. But let's try not to wake up your Aunt Deb. That means we don't have to brush our teeth. That okay with you?"

Teddy and Clay dressed, headed out to the shed, and geared up. They wore headlamps down to the river, scared a big doe who'd bedded down near the trail, and watched her bound away.

"Wow," said Clay. "We were almost close enough to touch it."

"They're beautiful animals," said Teddy. "That's why I can't hunt 'em."

"I don't want to hunt 'em either."

"Better to piss off some trout and let 'em go."

"Yeah . . ."

Teddy watched Clay stare off in the direction of the doe, who was now out of sight, hidden by the trees and brush. They continued down to the stream and cast mouse patterns for trout. Huge flies compared to the insect patterns. The size of a real mouse, they were made of spun deer hair, foam, and a length of stripped rabbit for the tail. Clay and Teddy couldn't see their flies and had to listen and feel for the strike. The big trout became uninhibited in the dark, leaving the safety of the depths to hunt the surface.

Clay missed two strikes. Teddy hooked one, but the heavy fish broke off before he could get it in the net. Clay hooked up on his next strike. The fish made several runs, taking Clay's line into the backing, but Clay, at thirteen years old, had learned how to fight a big trout. Let it run to tire itself out and so it doesn't break the line, but keep the rod tip up to steer the fish away from the fast water where it can use the current to its advantage.

"Attaboy," said Teddy on his way over to help. Clay managed to get the trout's head out of the water and skate it into Teddy's net. He'd landed a twenty-inch brown, the biggest fish Clay had ever caught.

"Take the hook out first," said Teddy. "Then reach into the net, hold the tail firm, and gently cradle the belly."

Clay followed his uncle's directions. Teddy removed a cheap disposable camera from his vest pocket and snapped a picture, blinding Clay with the flash.

"Now let that big one go the way I taught you. He's going to be plenty tired after that fight, so give him some help."

Clay faced upstream, then lowered the big trout into the water, holding it steady so the current would flow through the fish's gills. Then Clay gently rocked it back and forth to increase the trout's oxygen intake. After half a minute, he could feel the fish's strength return. It struggled to escape, and he let it go.

The stars disappeared as the sky lightened to periwinkle and then a rich azure. They decided to call it quits, hike back up to the trailer, and dive into bacon, eggs, and toast. It was a perfect morning, thought Clay. At least that's what he thought before he saw his father's squad car parked in front of Teddy's trailer. That's when Clay knew his mother was dead.

And now, thirty years later, Clay sees another squad car he didn't expect to see, this one parked in front of Judd's house. Different house. Different car. Different millennium. But Clay gets the same sick feeling.

CHAPTER 24

Clay is the first one out of Mike's car and the first one to the door. He grabs the knob, twists, and pushes. It's open. He steps into Judd's small foyer and then the living room. Chief of Police Zoey Jensen sits in Judd's recliner, her expression solemn. Straight-mouthed with eyes staring right at him. Clay goes numb, as if the world has stopped spinning and is about to explode. He opens his mouth to speak when Zoey's eyes look to her left. Clay follows them to see Braedon stretched out on the couch, fast asleep under a blanket. He snorts, then rolls over onto his side. Clay responds by motioning for Zoey to step outside.

Judd, Mike, Clay, and Zoey walk away from the house and speak in hushed voices, hoping they blend into the sounds of the night and Braedon doesn't wake.

"What happened?" says Clay.

Zoey looks at Judd and then Mike and then back to Clay and says, "When I ran into you earlier tonight, I knew you were up to more than just looking for Teddy. Something was happening or was about to happen. You were acting a little too casual. There was no desperation in your voice. No frustration. It was like you had everything under control, or at least thought you did."

Clay doesn't respond. Neither does Judd or Mike.

"So after you left the bar, I followed you. First to right here, and then again when you were tailing Judd."

"How did you manage to tail me?" says Clay.

"It's amazing how difficult cars are to see when all their lights are off. Especially when your focus was on following Judd. I parked a couple hundred yards behind you. Too far away to know what you were doing. Then when you took off toward the bridge, I moved up and watched you help Judd."

"And you didn't come to our aid," says Judd.

"I was going to," says Zoey. "But I witnessed your truck being stolen and I had to make a choice. And since whoever bopped you on the head most likely had something to do with Teddy's disappearance, I decided to follow them."

"And?" says Clay.

"And first of all, I had no intention of just leaving you there. While in pursuit of the suspects, I called both Officers Wahlquist and Kimmich. They did not answer their phones. I woke up Sue at home. She couldn't track them down either." Zoey turns toward Wahlquist and, for the first time since he's met her, Clay sees pure police in her eyes. No quirky offbeat personality. No playful smile. "Where the hell were you, Mike?

I saw you at Knut's handing out meat raffle tickets. But when I called the bar a little later, they said you'd left."

"On patrol," says Mike. "Could have been on the road along Shady Creek. No cell reception there."

"No radio reception either?" says Zoey. "'Cause Sue went to the station to try you."

"I didn't get a radio call," says Mike.

Three pairs of eyes swing toward Mike. And three pairs of eyes know he's lying.

"Let's put a pin in that for now," says Zoey. She takes in a big breath and exhales disappointment. She then turns toward Clay and Judd and adds, "I remained in pursuit of the suspects who led me into town. And that's where things got a little dicey."

Clay looks back toward the house where Braedon sleeps. He feels it in his body before he understands it in his head, but his brain catches up in a fraction of a second. "The boys on the bikes," he says. Statement. Not a question.

"Uh-huh," says Zoey in a flat monotone.

"What does that mean?" says Judd. "The boys on the bikes."

"We're talking about some kids who knocked you unconscious, threw your cell phone and keys into the river, and took Clay's truck. And just before they left, they pulled three bikes out of the brush and threw them in the truck bed. Don't worry, Clay. No damage to the vehicle. It's parked safely around the corner from the community center. And your canister of cash is in evidence lockup at the station. How much is it? I didn't have time to count it."

Judd hesitates, then, verging on embarrassment, says, "Forty-five K. And there were three of them? Now that number makes sense. A multiple of three."

"What?" says Mike. "Why didn't you—"

"Later, Mike," says Clay. Now it's Clay's turn to take a big breath. What he exhales is dread. "How was Braedon involved?"

"The boys called Daniel and demanded a favor. Braedon tagged along because, well, he panicked. He knew it was wrong but didn't want his friend to go alone. He'll fill you in. Just know that when Braedon tells you they had a gun—"

"What?" Clay can't tamp down his fury. "They pulled a—"

"Hear me out," says Zoey. "It wasn't loaded. Didn't even have a clip in it. The chamber was empty—I checked."

Clay hears Zoey's words but his heart still races.

"The short of it is," continues Zoey, "all three boys are in custody. Their story is they were out mountain biking and found a work glove, an electric saw, a Replacements hoodie—"

"The band the Replacements?" says Judd.

"Exactly. And with that stuff, Teddy's earring."

"What do you mean, they found that stuff?" says Clay. "On the mountain bike trail?"

"Just off it," says Zoey. "They knew Teddy was missing. So they hatched their plan to pretend they kidnapped him, took the earring as evidence, left the other stuff where they found it, and you know the rest."

"What are you talking about?" says Mike. "I don't know anything."

"No," says Zoey, her voice flat and unforgiving. "You don't."

"A glove, Teddy's Replacements sweatshirt, a saw, and his earring?" says Judd. "Just those four things? No other sign of Teddy?"

"That's what they said," says Zoey. "I didn't ask for more details. I want separate interrogations for that."

"Let's do it," says Mike.

"I'm going to let you sit this one out, Mike," says Zoey. "But thanks."

"But who—"

"I'm bringing Judd out of retirement for this one." She then turns to Clay and says, "And you went to West Point. They must have taught you something about enemy interrogation when you weren't playing soccer."

Clay wonders if she knows more than that, but how could she? She couldn't. She doesn't. He simply nods and says, "A little. Happy to help."

"Good," says Zoey. "Consider yourselves deputized. And thank you. I've spoken with each of the boys' parents. They're not real happy with their sons at the moment and waived the right to have an attorney present at questioning, so let's get to it. Sue and Carol are expecting you to drop Braedon at their place. Then I'll meet you at the station at . . . let's say three o'clock. Figure by the time we're done, we can go out for breakfast."

"I really screwed up, Dad. I'm sorry." Braedon leans against the passenger door half asleep. "I'm willing to accept whatever punishment you give me."

Clay is tempted to say, *Oh, you're willing? Thank you for your permission and generosity.* But this is the first real trouble Braedon has ever been in, and Clay wants to get the parenting part right. When Clay was a boy, Judd didn't handle this kind of thing well. All it did was drive Clay underground. Make him more careful. More secretive. Especially when Clay was twelve years old and hadn't yet found his place on the soccer team at Dorset-Cornwall. He did his share of sneaking out of the house and other mischievousness, and he became damn good at hiding it from his father. Maybe that's why he became a spy.

More lies is the last thing he wants to instill in Braedon. He doesn't want to seed clandestine thinking in his son. He wants to seed honesty and transparency. "I hear that you know what you did was wrong," says Clay.

"I really do," says Braedon.

Clay believes him. One thing Braedon is not is a bullshitter. "And I appreciate you saying so. Still, I may come up with some kind of punishment. Something that will give you some thinking time."

"Like what?" says Braedon.

"Maybe repainting the shed out back. It's looking kind of rough. What do you think of that?"

"That sounds fair," says Braedon. "I helped paint my room. I think I can do a shed."

"There you go. Good attitude." They drive in silence for a minute, then Clay says, "So when that Graham boy pulled a gun on you and Daniel, did it feel like he might really pull the trigger?"

Braedon shrugs. "I don't know. But I didn't feel scared when it happened. That's why I grabbed the bottle from Daniel. I guess I figured he wouldn't really shoot us. Later, after Chief Jensen came, I felt kind of scared. Like something bad could have happened. But I was okay when it was happening."

Clay nods. "I know the gun wasn't loaded. But a gun is a gun. Some people treat them with respect and a healthy amount of fear. And some people think they're a license to act tough. Or worse. I guess what I'm asking is, do you think any of those boys are capable of killing a person? Or do you think they're just kids being kids, screwing around?"

"I don't know," says Braedon. "Probably kids being kids. They act tough but they're not scary."

Clay says in his best Irish accent, "Not like the lads of Ireland, aye, sonny Jim?"

Braedon laughs. His brogue blows away Clay's. "No, Da. The hard lads of Ireland are proper brutal, yeah?"

Clay and Braedon laugh their way into Sue and Carol's driveway. It's the same house where Clay sometimes spent the night or even a week while his mother was going through the worst of it. It hasn't changed much. It's a hundred-year-old saltbox two-story with white clapboard siding, a white picket fence, and a flower garden bordering the house. Half barrels of more flowers are scattered about. The lights are on inside and out. This is something Sue and Carol did for Clay, too. To make him feel like he wasn't being a bother getting dropped off in the middle of the night when his father had to rush his mother to the hospital.

Seeing the place again, especially at this hour, pulls at Clay's heart. He can't take his eyes off it but keeps both hands gripping the steering wheel lest he get sucked into a vortex that pulls him back to those terrible days. Sue and Carol did their best to ease Clay's pain. In some ways, they were both the mothers Pam couldn't be. Not on her bad days, anyway.

"You okay, Dad?" says Braedon, watching his father lost in another time.

Clay manages a smile. "Yeah, Brae. I'm good. Sue and Carol meant a lot to me. Still do. You'll be in good hands here. Now let's go. My guess is there's going to be hot chocolate and cookies waiting for us."

CHAPTER 25

The Riverwood Police Station is not a big place, so sitting the boys down in three separate rooms pretty much fills it out. Clay is surprised to learn that one of the three boys is Thomas Becker, Steph and Wags's son. Clay figures it's best if he doesn't interrogate Thomas—let someone else do that.

Judd questions Thomas Becker at the facing desks Mike and Andy use. Zoey questions Markey Franzen in her office. Clay questions Graham Collins in the basement storage area. All three boys are cuffed at the ankles and wrists, but that is the extent of their confinement. Zoey hasn't even put them in a cell. Nor has she arrested them, though she has every right to since they assaulted Judd and stole forty-five thousand dollars, and she witnessed Graham point a handgun at Braedon and Daniel, even though the handgun was not loaded.

Judd allows Thomas Becker to sit at Mike Wahlquist's desk

while Judd sits in Andy Kimmich's. This is Judd's way of making Thomas feel he has some importance and control in the conversation. That's how Judd defines it to Thomas. "This is just a conversation. That's all. No big deal . . ."

Thomas Becker is one of those fifteen-year-old boys who could pass for eighteen. He's six feet tall, has to shave every day, and has deep-sunken brown eyes and olive skin like his father. He also has Wags's black hair that falls down the sides of his face to his jawline. He tries to look like a man, but Judd sees the boy. Thomas has the cheeks and forehead of a child. His hands are delicate as if the kid were a concert pianist. His eyes are not yet hardened. Judd sees fear but also inquisitiveness, an eager anticipation of what's about to happen.

"Where exactly did you find my brother's things?" says Judd.

"I already told all this to Zoey," says Thomas, whose voice is deep but without much resonance in his tiny chest.

"I know," says Judd, "and I appreciate that. But humor me. I want to hear it right from the source."

Thomas sighs. "All right." He fidgets a bit with the handcuffs on his wrists and adds, "We found the stuff halfway up the mountain bike trail on Miller's Bluff. We ride there a lot."

"Could you lead us back to that exact same spot when it gets light?"

"Yeah," says Thomas. "Easy."

"How did the stuff look when you found it? Was it all over the place or stacked in a neat pile or some combination of the two?"

Thomas takes a moment and looks up into his brain as if

the answer is posted there and he just has to read it. "It was in a messy pile, kind of . . . like the hoodie was just tossed on the ground with the saw and glove and earring on top of it."

"And did the earring have the little pink back on it or did you find that separately?"

Thomas looks down for a moment and then up. "Off, I think. Like crumpled up in the sweatshirt."

"Okay," says Judd. He's trying to convince himself that this is just another questioning of a suspect who'd found a random man unconscious on a trail. Not his own brother. Judd tries his best to mask the urgency he's feeling. "And whose idea was it to take the earring?"

"That was Graham."

"Was this fake kidnapping and ransom note his idea?"

"I guess," says Thomas.

"You guess or you know?" says Judd.

Thomas shifts in his seat. "I suppose I know."

"And you and the other guy, Markey, you went along with it."

Thomas nods.

"Why didn't you take the saw and glove and hoodie?"

Thomas shrugs. "Once Graham thought of the kidnapping idea and using the earring, we were kind of focused on that, I guess."

Judd nods. "What was the split? Fifteen thousand each?"

"Yeah," says Thomas.

"What were you going to do with the money?" says Judd.

"We were going to buy cars when we turn sixteen. You know, used ones. You can't get much for fifteen thou."

"That's practical," says Judd.

"Well, Markey works at the marina. And he heard you saying you had fifty grand to spend on a new boat. And when the salesman asked you about financing, you said you were going to pay cash. That's how we knew you had that much."

"But it was easier to divide forty-five by three than it was to divide fifty by three?"

Thomas responds with a shrug.

"When did Graham come up with the kidnapping plan?" says Judd. "Before or after you guys found Teddy's earring?"

"What do you mean?"

"Well, did you see the stuff and think you could use it to say you kidnapped Teddy? Or did you find the earring and then get the idea?"

"Well . . . when we saw the hoodie and stuff, we were wondering if there was a wallet and phone in there. Kind of to know who it belonged to, but also kind of like we wanted the stuff. Graham was kind of pissed there was nothing valuable. But then we found the earring . . . yeah . . . and we thought it was Teddy's. So Graham said he was going to take the earring as a consolation even though we knew it was a big deal because that guy from the Clash supposedly gave him that earring. Everybody in town knows that story. So Graham thought maybe we could ransom it back to Teddy.

"But the next day we heard Teddy was missing and you and other people were looking for him. So Graham said fuck trying to get money for the earring—excuse my language, but that's what he said—we can get a lot more money if we say we kidnapped Teddy and use the earring as proof."

Judd doesn't speak for a minute. He wants Thomas to feel comfortable but not too comfortable. A good pregnant pause does wonders to unsettle a suspect under interrogation. "Anything else you remember about the glove and saw and hoodie?"

"Like what?" says Thomas.

"Did anything look dirty? Maybe smudged with blood? Was the electric saw intact or broken? Was the battery attached?"

Thomas looks up into his brain again and says, "It just looked like it had been dropped on the ground. That's all I remember."

"Was the glove for a left or right hand?"

Thomas shrugs. "No clue."

"Tell me more about the saw," says Judd. "Was it a circular saw, jigsaw, reciprocating saw?"

"Oh!" says Thomas, brightening. "That I do remember. It's the kind with a blade pointing out the end. Like a swordfish. My dad has one. He can put different blades in it to cut different stuff. Like metal or wood or a concrete block."

"Got it," says Judd. "That sounds like a reciprocating saw. Also called a sawzall. If we go to the hardware store when it opens, maybe you can point out what you saw to me?"

"Yeah," says Thomas. "I can do that." He lowers his cuffed hands from the desk to his lap and adds, "Are we under arrest? Are we going to jail?"

"The arrest part is up to Chief Jensen," says Judd. "If she does arrest you, the jail part will be up to the district attorney and a judge or jury. Do you think you deserve to be arrested?"

Thomas shrugs. "I know what we did was pretty bad. But we didn't hurt anyone."

"Really?" says Judd. "Because I got a bump on the back of my head that says otherwise."

In the basement of the police station, Graham Collins sits in an old office chair made of oak. It's on wheels and can swivel back and forth and that's just what Graham does as if he has a nervous tic or restless leg syndrome. He has a boyish haircut, as if his mom still sits him down in the kitchen and hovers over him with electric clippers. It's still blond as a child's, and his blue eyes are *blue* blue, not gray. He wears cargo shorts and a ratty gray University of Minnesota sweatshirt. His socks don't match each other and neither do his Converse sneakers. One blue, one white. His buddy, Markey, who's upstairs talking to Zoey, wears the other white and blue sneakers.

Clay leans against a wire cage where Riverwood law enforcement sometimes keeps stray or dangerous dogs taken away from crime scenes or homes where someone had been bitten. "Tell me about the gun," says Clay. "Where did it come from?"

"It's my brother's," says Graham. His voice is high-pitched. It hasn't changed and maybe never will. "He's in the army. He keeps it locked in a box in his room but I know where the key is."

"Why didn't you load it?"

"He keeps his ammo and clips in a safe with a combination lock. I don't know the combination, so I just carried the gun in case something went wrong and I needed to scare someone with it."

"You realize you're in a lot more trouble because you threatened someone with a gun."

"But it wasn't loaded."

"Doesn't matter. You're in trouble with the law. And you're in trouble with me. You pointed that gun at my son."

Graham winces with fear and averts his eyes from Clay's. "Like how much trouble?"

"That's up to the police and the courts," says Clay.

"Hey," says Graham. "You're not the police. Why am I talking to you?"

"Because I've been asked to help by Chief Jensen. She has the authority to do that."

"But why? I thought you were a soccer player."

"I was. I was also in the army. Now, you told Chief Jensen that you found Teddy's sweatshirt, a glove, an electric saw, and his earring."

"Yeah," says Graham. "Because we did."

"And you only took his earring."

"Right . . ."

"Why should we believe that? Why shouldn't we think that you abducted Teddy for the purpose of extorting a ransom? You certainly seem capable of it."

"Because we didn't do it," says Graham. "We just found his stuff. Plus, all we needed was the earring. It's not like we needed to take Teddy so we could chop fingers off him and tie those to a rock and throw them through your dad's window."

"That's your reasoning?" says Clay.

Graham swivels on his chair. "What's wrong with it?"

Clay stares hard at Graham. "The police and prosecuting attorney will consider your attitude and willingness to cooperate when deciding what to do with you."

Graham drops his eyes and doesn't respond.

"Not that it matters legally," says Clay, "but whose idea was it to send the ransom note and earring to make it look like you'd kidnapped Teddy?"

Graham keeps his eyes down. "Mine."

"By the way, who wrote that ransom note? It doesn't read like any of you three wrote it."

"We had AI write it so it didn't sound like us."

Clay nods. Makes sense. "So you find a guy's earring and think, *Hey, let's make it look like we kidnapped him and make a quick forty-five thousand?*"

"It didn't happen like that," says Graham.

"Then how did it happen?"

Graham lifts his eyes. "I just wanted to take the earring. You know, 'cause Joe Strummer supposedly gave it to Teddy. I thought it might be worth some cash. Then when we heard Teddy was missing, I had the idea to make it look like we kidnapped him. Figured we could get a lot more money that way."

"Yeah," says Clay. He leans back into the chain-link. "Forty-five thousand dollars is a lot of money. What were three fifteen-year-olds going to do with that kind of money?"

"Buy cars when we turn sixteen," says Graham. "Well, Markey wanted to buy a car. A Mustang. Rugburn—"

"Who?"

"Thomas Becker. I call him Rugburn. He wanted like a Ford Escape or some other small SUV. And I wanted a pickup. Kind of like what you got. Sweet ride."

"Yeah," said Clay. "Are you the one who drove it away from the bridge?"

Graham looks away again and nods.

"Thanks for not banging it up."

Graham shrugs, reluctant to take the compliment.

"Which one of you picked up the earring from the ground?"

Graham exhales as if it's a stalling tactic. As if he won't have to take another breath for half an hour. But he does take another breath and says, "Me."

"Was that little back thing on it when you found it? The pink clasp?"

Graham shakes his head. "No. But near it. Like Teddy took it off fast and dropped it with the other stuff."

"A hoodie, a saw, a glove, and an earring . . . That's a weird four things to find together. And I assume once you saw the earring, you thought it might be Teddy's."

Graham nods. "Yeah . . ."

"Did you think he might be nearby? Did you call out to him or anything like that?"

Graham bites his lower lip and shakes his head.

"Did you look around for him?"

"No. We just wanted to get out of there with the earring."

Clay nods as if this makes sense. "Any other details you remember?"

"Like what?"

"Were the hoodie and glove dirty? Were they wet? Did they have any kind of odor?"

Graham shakes his head, but then stops and says, "There is one thing that was kind of odd. When I knelt down to pick up the earring, the hoodie smelled like smoke. Like it'd been hanging around a campfire or something. It wasn't exactly that kind of smell but it was like it, do you know what I mean?"

"Not really," says Clay. "Are you saying the hoodie smelled like woodsmoke?"

Graham thinks about this. "Maybe . . ." he says. "Kind of like that but not that."

"Like car exhaust?" says Clay.

"Maybe . . ." says Graham.

"What did the glove look like?"

"It was a work glove."

"What color?"

"Brown leather . . ." Graham thinks for a few more seconds, then adds, "Yeah, pretty sure it was brown. So what's the deal here? Am I under arrest or what?"

CHAPTER 26

After the boys have been questioned, Zoey locks them in a jail cell so they get a taste of it. A glimpse into a future they'll want to avoid. She then joins Clay and Judd in her office. Judd has brewed a pot of coffee, which seems necessary as the sky lightens outside Zoey's office window. They compare the boys' stories and find them consistent.

"My guess is they're not lying," says Zoey. "Their bulbs don't burn bright enough to concoct those details, memorize them all, and recall them under pressure."

"Seems that way," says Judd.

"I want to hold off with charges," she says. "At least for now. It may be unavoidable, but I hate for kids to have that on their record. That's partly up to you, though, Judd, since you were the one who was assaulted. Clay, your truck was stolen. You're free to press charges now and that will be that."

Clay watches something change in his father. Soften. Maybe it's just fatigue—they haven't slept in twenty-four hours. But Judd seems to have embraced Zoey's ability as a police officer. Or if not embraced, then accepted.

"No need to press charges right now," says Judd. "We can think about it for a little bit. The boys may know more than they've told us. I don't think they're holding back—they just might have overlooked something that could be important. Let's stay on their better sides as long as we can manage."

"We'll take them to where they found Teddy's things," says Zoey. "See if the stuff's still there. And I'll talk to them about the stolen bike and tell them to stay clear of Braedon and Daniel. Then we'll drop them at their homes and I'll talk to their parents and tell them that, for now, the boys are cooperating with our investigation. I won't go into more details. Hopefully, those three boys will feel indebted to us and who knows, like Judd said, maybe help us out down the line."

"Clay," says Judd, "you want to take home the Becker boy? Talk to Steph personally?" Zoey throws an inquisitive glance at Judd. "Clay knows her pretty well. They dated in high school. Now he gets his hair done at her beauty parlor."

Zoey turns toward Clay. "Nails, too?"

Clay offers Zoey a flat, "Fingers and toes." He then turns to his father and says, "Zoey should talk to all the parents. Including Thomas's. Better that they hear it from a uniform."

"You sure?" says Zoey. "I don't want to douse the flames of a rekindling romance."

"I'm sure," says Clay. "And there is no rekindling romance.

I think Steph may have found a new beau already. And by beau, I mean boy. I saw them looking at each other at Knut's."

"As long as he's over eighteen," says Zoey, "that's none of my business. Okay if we take your truck, Clay? It won't help matters if they're seen being dropped off in a squad car."

Miller's Bluff was also named after the bigamist Leon Miller. Since Liar's Creek flows right by it, the townspeople thought it appropriate to use another meaning of the word *bluff* to further disparage Leon Miller's lack of veracity. A small park sits at the base of Miller's Bluff. It has a basketball court, horseshoe pit, picnic tables, and three built-in grills. Liar's Creek runs along the base of the bluff, crossable over an arched wooden bridge for foot and bike traffic only. The bridge provides access to two trailheads, one for hikers and one for mountain bikers. It's a beautiful bluff unless you make it to the top where you're greeted by a cell phone tower and defunct power line.

Graham leads them up the bike trailhead on foot. Markey and Thomas follow close behind, and two steps behind trudge Clay, Judd, and Zoey. It's about a fifteen-minute hike up to the spot where the boys found Teddy.

"It's gone," says Graham. "It was right here."

"You sure this is the spot?" says Judd.

"Positive," says Graham. "The stuff was right on that area of small stones. That's where I knelt down to pick up the earring."

Judd lowers himself to the ground and, on his hands and knees, looks closely at a bed of small stones that were most likely helped down the bluff by recent rains. "Don't see any blood," says Judd. "Or anything else."

Now Clay is down next to him. He crawls around the stones and goes up the hill.

"Careful," says Zoey. "I'll order a forensics team from Rochester. Have them comb through it for hair and fibers."

"There are broken branches up here," says Clay. "Teddy could have fallen through this area and landed on the rocks. Somehow shed the hoodie and earring . . ." Clay shakes his head. Again he turns to the boys and says, "Are you sure there wasn't anything other than the things you found?"

"Like what?"

"Like a beer can," says Judd. "Maybe a whiskey bottle?"

"No," says Graham. "We didn't find anything like that."

"Well," says Zoey, "if Teddy came to and walked down the bike path, his footprints could have been erased by bike tires. This trail gets a lot of use this time of year."

Judd looks at his watch and says, "Hardware store should be open. Let's go see if we can identify that saw and get you boys home."

Braedon opens his eyes and looks at the digital clock on the nightstand. It's 8:14 AM. Something smells delicious. He slips out from underneath the quilt, puts his feet on the floor, and stands. Clay told him this room hasn't changed one bit since Clay was Braedon's age. Sue and Carol call it the Map Room because framed maps cover the walls. Maps of where, Braedon isn't sure. They're old. Not Middle-earth old, but old.

He slept in his clothes, which at twelve is more of a treat than uncomfortable, so he pads out of the room in stocking feet, descends the stairs, and follows his nose into the kitchen.

"Hey!" says Sue. "There he is. What'll it be for breakfast, young man?"

"Whatever you're making smells great," says Braedon.

"That would be my famous pancake sandwich. One big sausage patty between two pancakes and the whole thing smothered in butter and maple syrup. They're your dad's favorite. And what'll you be washing your pancake sandwich down with? Orange juice? Coffee? Milk? A cuppa? Isn't that what you call it in Ireland?"

"Yes," says Braedon. "But orange juice, please."

"The prince has awoken!" This from Carol as she enters the room carrying a bouquet of fresh-picked flowers from the garden. She has perfect silver hair that falls to her shoulders, long and thick and bright like metal. Soft green almond-shaped eyes in browned skin from her hours in the garden and on the river. "For you, my liege," she says, handing Braedon a daffodil.

Braedon can't help but laugh. "Thank you."

"I got Marty opening up the shop this morning, so I figure you and I might find something fun to do."

"Yeah," says Braedon. Although he barely knows Sue and Carol (he's met Sue a few times at the police station and Carol a few times at the fly shop), he feels like he belongs in their home. Both women were and maybe still are surrogate mothers to his father, and that makes them surrogate grandmothers to Braedon. That's where the belonging feeling comes from. Sue and Carol are like family. When you meet a relative for the first time—even at the age of eleven or twelve or thirty-five, there's an immediate comfort level.

"I was thinking," says Carol, "we could spend some time at the fly-tying bench."

"Sure . . ." says Braedon, trying to sound upbeat about the idea.

"I know you're not a fly-fisher. Your dad complains to me about it every time he's in the shop. You like fishing with your grandpa Judd, right?"

Braedon nods.

"Well, guess what. Fly-tying isn't just for making flies. You can also make lures for fishing the way you and your grandpa do. Lures to catch bass, walleye, northern pike, even muskies. Big old honkers made of buck tail and silver spoons and colored beads and feathers. We can make 'em in brown, olive, chartreuse, white, yellow, red. There is no shortage of supplies in this house. What do you think about surprising your grandpa Judd with a whole mess of them? Handmade by the prince himself!"

Braedon laughs. "I don't know how."

"I'll teach you. I got a book about making plunker lures around here somewhere. Otherwise we'll resort to YouTube."

"One pancake sandwich hot and ready to be eaten," says Sue. She sets the plate on the kitchen table and retrieves a carton of orange juice from the refrigerator.

"Thank you," says Braedon. He sits at the kitchen table and feels so grateful he might cry. Grateful for Sue and Carol. Grateful for his grandpa Judd. Grateful for his father moving them to Riverwood, Minnesota. He's a boy who's never had a mother. His father tries to be both, father and mother. And he had Siobhan, his full-time nanny for the first eleven years of his life. She was motherlike, but she never loved him the way a person does when they choose to be your mother. Loving Braedon and being there for him was Siobhan's job. Not her pleasure. But Judd and Deb and Teddy and Sue and Carol, they not only love Braedon, they love loving Braedon. Like a real mother would. He misses Emily and his other friends in Ireland. He misses the language and the sea, the League of Ireland Premier Division on the telly. He misses the culture and pride of the Irish people. But the abundance of love Braedon feels in Riverwood fills him with more warmth than just-out-of-the-oven soda bread and beef stew. Even with the trouble he had last night, he can't imagine living anywhere else.

CHAPTER 27

Braedon texted Clay to ask if he could spend the whole day with Carol. Apparently they're working on some kind of special project and won't be done until evening. Normally Clay wouldn't want to put that responsibility on Carol and Sue—spending an entire night and day with Braedon—but he seems to be having a good time. And Carol chimed in with a text of her own saying she had big plans for Braedon that day. Clay gives his permission—he can definitely use some quiet time to catch up on sleep.

But first Clay, Judd, and Zoey eat breakfast at Nick's Bar & Grill, known for their everything-is-fried-in-bacon-grease breakfast, which doesn't disappoint. They recap the last twelve hours to see if any of them missed anything, make a plan to go update Deb, and then head to their respective homes for naptime.

Deb welcomes them into the doublewide with no news. She

hasn't heard from Teddy. Nor has she heard from the dozens of people she's asked to keep a lookout for him. Friends in town. Friends up in Rochester. Friends in the Twin Cities.

They gather around the kitchen table. A platter of fresh-baked-from-frozen cinnamon rolls proves too tempting along with the fresh pot of coffee Deb brewed. They haven't missed a meal in the last twenty-four hours, but pulling an all-nighter makes them feel like they have, and Deb's offerings are a welcome second breakfast.

"Do you know if Teddy likes to hike Miller's Bluff?" says Judd. "Because he's never mentioned it."

"No," says Deb. "Teddy didn't hike for the sake of hiking. He hiked to get to his favorite fishing spots, and as far as I know, there's no water up on Miller's Bluff."

Zoey picks a layer off her cinnamon roll and puts it in her mouth. No need to chew—it just melts. "Do you know if he's had any health problems that either Clay or Judd might not know about?" says Zoey. "Any light-headedness? Fainting? Is it possible he's had heart trouble or suffered any small strokes?"

"No," says Deb. "Why do you ask?"

"I think Zoey's wondering if a health issue could cause Teddy to lose consciousness," says Clay, who sips his coffee. "Has he ever complained of dizziness after standing up too fast?"

"No," says Deb. "But I suppose anything's possible. He's sixty-three years old. Things start happening. Billy Hoffmann graduated with us and he dropped dead of a heart attack over the holidays. He was thin and ran every day. And fainting doesn't explain why Teddy might have left his things where those boys found them. Especially the earring. He never took off that earring."

"About the saw," says Zoey, holding out her phone to show Deb a photograph. "Does this look familiar?" In the hardware store, Graham identified the sawzall that looked exactly like the one they'd found on the ground. "Is it one of yours?"

Deb shakes her head. "We have a mower and a Weedwacker for the lawn and that's it. Teddy and I both prefer nature to do its thing on the rest of the property."

"Ever see a tool like this before? Could Teddy have maybe borrowed it from a friend?"

Deb studies the picture for a while and says, "You know, I think Ash has tools that look like that. My cousin loves things that match. It's all about appearances. He has a pretty big shop in his pole barn. Sometimes Teddy will borrow tools from Ash. You could ask him if anything's missing. I think he's home. He got that new truck he's been talking about and honks every time he leaves or gets back as if he thinks I'm dying to see it one more time."

"All right," says Zoey. "One more person to talk to. Our beds can wait."

"Thank you," says Deb. "Thanks for all you're doing to find Teddy. I'm sorry that he does things like this."

"Like what?" says Zoey.

"Like disappearing for a few days. Like getting himself into trouble. He's a sweet man, my Teddy. He really is. But sometimes he just can't help himself."

Ash answers the door wearing khaki pants with the cuffs rolled up, revealing a blue-and-pink-striped lining. Red Wing work boots are on his feet, although they've never seen a day of work. They look new or maybe just well-kept and cared for. Ash wears a sky-blue cable-knit sweater over a pink polo shirt to match the lining of his pants.

"Oh, no" are the first words out of his mouth. He looks at Clay and Judd and says, "I'm so sorry."

"Sorry for what?" says Judd.

"Teddy. Isn't that why you're here with a police officer?"

"No," says Clay. "We're just here to ask a question."

"Thank God." Ash half laughs. "Guess I've been listening to too many true-crime podcasts."

"Guess you have," says Zoey. She holds out her phone and shows Ash the photograph of the sawzall. "By any chance do you have a tool that looks like this?"

Ash looks at Zoey's phone. He stares a long time. Too long as far as Clay's concerned.

"Hmm . . ." says Ash. "I might. I don't do as much work around here as I used to. Could have something like that out in the pole barn."

"Mind if we take a look?" says Judd.

Ash twists his face into something unnatural. "Not at all. Hold on. I'll get the key." He turns and disappears into the house.

Zoey watches him go, then says in a hushed tone, "Is he always this weird?"

"Yep," says Judd. "The guy fell ass-backward into money and acts like he earned it. I don't know where the hell he buys his clothes."

"I do," says Zoey. "1980."

Clay laughs but stops when he hears a woman's voice. She sounds like she's complaining. Ash scolds her and she snaps back at him.

"Sounds like Ash has a lady friend," says Judd.

They hear footsteps and all take a step back from the screen door.

"Got the keys," says Ash. He steps outside and closes the door behind him. He descends the porch steps and heads for the pole barn. Ash looks flushed, and Zoey makes out a handprint on his left cheek.

"We catch you at a bad time?" says Zoey.

"Not at all," says Ash. "Was just giving a few directions to my new maid. I'm a stickler for cleanliness. Always have been. Want to make sure she does things right."

Judd and Clay share a glance but say nothing. Their feet crunch on the gravel path until they reach the pole barn, a metal garage–looking building with one large door for vehicles and a regular-sized door for people. That's the one Ash unlocks and in they go. He flicks on the fluorescents that blink to life. There are three vehicles. A brand-new Ford F-150, atlas blue with an extended cab. The other two are covered in tarps, but Clay knows one is an old 2002 BMW and the other is an MG Roadster. There's also a speedboat on a trailer, an ATV, and a John Deere Gator utility vehicle.

"Tools are over by the workbench," says Ash.

They walk to the far end of the pole barn. A ten-foot-long workbench sits against one wall under eight-foot fluorescent tubes in a fixture that hangs by a chain from the ceiling. Above the bench and against the wall is a pegboard where tools hang on hooks. They all match each other as if they were purchased as a set. Some are power tools and some are hand tools but they're color coordinated with lime-green-and-blue handles, just like the tool Graham identified at the hardware store. Someone drew Magic Marker outlines around the hanging tools so there's no doubt where each tool goes. One outline looks like a sawzall, but the tool is missing.

"I think we've found what we're looking for," says Zoey. "Or at least where it came from."

"Did Teddy borrow your sawzall?" says Judd. There's an irritation in his voice because this is something Ash should have shared when he learned Teddy was missing.

Ash hesitates, then says, "No. I mean, sometimes he's asked to borrow tools and I always say yes, but he never asked to borrow that saw. Teddy or someone else must have just taken it."

"Why do you have these tools?" says Clay.

"What do you mean?"

"You're not exactly the handy type. You don't seem like the kind of guy who would have a well-supplied workshop, so neat and organized."

"It's . . ." starts Ash, then trails off. He starts again. "My grandmother bought all these tools for her groundskeeper. She loved living on this piece of property, but she was too busy driving around in her pink Cadillac selling cosmetics to take care of it."

"You're saying these tools came with the place when you inherited it?" says Judd.

"That's right," says Ash. "I can't remember her groundskeeper's name, but he must have organized everything like this."

"Who uses the tools now?" says Zoey.

"Alejandro," says Ash.

"Who's Alejandro?"

"He's the man I hire to take care of things now."

"What's his last name?"

Ash pops the collar on his polo as if feeling it on the back of his neck gives him comfort. "No idea. I just call him Alejandro. I never asked his last name."

"So you pay him in cash, not electronically or with a check?" says Clay.

"That's right," says Ash. "I'm not even sure where he lives. He just shows up once a week. He has that old sage-green Chevy pickup. You've probably seen it parked up here."

"I have," says Judd, his eyes on the pegboard. He can't help but marvel at how well he and Clay and Zoey are working together. They way they're tag-teaming Ash with questions, it's like they're reading each other's minds. "And just so we're clear, Alejandro didn't have anything to do with acquiring and organizing these tools. Your grandmother bought them and her old groundskeeper organized them."

"Right," says Ash. He shoves his hands into the pockets of his khakis and rocks back on his heels.

"Does Alejandro have a key to the pole barn?" says Clay.

"He does," says Ash. "That way he can come work whether or not I'm home."

"Does anyone else have a key?" says Zoey. "Did Teddy? Or Deb?"

"No," says Ash. "No one. I have one key. Alejandro has the other."

"When is Alejandro scheduled to work here again?" says Zoey.

"Thursday," says Ash. "He works on Thursdays."

"The day before Teddy disappeared," says Clay.

"I guess," says Ash.

"Do you keep your key to the pole barn in the house?" says Judd.

Ash holds up his key ring. "I keep the key right here." He smiles. "You just saw me use it to open the service door."

"And you don't have a spare in the house?" says Zoey.

Ash thinks about this. Thinks about it a little too hard and too demonstrably like a cartoon character before answering a question, looking up and twisting his lips. "Well, there might be a spare in the junk drawer. I haven't cleaned that thing out in years."

"And who has a key to the house other than you?" says Clay.

"No one."

"Not even the maid?" says Zoey, pointedly looking in the direction of the house.

"No," says Ash. "She's new. I don't trust her with a key yet."

Clay says, "But you gave Alejandro a key to the pole barn even though you don't know his last name or where he lives."

Ash seems to realize the inconsistency if not flat-out ridiculousness of this. "Yes," he says.

"What about Teddy and Deb?" says Judd.

"What about them?" says Ash.

"You didn't give a spare house key to Teddy or Deb in case you're on vacation and you wanted them to take in the mail or a package or let the maid in?"

Ash shakes his head. "I don't like people in my house when I'm not home."

"So to confirm," says Zoey, "you didn't lend your sawzall to Teddy. Either Alejandro used his key to take it, or Teddy somehow broke into this place and stole it."

Ash rocks back on his heels again and says, "I guess. I don't know what else could have happened."

"He's lying," says Judd.

The three of them are standing outside Clay's truck in front of Deb's house.

"I agree," says Zoey. "That Ash is a fidgety one. Just not sure what he's lying about."

"I can tell you one thing for sure," says Judd. "His grandmother didn't buy those tools. And her groundskeeper didn't organize them."

"You sound pretty certain of that," says Clay.

"That's because Ash and Deb inherited their respective pieces of property in 2001. I remember because I was helping Teddy tow that first trailer they used to live in onto the property when the first plane hit the tower in New York. We were glued to the truck radio. I'll never forget it."

"And?" says Zoey.

"And that brand of tools didn't come out until probably 2010. I remember that because I bought a bunch of them when Clay was playing soccer in Europe. And I know that because I specifically remember wondering whether I should keep my old tools for him, but figured he wouldn't be moving back."

"Anything else that you're certain Ash just lied about?" says Zoey.

"Not certain," says Judd.

"Me either," says Clay. "But I'd be damn surprised if the woman in Ash's house is his maid. Not unless he's paying her to scold him like a child."

"Some men like that," says Zoey. Both Clay and Judd stare at her. She seems to feel their eyes on her and adds, "That's what I've been told."

CHAPTER 28

Carol's fly-tying bench is in the sunroom. Shelves line the one wall not full of windows. The old house has high ceilings—ten feet tall—and the shelves go all the way up. They're filled with clear plastic shoeboxes but the boxes don't hold shoes. They hold fly- and lure-making materials, each labeled in Carol's neat hand. Braedon reads: DRY-FLY HOOKS, STREAMER HOOKS, JIG HOOKS, PLASTIC BEADS, METAL BEADS, TUNGSTEN BEADS, ROOSTER FEATHERS, HEN FEATHERS, TURKEY FEATHERS, TURKEY BIOTS, PARTRIDGE FEATHERS, CHENILLE, SYNTHETIC FIBERS . . . The boxes keep going and going.

A ladder slides along a track in the floor. The top of the ladder has pulley-like wheels that run along a track up near the ceiling. If you wanted say, rabbit zonkers, you pushed the ladder to the left side of the wall, climbed up a few rungs, and grabbed it off the top shelf. Zonkers are strips of rabbit fur, skin intact, usually dyed. Braedon's lashing a rust-colored one to a hook with thread.

"Your grandpa Judd's going to love these," says Carol. "You're a natural."

"Thanks," says Braedon. "Should I tie this all the way up to the hook-eye or leave some room?"

"Leave a little room. That'll give you space to make a nice head out of thread wraps."

"And we'll coat that with resin?"

"You got it," says Carol. "You might want to consider making lures as a career."

Braedon smiles. "I don't know what I want to be yet."

"What about a professional soccer player like your dad?"

"I don't think so," says Braedon. "I'm not good enough."

Sue enters the room and says, "You're not good enough for what?"

"Playing soccer," says Braedon. "At least for a job. But I might want to be a police officer like my grandpa."

"We'd love to have you down at the station," says Sue. "Get you a uniform, maybe your own police bike. You can wear a helmet with a siren on top."

Braedon laughs. "Maybe someday. It just seems like a job where you get to be out doing stuff all the time. Talking to people. Looking for bad guys. Don't have to be in one place."

"That's the way it used to be," says Sue.

"Used to be?" says Braedon. "It's not anymore?"

"Technology has changed things. Most police officers nowadays have their face in front of a computer more than they do real people. They can get more done that way. When I started out—this was back before your dad was born—if the police were looking for a suspect, they had to drive around and talk to people all day and all night. Now the first place they check is Google. In less than an hour, they can accomplish what used to take a whole week."

"Like, what do you mean?" says Braedon as he coats the head of the lure in UV resin.

"Well," says Sue. "Let's say someone robs a gas station. And a security camera captures their picture. In the old days, the police would take that picture all over town, show it around, maybe have it printed in the newspaper or broadcast on the TV, and they'd just hope someone would recognize and identify the culprit. But today, all the police have to do is a reverse-image search online. If that person's image exists on the internet, either on social media or maybe on their workplace's website, or maybe they appear in someone else's post and they're tagged . . . Then it's over. The police have their suspect."

Braedon shines a UV flashlight on the resin and says, "Really? Police just look at their computer all the time?"

"Not all the time," says Sue. "They still go out on patrol. But a whole lot of their investigative work is done online now. All I'm saying is if you want to be a police officer, I hope you have a comfy chair."

Clay's night finally ends at 11:15 AM. If he had heard Sue's speech to Braedon about investigative work being done online, he would beg to differ. Clay hopes to sleep until five o'clock or so, then he'll pick up Braedon, make dinner, watch a little TV, then get to bed before midnight. He used to pull all-nighters all the time. Soccer by day. Slip out of the team's hotel to moonlight for the US government, then another day of soccer. He'd catch up with little naps where he could. Flying to the next city. Riding on the team bus. During an hour or two of quiet time in the hotel before heading to the stadium.

But now he's out of practice. Or maybe he's simply forty-two years old and can't do what he used to. Clay brushes his teeth and looks at himself in the bathroom mirror. He can't stop picturing Teddy on Miller's Bluff. Maybe Teddy slipped and hit his head and, when he came to, had amnesia. In his confusion, he took off his earring and hoodie. But that doesn't explain the sawzall and glove. Plus Clay has seen amnesia a lot in TV shows and movies, but in all his experience in the army, on the soccer pitch, and as an intelligence agent, he knows of plenty of people who hit their head one way or another, but not one forgot who they were.

Another possibility is Teddy thought he was under suspicion for a crime. Either a crime that Clay doesn't know about or he's involved with the thefts up at Dorset-Cornwall or the recent spate of catalytic converter thefts. Maybe Teddy's hiding out on Miller's Bluff until things settle down. Maybe he doesn't want to put Deb in the position of having to lie for him, and that's why he hasn't contacted her. Or Judd. Or Clay, for that matter. Or maybe he's just ashamed.

It's all plausible but something doesn't feel right, and Clay's too tired to figure out what that is. He goes into the kitchen and drinks a big glass of water in an attempt to dilute the salt and sugar in his blood from his first and second breakfasts, then walks into his bedroom when the doorbell rings.

The house is not large but, in Clay's sleep-deprived state, the walk to the front door feels like a mile. He opens the door and says, "Steph." It sounds stupid but he doesn't know what else to say.

"Hi, Clay. I'm sorry about Thomas. I can't believe he did what he did."

Clay says, "It's hardly your fault. Come on in."

Steph Becker steps into Clay's home for the first time. She wears her blond hair long and unbound. It falls like curtains on the front of her shoulders. She scans the open, modern house and says, "Nice place."

"Thank you. And I apologize if I sound a little out of it—I haven't slept yet."

Steph walks from the foyer into the living room and sits on a leather lounge chair. Clay follows and takes the couch.

"Can I get you anything?" he says.

She shakes her head. "Listen. I'm sorry this is so weird. I can't believe Thomas was involved in a fake kidnapping plot. And that he just stood there and did nothing when that Graham pulled a gun on your son."

"Yeah," says Clay, "I'm not crazy about that either."

"I hate that Graham," says Steph. "Whenever Thomas gets in trouble, Graham's somehow involved. I hate to think a fifteen-year-old boy is rotten. But I'm getting pretty close with that one."

"Appreciate that. And I appreciate your commiseration."

Steph doesn't respond right away. She drops her face into her hands, stays that way for ten long seconds, then says, "I want to come clean about something."

Clay stares hard at the top of Steph's head. "Okay."

Steph sits back up and drops her hands. "I haven't seen you very much since you moved back. Mostly just when you need a haircut. But whenever we do see each other, it feels kind of flirty. Do you think that?"

Clay considers Steph's question, then says, "Friendly. I'd say it's friendly more than flirty."

"Okay . . . But there's something, right? I know high school was a long time ago but we definitely had something between us then. Something kind of special, I think. And some of those feelings are still there. Is it just me who thinks that? Because it seems to me like you feel it, too."

This is the last conversation Clay expects or wants after being awake for thirty hours straight. He's not sharp and fears he'll say something stupid or, worse, hurtful. "We always got along great," says Clay. "And yeah, it feels like we still do."

"Of course," says Steph. "I agree. So it's . . . I guess the reason I'm here is . . . Last night I saw you at Knut's. I was going to come over and say hello but then the chief of police sat next to you. And she wasn't looking like the chief of police—she looked like she was on a date. With you."

"Ah," says Clay, more to buy time than because he understands. "We were not on a date. I ran into Zoey there. We talked for a little bit, then I left."

"I know you left," says Steph. "And about a minute after you left, so did Zoey. Did you two go somewhere together? I know, I know. It's none of my business. We're not dating. You're free to see whoever you want to see. I just . . . I'm not in a great place right now. I'm super vulnerable with the divorce and with everything that happened with Thomas last night . . . So I guess

I just don't want to assume anything and make up stories in my brain. My therapist says I really have to work on that. So about an hour after you left, I was feeling very anxious about you leaving with her."

"I didn't leave with—"

"I know. Technically you didn't leave with Zoey. You left a minute before and then she left. That's what people do in small towns hoping there won't be gossip. But it is a small town. We all know what leaving a minute apart means."

Clay rubs his forehead. "Zoey ended up following me but not for romantic reasons. We were talking about Teddy. I told her that I was leaving because my father and I were going to ask around to see if anyone had spotted Teddy, but Zoey thought I might be up to something else. Which I was. So she followed me. Without me knowing it, which is not easy to do. That's how she was nearby when Thomas and the other two boys assaulted my father and stole my truck. Then she followed the boys to the mess with Braedon and Daniel and took them into custody."

"Oh," says Steph. "I see. Oh, boy, Clay. I'm sorry I came over like this. I tried calling but it kept going straight to voicemail. Like you blocked my number or—"

"My phone is in the river," says Clay.

"What?"

"My phone went straight to voicemail because it's underwater. Thomas and his pals tossed my phone in the river after they stole my truck. When they were going over a bridge near Chatfield. It's probably in La Crescent by now."

"Oh, God," says Steph. She's on the verge of tears and tries to blink them away. "I'm so sorry, Clay. I've had no real trouble with

Thomas, and then out of the blue this happens. I'm shocked. And so embarrassed. He is never hanging out with that Graham again. That friendship is officially over."

"That's probably a good idea," says Clay.

"Thomas is going to jail, isn't he?" Steph can no longer hold back her tears. "My baby's going to jail and there's nothing I can do about it."

"That hasn't been decided yet," says Clay. "The police will investigate the incident further, and then they'll decide if they want to press charges."

"Of course they'll press charges!"

"Not necessarily. For one thing, my father and I are not pressing charges."

"You aren't?" says Steph. "They knocked Judd unconscious, stole forty-five thousand dollars, and your truck."

"We are aware of that," says Clay. "But they're fifteen. A criminal conviction would be quite a hardship for all three. We would rather give them a chance to turn things around. The important thing right now is that we find Teddy. Maybe the boys can be of some help. We'd rather keep them in a mindset where they might remember something rather than worrying about who their cellmate will be."

"Oh . . ." Steph places her palm over her chest. "That is so kind of you. So kind . . . And considerate. Thank you. Thank you so much." Steph drops her face into one hand and adds, "I've made such a fool of myself."

"No you haven't. I got duped by three fifteen-year-old boys. That's making a fool of yourself."

Steph looks up at nothing and taps her foot in the air, one

leg crossed over her opposite knee. She shakes her head and says, "I'm a piece of work, huh? I just freaked out like I'm the victim in all this. But you're the victim. You and your dad. I guess I just couldn't believe you weren't answering my calls or returning my texts this morning and . . . Okay, I'll shut up. I know you need sleep. I'll go." Steph stands.

Clay considers telling Steph that after they find Teddy, he's open to discussing the idea of him and her and . . . But he can only think clearly enough right now to know that he isn't thinking clearly. Plus he's pretty sure she has something going on with Eli Hensel. Maybe it's best not to say something he might feel differently about after he gets some rest.

Instead he says, "I'm glad you came by."

"You are?"

"It's better you got the truth than thinking the worst of me."

She smiles. "Thanks for saying that."

He walks her to the door, gives her a hug, and adds, "I'll see you soon."

He can feel her nod into his shoulder, then she turns, opens the front door, and leaves.

CHAPTER 29

Judd wakes to his doorbell. He looks at his watch. It's just after 5:00 PM. The sidelight window next to the front door is covered in cardboard. He can't see who is on his front step. His inner cop won't allow him to open the front door without knowing who's on the other side.

"Can I help you?" he says to the door.

"Judd. It's me."

Judd unlocks and opens the door to see Mei standing in her scrubs. The look on her face walks the line between pissed off and relieved.

Mei says, "Why haven't you responded to my calls or texts?"

"Lost my phone. Why didn't you call me on my landline?"

"I didn't know you had a landline," says Mei. "Where do you keep it? Next to your steam engine and washboard?" She sighs something sad. "I'm sorry. You're going through hell right now.

I just . . . I was worried. I *am* worried. Why do you look like you just woke up?"

"Because I just woke up," says Judd. "Come on in. I have a lot to tell you."

The invitation to Clay has to be delivered in person. Deb reaches Judd on his landline. Deb reaches Zoey through Sue. And Zoey stops at Clay's house and rings the doorbell. He answers it wearing joggers and a sweatshirt and hair pointing in all directions.

"Rise and shine," says Zoey. "Deb wants us over there for pizza and to share some new information."

"What kind of information?" says Clay.

"She figured out Teddy's password on his cell phone. She's in. Now come on. Go pretty yourself up. I can't be seen with someone looking the way you do. I have a reputation in this town. And brush your teeth. I don't want any bad breath fogging up my windshield."

When Clay walks into the doublewide, he notices something missing—it's the hope in Deb's eyes. He and Zoey enter the living room and sit on the couch. Deb has brought in a chair from the kitchen for herself. She holds Teddy's cell phone. Judd and Mei have squeezed into Teddy's old recliner but keep it unreclined with their feet on the floor.

"Thanks for coming," says Deb. "I've found some disturbing emails and texts in Teddy's phone."

"If you don't mind sharing," says Zoey, "what was the password? It may give us some insight into Teddy's state of mind."

Deb looks down at Teddy's phone, then lifts her eyes to Zoey. "91279."

"Any significance?" says Zoey.

Deb nods. "It's the day Teddy and I drove up to St. Paul and he talked his way into backstage passes at the Clash concert. That's when Joe Strummer gave Teddy the earring. After the concert, we walked down by the river, and Teddy proposed to me. We were seniors in high school so we kept it secret until we graduated." Deb manages a sad smile. "I don't know why I didn't think of it before. We celebrate the anniversary of our first date. We celebrate our wedding anniversary. But we never celebrate the anniversary of Teddy's proposal." She wipes away a silent tear. "Apparently, the date was still important to Teddy."

Clay glances at his father, looking for the same despair that he sees in Deb's eyes, but what Clay sees in his father is curiosity. Judd doesn't know what's in Teddy's phone. Deb has waited to tell them together.

"Teddy's been gambling," says Deb. "One of those sports gambling sites. He downloaded the app—I can see all his winnings and losses—and the losses far outweigh the winnings."

"Oh, boy," says Judd. "Why do people fall for that? Just because they advertise on TV every ten seconds? It's like Vegas. Think they build those big hotels and give you free drinks because they're losing money?" And then, almost to himself, he adds, "Come on, Teddy. You know better than that."

"Where's the money coming from?" says Clay.

"It appears," says Deb, "that Teddy opened a checking account I didn't know about. It also appears that Teddy uses the same password for our regular bank account. I've logged into his secret account. All expenditures are for the gambling website. And all deposits are cash. They range from twenty dollars up to a thousand dollars." Deb looks from her phone to Judd. "Has any of that cash come from you?"

"No," says Judd. "Teddy hasn't asked for money in a few years. And that was for getting his car fixed, which he did. I paid the mechanic directly."

"Clay?" says Deb.

Clay shakes his head. "Teddy doesn't ask me for money, and I've never offered it."

"Is it possible Braedon has given Teddy money? I hate to even mention it, but he's a sweet kid, and he adores Teddy. If Teddy asked—"

"No," says Clay. "Braedon has a savings account, but I have access to it. The only thing he's withdrawn money for is to buy a fishing rod and reel and some tackle." Clay shifts positions on the couch to face Judd. "So he can impress his grandfather up north."

"So," says Zoey. "Teddy has a secret source of cash. Someone's been paying him under the table to do something we don't know about."

"It looks that way," says Deb. "I have no idea who that person is, but I'm pretty sure I know their phone number. There's a text chain in here . . . The contact is just a phone number, no name or anything."

"Probably a burner," says Clay.

"And each text just contains a date and time," says Deb. "The response is either a thumbs-up or thumbs-down. Sometimes initiated by Teddy. Sometimes initiated by whoever the number belongs to."

"When is the most recent text?" says Zoey.

"Saturday," says Deb.

"A day after Teddy disappeared," says Judd.

Mei takes Judd's hand in hers and gives it a squeeze.

"Yes," says Deb. "It's from the same number. Teddy's last text is at one AM on Friday. It just reads *2:30*. And the response came two minutes later: a thumbs-up. Teddy must have left the house shortly after."

"If we knew their meetup location," says Clay, "we could send a time and date and show up to find out who it is. But we have no idea where they've been meeting. Zoey, can you start the process of getting records for that phone number? Maybe location stamps for the texts? Find out what other apps the person is running that may reveal personal information?"

Zoey looks hard at Clay with her mouth half open.

"What?" says Clay. "You think it's a bad idea?"

"No . . ." says Zoey. "I think it's a good idea. I'm just wondering how you thought of it."

"It's a phone," says Clay. "Isn't it common sense?"

"Yeah . . ." says Zoey. She eyes Clay with suspicion and doubt. "Sure . . ." she says. But her expression does not change.

Judd takes this in, and Mei watches Judd. Deb is too preoccupied with Teddy's phone to pick up on anything else.

"Anyway," adds Zoey. "If that phone number does belong to a burner, it was probably paid for with cash. We can subpoena the company for locations and additional information on that phone, but the process takes time. And we don't have time."

"What we do have," says Judd, "is a time stamp for Teddy's last text and a time for whenever Teddy and whoever were supposed to meet. Teddy left his phone and wallet and car here, so either he walked to the meetup place, got picked up in a vehicle, or had a bike stashed on the property that we didn't know about. The dogs tracking Teddy down to the creek doesn't mean much. That could have been from a day or two before he disappeared. The time difference between the text and the meetup is ninety minutes. If Teddy walked, we can figure out the radius of where he could get to on foot in that amount of time. Same if he biked. If he was picked up in a car, that could get him almost to the Twin Cities. Or to Wisconsin or well into Iowa."

Zoey takes out her cell phone. Clay asks what she's doing, but Zoey doesn't respond. She thumb-types, waits, and thumb-types some more. After about ten seconds, she says, "My map program says it takes one hour and fifteen minutes to walk to Miller's Bluff. Think that could be the meetup place?"

"If it is," says Clay, "we could use a Stingray device to emulate Teddy's phone to set another meeting."

Zoey stares at Clay.

"What?" says Clay. "You think *that's* a bad idea?"

Zoey says nothing.

"What? We used IMSI devices all the time when I was in the army. That technology goes back to the early nineties."

Zoey keeps her eyes on Clay. Dubious eyes. Dubious with a hint of playfulness. She smiles and shakes her head.

"We don't need to emulate Teddy's phone," says Judd. "We have it right here. And speaking of phones, Clay and I need to replace ours." He looks at his watch. "Let's head up to Rochester now so we're all back in communication with each other. And thanks, Deb. Thanks for getting inside Teddy's phone and sharing what you've found."

Deb shrugs. "I wish I could do more. I feel frozen. Like I have to stay here in case . . . for when Teddy comes home. Thanks to all of you for being out there looking for him."

The pizza arrives. They eat and discuss more theories about where Teddy might be. Then Clay heads up to Rochester in his truck. Judd wants to drive separately so he can spend more time with Mei, which Clay interprets as spend the night. Deb is the most upset she's been since Teddy disappeared. Part of that is from more time having passed. The longer Teddy is gone, the more likely he got himself into some real trouble. And gaining access to Teddy's cell phone isn't helping Deb's mental state. The man has an addictive personality. Sometimes that means substituting one drug with another. Or one activity with another. It's all about chasing the same high, whether that high comes from alcohol or gambling or whatever.

Judd kisses Mei goodbye at her car and makes a plan to meet at her place. Zoey is about to get in her squad car when Judd calls out to her.

She stops, one leg in the car, the door open. "Yeah?"

Judd walks over and says, "Why are you keeping Mike and Andy out of this?"

"I'm not," says Zoey. "Finding Teddy is their number one job at the moment."

"Yeah, but how come you're working primarily with Clay and me and not them?"

Zoey swings her other leg into the car, shuts the door, rolls down the window, and says, "I don't trust Mike and Andy."

"What does that mean?" says Judd. "You think they're involved in Teddy going missing?"

"Not necessarily," says Zoey. "But they're up to something. Their communication with me is dodgy. They come and go at odd hours and in strange ways. For example, why did Wahlquist choose to drive home on such an obscure route the night he found you and Clay walking home after the bridge incident?"

"Yeah," says Judd. "I've been wondering the same thing."

"I saw him earlier that night at Knut's," says Zoey. "Then he left to go on patrol but he made some lame excuse about being down in a river valley and out of service."

"It can happen," says Judd.

"I know. But Sue tried radio contact for over an hour. Those out-of-contact spots are small. Just at the lowest elevations. What was Wahlquist doing in one for over an hour?"

"Wahlquist and Kimmich are good cops," says Judd.

"They can be," says Zoey. "But they're not always good cops. I've seen that firsthand. And my guess is you have, too."

Judd doesn't respond directly. He's never held his friends Mike Wahlquist and Andy Kimmich to the standards he sets for himself. Maybe that's part of being Teddy Hawkins's twin brother. Always expecting less from others. Making excuses for them. Bailing them out of whatever trouble they might get into because, hey, they did not fall short of expectations. At least Judd's expectations. Maybe the only person he's ever had high expectations for is Clay. And Clay met Judd's expectations and then some. Not exactly in the way Judd would have preferred, but Clay is one capable human being.

He can't help but wonder if all that animosity toward Clay stemmed from a fear of losing the boy. Losing him like he lost Pam. Maybe Judd kept his son at arm's length so Clay couldn't hurt him the way Pam did. The idea is just hitting him now in the moment, and it's making his stomach churn. He's got to put that to bed. Accept Clay for who he is. Because Clay is pretty damn amazing. His violin playing. Going to Dorset-Cornwall. Working for his country using pro soccer as a cover. And Clay's raising one hell of a boy. Gave Judd his most treasured gift.

And it was Clay who noticed Zoey's skilled police work. Maybe, if Judd is honest with himself, he saw it, too. But he didn't want to, and Clay opened Judd's eyes. Because Zoey Jensen is a hell of a cop. Her investigation of Teddy's disappearance is top rate. Hell, she's even sniffed out Clay's secret agent work while he played professional soccer in Europe. Or she's damn close to doing so.

Judd doesn't much like himself at the moment. But he swallows it all down and says, "So what do you think Wahlquist and Kimmich are up to?"

"Not sure," says Zoey. "Clay said Wahlquist is going to run for mayor. Maybe it has something to do with that. Or it might just be that they're trying to find Teddy on their own to show me up. I hope that's what they're doing. I know they feel slighted that one of them wasn't promoted to chief. They're not outright hostile toward me. But there's an undercurrent of tension at the station. Ask Sue. She's noticed it, too.

"The most important thing right now," adds Zoey, "is that whatever they're up to, I don't want it distracting from the work you and Clay and I are doing."

"All right," says Judd. "Fair enough. I'll talk to them. See if I can sniff out anything. And hopefully you're right. They're just trying to be the heroes so they can embarrass their boss." Judd looks down, as if he has to muster up the courage to say what he's about to say. "But don't worry about them. You're a good cop, Zoey. Riverwood is lucky to have you."

Zoey feels Judd's compliment in her throat and behind her eyes. And it takes all her strength to keep that feeling from spreading. "Of course you'd say that," she says. "You trained me." Zoey manages a hint of a smile, then rolls up her window and drives away.

CHAPTER 30

"Is it okay if I stay over one more night?"

Clay tests his new cell phone with a call to Braedon. He told his son he'd pick him up at 8:00 PM but Braedon has other ideas.

"Yesterday you said you didn't want to stay with a couple of old ladies," says Clay. "Now you don't want to leave?"

"It's just . . . I'm making the coolest lures for when me and Grandpa go fishing up north. Carol has books on how to make everything, and Sue gave me a ride to the house to get clean clothes and my computer so I can watch YouTube videos on lure making. I even made you some woolly buggers."

"Thank you, Brae. Woolly buggers are a go-to fly. I appreciate that."

"They're not hard. Just marabou, chenille, and hen hackle.

Oh, and a bead head and lead wire that isn't really made of lead because lead's toxic."

"That's perfect," says Clay. "What color?"

"I made you some black ones and olive ones and yellow ones. And a few white ones, too."

"Those are the best colors," says Clay. "I appreciate it, bud."

"Yeah," says Braedon. "That's what Carol said. And tomorrow I'll make you some purple ones because Carol says that's what the rainbow trout like the best even though there aren't many rainbows around here. So can I spend another night?"

"Put Sue on, would you?"

Clay hears rustling and muted conversation. He's waiting to hear Sue's voice when he notices a pair of headlights in his rearview mirror. They are dim and warmer in color than most headlights. Clay assumes the vehicle is older. Highway 52 is two lanes with a lot of ups and downs as the northern plains transition into the hilly driftless area with its streams and bluffs. A yellow dotted line bifurcates the road. It's okay to pass here. Clay pulls toward the shoulder and keeps his speed steady.

"Don't you take him home tonight," says Sue over the speakers in his F-150. "Carol hasn't had this much fun in years."

"All right," says Clay, "just making sure he's welcome."

"Carol's off carbs," says Sue. "I haven't had anyone else to eat cake with. He's welcome to stay as long as he likes."

"Thanks for going over to the house to get his stuff."

"Not a problem," says Sue. "You have a good night. Maybe go on a date. You've been home for months. It's time you found yourself a girlfriend."

"All right," says Clay. "I'll put it on my list. See you tomorrow."

Clay ends the call and checks his rearview mirror. The vehicle remains several car lengths back and shows no inclination to pass. They're about ten minutes north of Riverwood. There are no streetlights. Clay takes his foot off the gas, slowing down without activating his brake lights.

Now he's going forty miles an hour. The speed limit is fifty-five. The car comes closer then falls back, refusing to pass. Old habits are hard to break. One of those is having access to a gun. This is Minnesota. Clay could get a permit to carry a concealed weapon, something that would have been difficult if not impossible in Europe. Plus it would have attracted the attention of European government officials and law enforcement, and that's the last thing Clay wanted while moonlighting as an agent.

But in potentially dangerous situations, he always knew a weapon was nearby. That responsibility fell to his colleagues. Usually operatives Clay never had and never would meet. Before every night on the town, Clay would receive a coded message on his phone. To anyone else it would have looked like text spam. A sale on this or that. A request for a political donation. A reminder of an upcoming dentist appointment.

After Clay decoded the message it said there's a lockbox under the countertop in the men's bathroom. A lockbox against the wall in the coatroom. A lockbox behind the fire extinguisher in the kitchen. Always a lockbox that Clay could open with his fingerprint. Never an unsecured weapon that anyone might find.

Clay speeds up. The car speeds up with him to keep pace.

Clay reaches under the driver's seat of the Ford truck and removes a safe the size and shape of a cigar box. A digital panel lights up on the front edge. Clay can either enter a PIN or touch his finger on a sensor to the right of the display. He chooses the latter, and then hears the box unlock.

He sets the box on the passenger seat, opens it, and reaches in with his right hand, which he places on a SIG Sauer P226. The gun feels like it wants to be picked up, as if it can change its shape to fit one's hand perfectly. Clay checks his rearview mirror again. The headlights behind him follow at the same distance. Whether he speeds up or slows down, so does the car behind him, as if Clay and his follower are linked by a pole. The headlights appear to belong to a car, not a truck. Clay makes that deduction based on their relatively low position to the road, and that they appear too close together to belong to a truck.

There are a number of plausible explanations for why the driver of the car has chosen not to pass him, even though Clay is now going thirty-five miles per hour in a fifty-five mile per hour zone. The driver may be frightened to pass at night. The driver may be concerned about a deer leaping from the ditch on the opposite side of the road and having no place to bail out. Then again, maybe the driver has less safety-oriented concerns.

Clay approaches the top of a hill and punches the gas. His truck lurches forward. He crests the hill and flies down, leaving his tail still climbing behind him. There's an intersection at the bottom. Clay pumps his brakes and takes a hard right off Highway 52. He floors it for a quarter of a mile, then turns up the drive toward a farmhouse. He kills his headlights, does a three-point U-turn, and waits in the dark. A minute later, the car with the dim headlights crosses in front of him. Clay pulls out onto the road—he's now tailing the car. He turns on his lights and speeds up until he's two car lengths behind his former follower. Clay recognizes the car, accelerates, and flips on his brights. The car does not pull over.

He presses closer to the car, sets the gun on the passenger seat, and checks to make sure his new phone has finished updating from the cloud. It has, and he calls Zoey's cell phone. She answers on the first ring.

"We've got to slow down," says Zoey. "I just spent the night with you and half the day. How about a little break to whet our appetites?"

"I picked up a tail between Rochester and Riverwood."

"A tail or *some* tail?"

"Zoey," says Clay. "Not now."

"Fine. Any idea who it is?"

"I know exactly who it is, but he may not be smart enough to realize it. If he has a full tank, this could go on for hours. Want to lend a hand?"

"Well, when you get all mushy and romantic, how can I say no? All right, all right. Not now. Where are you?"

"I'll share my location, and you can think of something fun."

"Hold on," says Zoey. "Who's driving the car?"

"You want me to spoil the surprise?"

"Not that as much as I'd like to know if the person might be armed and dangerous. That's police lingo for carrying a gun and being willing to use it."

"Thank you for the explanation," says Clay. "And I don't think he's dangerous."

"You don't *think* he's dangerous? That does not fill me with confidence."

"Just set up a roadblock," says Clay. "He'll be thrilled to see a cop."

"Sarcasm?"

"Not one bit. Trust me."

"*Trust me,*" says Zoey. "That old line."

"I have a soft spot for the classics."

"I bet you do. Okay, ping me your twenty. See you soon. And one more question."

"What?" says Clay.

"Is it Ash Solbakken?"

Clay laughs. "How'd you know?"

"That creep is hiding something. He probably tailed you to find out if you know what it is. I bet he just drives home so he can claim he was out and about minding his own business. He didn't even know that it was you he was driving behind."

"You have experience with weaselly men," says Clay.

"I do," says Zoey. "Maybe that's why I'm so comfortable with you."

Clay can hear the smile in her voice; otherwise, he might be offended.

CHAPTER 31

Chief of Police Zoey Jensen is right. Clay tails Ash directly to his hundred-acre parcel of land with its horses and llamas, its grand old house and metal pole barn, all of which sits adjacent to Deb and Teddy's place. When Ash starts down his long gravel driveway, Zoey is already there, sitting in her squad car with the headlights on and the cherries off.

"Oh hey, Chief," says Ash. "What's going on?" He's out of his car and walking toward Zoey, who sits behind the wheel with her window down. Ash wears a deep V-necked cable-knit sweater in white over a red polo shirt, Nantucket red shorts, which are not red but pink, no socks, and Tretorn tennis shoes. Ash turns back to Clay, who's stepping out of his truck. "What the hell, Clay? Why are you following me?"

Zoey says, "This won't go well for you, Ash, if you keep saying things like that."

"Saying things like what? What did I do? I was just out running the MG because I haven't driven it in a while. Then this truck pulls behind me and—"

"Don't," says Clay.

"Don't what?" says Ash.

"I have a dash cam and a rearview cam. The whole thing is on video." This is a lie, but it's one of Clay's favorites. He used it all the time when confronting Russian assets. Not spies, but the stooges they hired as couriers and lookouts. No amateur wants to be confronted with video evidence. It's easier to just assume that the video exists and play ball rather than deny it and face the irrefutable truth.

Ash's shoulders slump forward like a child's who's just been sent to his room. Then he swings his eyes toward Zoey and says, "I was acting out of self-defense."

"When?" says Zoey. "And with whom? Teddy?"

"What?" says Ash. "No. With Clay. He has a very threatening presence and I don't like the way he's been looking at me lately."

"Clay is threatening," says Zoey. "That Clay? The skinny little fellow with long flowing locks?"

"He's not that skinny," says Ash. "So I followed him to see what he's up to." Ash's posture straightens the more he likes the smell of his excuse. "You know, to protect myself. Living outside of city limits. A guy has to take security into his own hands."

"Really?" says Zoey. "Did you decide that before or after someone stole the sawzall from your pole barn?"

Ash opens his mouth but no words come out.

"Why did you give the saw to Teddy?" says Clay. "What are you two up to?"

Ash says nothing.

"Maybe," says Zoey, "we should go down to the station and have a chat."

"Am I under arrest?" says Ash.

"You will be if you don't cooperate. Come on. Let's go. I'll drive you home after."

"No," says Ash with panic in his voice. "Not the station. Let's talk here. Please . . ."

Ash hasn't updated the house since he inherited it from his grandmother. There's a lot of honey-colored oak and floral print on everything that can have floral print. The wallpaper, the upholstery, rugs, and, in some rooms, the ceilings.

"Teddy needed money," says Ash. "He came to me and asked for a loan."

"How much money?" says Zoey.

"Ten grand. He told me he'd gotten himself in over his head on something and was in a real jam."

They sit around a kitchen table that looks like it might have been in a Cracker Barrel at one time. It features intricate chisel work and spindly legs.

"Did you lend him the money?" says Clay.

"Yes," Ash says. "Because he's family . . . and he promised he'd pay it back in a month."

"You've known Teddy your entire life and you lent him money based on a promise to pay it back?"

"Yeah . . ." says Ash, his voice rising and fading in a lack of confidence.

"When did you lend Teddy the ten grand?" says Zoey.

"A little less than a year ago, I think."

"Did Teddy ever pay back the loan?"

"No," says Ash. "He keeps saying he'll pay me back, but whenever I see him, he has an excuse. You know Teddy."

"Yeah," says Clay. "I do. Just like you do. Which brings us back to why would you lend him money."

"He's family," says Ash. "And a neighbor. What else could I do?"

"Say no," says Clay.

"What kind of interest are you charging him?" says Zoey.

"Excuse me?" says Ash.

"How much interest are you charging Teddy on the loan?" says Clay. "You know, the loan you agreed to because Teddy is family?"

Ash looks up at a cuckoo clock hanging on the wall next to a framed needlepoint that reads: PEARLS GO WITH EVERYTHING.

"Is that a hard question to answer?" says Zoey.

Ash sighs. "He's supposed to pay me back fifteen."

"Fifteen percent or fifteen thousand dollars?" says Clay.

Ash reddens. "Fifteen thousand dollars."

"You charged Teddy fifty percent interest?" says Zoey. "Not exactly the family and neighbors rate. Not to mention Minnesota usury laws."

Ash turns back to ashen. "What do you mean?"

"You broke the law, Ash," says Clay. "You can't charge that much interest. You could be in serious trouble."

"Real serious," adds Zoey.

"I didn't collect!" says Ash. "There's no deal. Teddy and me, we don't have a deal anymore. It didn't happen."

"But you lent him the money," says Clay.

"Yes," says Ash. "But then—" Ash stops himself as if he's forgotten the English language.

"But then what?" says Zoey.

Ash gets up from the table and walks to the pantry. He returns with a package of Oreos, slides out the plastic tray, and sets them before Zoey and Clay. Ash removes one, takes a bite, and says, with his mouth full, "I made a deal with Teddy. If he took care of something for me, I'd forgive the interest on the loan."

"Just the interest?" says Clay.

"Yes."

"And what was Teddy's quest, pray tell?" says Zoey.

Ash looks confused, as if he doesn't quite understand Zoey's question, then says, "I was in Lanesboro at the Root River Saloon. And there's this girl at the bar." It's like Ash can feel Zoey's eyes on him and says, "Woman. This young woman."

"How young?" says Zoey.

"Twenties. Maybe thirty. We get to talking. I ask if I can buy her a drink and she says yes, so I do."

"What did she order?" says Zoey.

"A Long Island iced tea."

"Twenties," says Zoey with an *I figured* expression aimed more at Clay than Ash.

"Probably," says Ash. "But over twenty-one—she was in a bar."

"Naturally," says Clay. "No one under twenty-one has ever set foot in a bar."

"Do you want me to tell you the rest or not?" says Ash. "Because if you just want to make fun of me, I'll be quiet and you can have at it."

Clay and Zoey share a look. They're tag-teaming poor Ash. But the look is more about their tag-teaming than it is Ash. Their teamwork feels natural, the two of them, and they both know it. Something transpires in this shared glance. Something bigger than Ash. Maybe even bigger than Teddy.

Zoey breaks eye contact first and says, "We apologize. Please continue."

"Anyway, we're talking—"

"Do you remember her name?" says Clay.

"Skye," says Ash. "Skye and I are talking and after a couple of drinks I ask her if she wants to come to the house to see the horses and llamas. And she gets this kind of sad look on her face. Really sad and like, kind of lonely or something like that. I expect she's going to tell me to take a hike, but no. She says she would like to see the horses and llamas. But not like in an excited way. Almost like it was something she had to do."

"And did she go back to the house with you?" says Zoey. "To see the horses and llamas?"

Ash nods.

"Did she spend the night?" says Clay.

"Technically no."

"Which means," says Zoey, "that you slept with her and then she left. So how was the sex?"

Ash's eyebrows rise almost all the way to his hairline. "Excuse me?"

"How was the sex? Was it tame? Was it wild? Was she into

it? What did she say? *You're the greatest lover I've ever had? Nobody has ever done it for me the way you do? You sure do know how to satisfy a woman?*"

Ash looks at Clay with an expression that says, *Do I have to answer that question?* Clay responds with a nod.

"Yeah," says Ash. "She said some stuff like that."

"And afterward," says Zoey, "how much money did she say you owed her?"

Ash reddens again. "Five hundred." He swallows hard. "Plus a tip."

"Did you pay her?" says Clay.

"I told her I didn't know she was going to ask for money. She never said she was a . . . you know . . . professional." And with downturned eyes, he adds, "I've picked up women before. Many times. None of them have ever asked for money after. Well, almost none of them. At least in the United States. And then she said it should have been obvious because look at her and look at me and I'm old enough to be her father. And why on earth would she choose me if it wasn't for five hundred dollars and a tip?"

Clay turns to Zoey and says, "Is five hundred the going rate around here? Sounds kind of steep."

"You're right," says Zoey. "It is steep. But look at the way he dresses." She rolls her eyes over to Ash. "He's screaming that he has money. Then she sees this big house with a petting zoo . . . She probably thought five hundred was about right." Zoey looks at Ash. "Did you pay her?"

"No," says Ash with a firmness in his voice. "Well, not right away. I said I didn't have five hundred dollars laying around the house. She said we could go to a cash machine in town. So I said

I lost my debit card because, you know, I shouldn't have to pay for it. I don't *need* to pay for it. Women like me . . . Some women like me. They do."

"Are any of them in their twenties?" says Zoey.

Ash pretends to think about this as if the answer is difficult, then says, "No."

"Did she buy the lost debit card excuse?" says Clay. "Or do you think it's possible she'd heard that one before?"

"She said," starts Ash, "that if I didn't pay her, I would have to answer to her boyfriend."

"Meaning her pimp," says Clay.

"I don't know . . . That was the first time I ever . . . I . . ." Ash deflates even further. "I don't know . . . Unless . . ."

Clay and Zoey share another look. Zoey helps herself to an Oreo, pops the whole thing in her mouth, and says, "Unless what?"

"You promise you won't tell anyone if I tell you?"

"I'm the police, Ash. Who are you worried about us telling?"

"Just, you have to promise." Ash sits up straighter to show them he means business.

"I can promise you this, Ash," says Zoey. "If what you're about to tell us does not involve criminal activity, we won't tell anyone. If it does involve criminal activity, and you're not involved, we won't mention your name."

"That works," says Ash.

"But I can't promise some lawyer won't subpoena you."

"Of course," adds Clay, "if it comes to that, you'll probably be in a lot more trouble then than if you just tell us now." Clay's hoping Ash doesn't think this through because it doesn't make a whole lot of sense. Again, trick of the trade.

Ash nods. It makes sense to him. "Okay. I'll tell you." He takes another Oreo, unscrews it, scrapes off the filling with his front teeth, and says, "I told Skye—I doubt that's her real name . . ."

"Really?" says Zoey in a flat, dull tone. "I hadn't considered that possibility."

Ash nods as if to say, *I'm almost sure of it.* "I told her that I would try to find my debit card and we could go get her five hundred dollars."

"Plus tip," says Clay.

"Yes, plus tip. If she promised that she would never tell anyone about our time together."

"Let me guess," says Zoey. "She promised."

"Yes. She did. Then I 'found' my debit card. We drove to a bank machine. I paid her. I dropped her back at the bar where I met her. Then never saw her again. But she broke the promise because a few days later—and this is the part you can never tell anyone—Andy Kimmich came to the house and told me if *I* ever told anyone about that night, he'd kill me."

"Andy Kimmich of Riverwood PD?" says Zoey.

"That's the only one I know."

"And he actually said he'd kill you?" says Clay.

"Kill me," says Ash. "His exact words."

"Okay," says Zoey. "So how is Teddy involved in all this?"

"Right," says Ash. "Okay. I told Teddy that if he did me a favor in relation to Andy Kimmich, I would forgive the interest on the ten grand."

"What was the favor?" says Clay.

"I told Teddy to tell Andy Kimmich that he saw an MC at

my house. This house. My house. You know, because Teddy and Deb's property is right next to this one. Teddy was supposed to say it in kind of an awestruck way, like I was in business with an MC. Just to let Andy know I wasn't somebody to mess with."

"An MC?" says Zoey.

"Motorcycle club," says Ash.

"You mean a biker gang? Guys with leather vests and loud Harleys and big handlebars?"

Ash nods.

"Holy shit, you have to be kidding," says Clay.

Ash shakes his head with dead-serious eyes.

"And you think," says Zoey, "that Teddy went to tell Andy Kimmich this, and that's why Teddy is missing."

Ash nods, and his lower lip begins to tremble. He wipes away a tear before it can start down his cheek. As he does, Clay and Zoey share a look of disappointment.

Zoey takes a deep breath and says, "All right. I'll have a talk with Andy."

"You promise you won't mention me, right? I mean, you promised."

"We promise," says Zoey.

CHAPTER 32

The old ladies didn't seem like old ladies until they went to sleep at nine o'clock. Braedon's wide awake, sitting up in the bed his father slept in when Clay was a boy. He tried texting Daniel. No response. Probably had his phone and computer taken away. He texted Emily, but it's 4:00 AM in St. Andrews. She's probably sleeping. He considers going downstairs and into the sunroom to make some more lures but he doesn't want to risk waking up Sue and Carol. YouTube is boring. Social media is boring.

Braedon second-guesses his choice to spend another night away from home. If he were with his father, they might be out looking for Teddy. He might be able to help. And then he wonders if what Sue said is true. When the police are investigating something, do they spend most of their time on the computer? Maybe Grandpa Judd retired before that happened, and Dad doesn't realize he should be using a computer. What does he know anyway? He's just a soccer player and coach. Maybe Braedon can be of some help after all.

He opens the photos app on his computer and scrolls through the pictures until he finds a good one of Teddy. He's sitting next to Judd on their birthday, a cake on the table before them, with a whole mess of lit candles on it. Braedon duplicates the photo, then edits out everything but Teddy's head. Long gray hair and a big smile. Braedon then copies the photo into Google and does a reverse-image search.

If Teddy went up to the cities to see friends, maybe one of them posted a picture of it on Instagram. If he got in trouble and got arrested in some other town, maybe his mug shot will show up. The kind of picture where a person stands in front of a height chart. Or if Teddy got conked on the head and has amnesia and wandered into some other town, maybe the local newspaper wrote an article about it. NEW MAN IN TOWN CAN'T REMEMBER WHO HE IS. That would be the headline and there would be a picture of Teddy under it. And then it will be Braedon who finds Uncle Teddy. Not his father. Not his grandpa Judd. Even though they're the ones out there looking for Teddy, Braedon will be the hero. Because he's the one who had the idea to do the reverse-image search. Thanks to Sue, that is.

But the search yields only a few results. All of them Instagram posts by Deb. The most recent one was last Christmas. No mug shots. No newspaper articles. No posts of Teddy at a concert up in the cities. Nothing.

Braedon sits with his disappointment for a few minutes. He's about to close the laptop and call it a night when the idea comes out of nowhere. *Of course*. It's so obvious. So sensible. So . . . duh.

Why didn't he think of it earlier? Braedon reopens his photos app and begins to search.

"Something feels wrong," says Judd.

"With us?" says Mei.

Mei's condo is a ten-minute walk from the Gonda Building of the Mayo Clinic. Three bedrooms, two and a half baths, and wall-to-wall white carpet throughout except for the bathrooms and kitchen. Not off-white. Not linen-white. White. Shoes have never touched it, nor have bare feet with their oils and barnacles. The walls are also white but covered in art, much of it Chinese, as is most of the furniture and things displayed in glass cabinets.

"God, no," says Judd. "Everything with us is . . ." He shakes his head.

"What?" says Mei.

"I hesitate to use the word . . . But everything with us is perfect."

"Oh, it is not," says Mei. "Don't say that if you don't mean it."

They're in Mei's queen-size bed in her king-size master suite, their naked bodies under the silk duvet as they lie on their sides facing each other. Judd reaches out and cups Mei's cheek in his palm.

"I do mean it. You're a doctor. That's job security. Plus if one of our *perfect* sessions in the bedroom gives me a heart attack, you'll know what to do. And you live and work half an hour away so I don't have to worry about you barging into my place all the time."

"Stop it," says Mei. She laughs and grabs Judd's wrist so

he doesn't take his hand away, then she pulls it toward her lips, kisses it, and puts it back where she found it. "So what feels wrong?"

"You know," says Judd. "Teddy. I don't know what it is but something's not adding up. Maybe it's a twin thing. I can feel it but I don't know what it is. My cop sense is on code red. My Teddy sense is on code red. But I'm not putting the pieces together. It makes me feel like the city council was right. It was time for me to move on. I can't do the job like I used to."

"Maybe it's a blessing," says Mei.

"How is not being able to find my brother a blessing?" He says this with a smile so she understands that his question comes from hope and is not belittling her idea.

"It's not that you haven't found Teddy that's a blessing. It's that you're not working as a police officer."

"Okay . . ."

"Let's start with the irrefutable evidence," says Mei. "Your relationship with Clay seems to have improved."

Judd wishes he could tell Mei that Clay worked as an intelligence agent while playing soccer in Europe, but that would not only be inappropriate, it could get Clay and him in a whole lot of trouble. In a way, Clay's admission helped heal things between father and son. That and Clay moving back and bringing Braedon with him. But more than anything, Judd's owning up to his parental shortcomings. He'll tell Mei about it sometime but not tonight. It's too late for that conversation. Instead he simply says, "Yep. Clay and I are getting along a little better."

"Have you two talked about it?"

"Our relationship?"

"Yes, your relationship."

"God, no," says Judd. "We don't talk about things like that."

"Why not?"

"Well, I suppose it's because we don't know how to. Clay and me, we've been at odds with each other since he was born. If he was crying in his crib and his mother picked him up, he settled right down. But if I picked him up, he screamed like I was pulling his fingernails out with pliers. And things between us deteriorated from there."

"Maybe," says Mei, "you just need some time in this better state, some time getting along, and then you'll be able to talk about your relationship."

"Maybe," says Judd, "but talking about it just might wreck it."

"Why would talking wreck it?"

"Eh, it's a guy thing," says Judd. "Sometimes the less said, the better. No risk of embarrassment."

"You don't treat me like that," says Mei. She nudges Judd onto his back and rests her head on his chest. "You told me you loved me after only knowing me four months. You opened yourself up to the possibility of all kinds of embarrassment."

"That's different," says Judd. "If you had rejected me, we would have gone our separate ways. Probably would've never seen each other again. Then I could have buried my shame deep, pretend I hadn't met you, go on living my life with dignity."

"Stop." Mei laughs.

Judd kisses her on the top of the head and says, "Let's talk about something else."

"Like what?"

"I don't know. Something fun. Want to go on a trip together?" Judd catches himself and adds, "You know, after we find Teddy." The light dims in his eyes, and he adds, "I just keep thinking he's going to walk into his doublewide and Deb will call to tell me he's back. This kind of thing, Teddy disappearing, it's happened a hundred times before. It happened when we were kids. He knew he was in trouble and would hide out in a friend's tree house or down by the river for a few hours. My parents called all over town trying to find out where he was. Teddy's real good at not being found when he sets his mind to it. But he always comes home. He's trained me into thinking that way." Judd shifts his head on the pillow. "But I'm scared to death that this time is different."

Mei doesn't respond right away in case Judd wants to say more. When he doesn't, she says, "Of course you're scared. You're a human being. And yes I want to go on a trip together when the time is right. But I don't want to stop talking about you and Clay. You two have a chance to heal your relationship through this crisis, and talking about that will only help."

"I don't want to dump my garbage on you."

"It's not garbage and you're not dumping it. You're opening up and sharing yourself with me. I'm here to support you. To help. Here." Mei lifts her head from Judd's chest and says, "Let's trade places." She rolls onto her back. "Put your head on my shoulder. Come on."

Judd looks at her. Dubious and uncertain.

"Do it, Judd. You're always taking care of everyone else. First Teddy, then Pam, then Clay. And the whole town of Riverwood. You deserve to feel what it's like when someone takes care of you." She pats her shoulder with her free hand. "Doctor's orders."

Judd lowers his head onto Mei's shoulder as if it's made of nitroglycerin. One wrong move and everything will blow up. But when he feels his weight sink into her, when his cheek rests against her skin, it feels impossibly right.

"There," says Mei. "That's better. Just stay like that for a while." Mei runs a hand over Judd's buzz cut and draws him into her.

He wants to say *thank you* but is afraid Mei will hear the tears in his voice. He tries to breathe through it when his phone buzzes on the nightstand. Judd keeps his head on Mei's shoulder while reaching over to grab it. He holds it at arm's length so his sixty-three-year-old eyes can see the screen clearly. Or at least clearly enough.

"It's Braedon," says Judd. "I'd better answer it."

CHAPTER 33

"What are you two doing here?"

Clay and Zoey sit at Wahlquist's and Kimmich's desks. Andy Kimmich has just entered to sign out after his shift. Wahlquist is still out on patrol having set a speed trap south of town.

"We were hoping to have a chat," says Zoey. She opens Kimmich's bottom drawer, removes a bottle of Scotch, and sets it on top of the desk. Johnnie Walker Red.

Kimmich smiles a sheepish smile. "What? I've had that in there for years. Once in a while, after a hard shift, I'll have a sip before heading home. Just to calm the nerves so I don't bring 'em into the house. It's all part of being a good husband and father."

"I don't want to talk about your Scotch, Andy. I want you to get three cups so we can sit and have a drink and ask you a few questions."

"Oh," says Andy. He makes a point of looking at his watch. "Now? Kind of late, isn't it? Maybe we can do it tomorrow."

"We might not have until tomorrow," says Clay. "This concerns Teddy."

"Why didn't you say so? Anything I can do to help find Teddy."

"You can get three paper cups from near the water cooler and join us," says Zoey.

That's what Andy does. Zoey pours Scotch into three cups, sets one before Clay and the other before Andy Kimmich, who's pulled up an extra chair.

"So what's up?" says Andy.

Zoey sips her Scotch and says, "Did Teddy recently talk to you about anything involving Ash Solbakken?"

The directness of the question catches Kimmich off guard. He forces a smile under his mustache and says, "Who told you that?"

"Deb," lies Zoey. "Teddy told her that Ash asked him to speak to you."

"Apparently," says Clay, "Teddy was supposed to tell you Ash has biker gang friends and you'd better be careful with Ash because his motorcycle friends had his back. Or something like that. We asked Ash about it, but he denied having an issue with you. Said everything was just fine. No problems whatsoever. So it's his word against Deb's, and who do you think we believe?"

Kimmich keeps his smile and says, "What exactly did Deb say?"

"Deb said that, according to Teddy, you threatened Ash.

Apparently he picked up a young woman over in Lanesboro, brought her home, had sex with her, and then money was exchanged. And then you threatened Ash. Said if he ever told anyone about it, you'd kill him. And to be honest, Andy, it sounds like something you'd say. Straight out of *Goodfellas*."

"Nah . . ." says Kimmich. "I never said nothing like that."

Clay leans toward Kimmich. "Then what did you say?"

Andy's eyes dart from Clay to Zoey then back to Clay. "Wait," he says. "What does this have to do with Teddy?"

"You buying time to come up with a good story?"

"No," says Andy. "I just don't see the connection."

"We just told you the connection," says Zoey. "According to Deb, Ash asked Teddy to deliver a message to you. It wasn't a favor. It was in exchange for Ash forgiving the interest part of a loan he'd made to Teddy. So we assume Teddy delivered the message. Then he disappeared. I'm sure you can understand that from where we're sitting, the message and the disappearance might be related."

"You're thinking I have something to do with Teddy disappearing?" says Andy. His voice sounds incredulous but his stupid, fake smile persists.

"We're thinking," says Clay, "that it's worth asking you about. So that's what we're doing. And as you know, time is an important factor after someone goes missing. So the sooner you're honest with us about what's going on, the sooner we'll be one step closer to finding Teddy."

The smile fades from under Kimmich's mustache.

"Who is she?" says Zoey.

"Who is who?" says Kimmich.

"Skye," says Clay. "Or whatever her real name is. The young woman who insisted Ash pay her for sex. Is she your girlfriend? Either voluntarily or on the clock?"

"What?" says Kimmich, who sounds genuinely outraged. "I'm a happily married man. I would never cheat on my wife."

"You say that like it's an impossibility," says Zoey. "Like there's about as much of a chance of you cheating as there is you playing in the NBA. Or time traveling. But let me tell you something I know for a fact: Sometimes happily married men do cheat on their wives. You know, just for fun. It doesn't mean anything. They still love their wives. They still want to be married. They just need a little excitement. Is there shame in that? Yeah. Probably. More like definitely. But we won't hold it against you. Your private life is your business."

"Is that why you threatened Ash?" says Clay. "You're worried that if word gets out about Skye sleeping with older men, someone will put it together that she's sleeping with you, too?"

Andy shuts his eyes, sips his Scotch, and shakes his head. "Did Deb really tell you all this? Or did that son of a bitch Ash talk?"

"Why?" says Clay. "You want to know if you need to make good on your threat?"

"This is . . ." Andy takes a healthy swig of Scotch. "This is not good."

"No shit," says Zoey. "I mean, it could be worse. And maybe it is. Because the way you've been acting, Skye is either your girlfriend or you're her pimp. Or both. Not sure why you'd threaten Ash to keep his mouth shut if you're her pimp because him talking would probably be good for business. Unless you're worried about

Ash being Teddy's brother-in-law and you thought word of your pimping somehow got to Deb or Teddy and then to Judd. Because—"

"I'm not her pimp," says Andy. His tone is firm and stern. "And I'm not her boyfriend. I'm her goddamn father."

Neither Clay nor Zoey responds right away. They just look at each other as if they're checking a truth barometer. *Do you believe Kimmich? I don't know—do you?* And right then and there, communicating with just their eyes, they agree that they do. No cop would lie about that. Not when they know a DNA test could prove them wrong. Then their eyes swing toward Kimmich in a plea for more information.

"I would never cheat on my wife. Now. But there was one time I did stray," says Kimmich. "I was up in St. Cloud with Aiden for a hockey tournament. Julie was here with the girls because they had activities of their own. Aiden's team and the parents, we all stayed in one of those Holiday Inns with an indoor pool under a glass dome. The kids loved the hotel more than the hockey tournament. And the parents loved it because we could just turn 'em loose in the pool area while we sat at tables drinking cocktails out of plastic cups.

"There were a few teams there. One from Duluth. One from the cities. One from Alexandria. The kids got to know each other at the pool, and the parents got to know each other at the bar. There was a single mom there from Duluth. She was lonely and I was drunk and the next thing I know we're in her room." Kimmich drops his eyes. "A couple months later she calls me and tells me she's pregnant and asks me to leave Julie. I say no way. It was a mistake. She says yes it was, and that's the last I hear from her."

"But you heard from Skye," says Clay.

"Yep. About a year ago. She wants a relationship with me. I don't want to mess things up at home so I say I can't do that. And then Skye—that is her real name, by the way—starts pretending she's a prostitute."

"Pretending?" says Zoey.

"That's not her real job," says Kimmich. "It's a cry for attention. Skye's a nursing student at Winona State. It's just that once in a while, she does what she did with Ash because she's trying to, I don't know, embarrass me? Get me to accept her and tell my family about her? I'm not sure. I just get these weird texts from her once in a while. I think . . . I think her mom's not so mentally healthy and Skye's had a rough go of it. She's acting out. And I have not been able to talk sense into her. Looks like I'll have to tell Julie and the kids. I don't see any way to avoid it."

"Then why did you threaten Ash?" says Clay.

"Because I want my wife to hear it from me. Not Ash Solbakken."

"Did Skye tell Ash that she's your daughter?"

"I don't think so," says Kimmich. "I think she's just trying to cause some major trouble. You know, big scandal and all that. And then she'll reveal she's my daughter, just to make a huge splash. The way she tells me by texting me a name. Nothing more. Just a name. But I know what it means. Girl's got a lot of anger. Can't say I blame her. Neither of her parents have done right by her."

"Who else in town has she slept with?" says Zoey. "And does she always demand money after the fact?"

"Oh, a few guys. I don't want to get them in trouble."

"Is one of them Teddy?"

"Not that I know of," says Kimmich. "He doesn't seem like the type anyway."

"Has she slept with Mike Wahlquist?" says Zoey.

Kimmich keeps his mouth shut, but his eyes answer with an emphatic *yes*.

Zoey shrugs. "Ouch. So circling back," she says, "Teddy told you Ash was consorting with unsavory characters and you'd better watch your back. Correct?"

Kimmich leans forward and says, "Worse than that. Teddy told me that Ash's new friends, his motorcycle gang buddies, thought Teddy was muscling in on their drug business because Teddy's growing pot plants on his five acres. I mean, technically it's legal, but the state is taking forever to license a dispensary. Most people still get it on the street. Teddy said he told them to go fuck themselves, and they beat him up pretty bad."

"And that made you lay off Ash about the whole Skye encounter?" says Clay.

"What? No way. I don't back down. In fact . . ." Kimmich hesitates, sips his Scotch, then says, "I didn't want to say nothin' until we had more proof, but Mike and I think we know where that biker gang established their southeast Minnesota headquarters. We've been staking the place out hoping to bring you visual evidence."

"And where's that?" says Zoey.

Kimmich lowers his voice to just above a whisper. "Lukas Keskinen's place down by Chatham Creek."

"You and Mike have secretly been staking out the Keskinens' house down by Chatham Creek?" says Zoey.

Kimmich nods, unable to hide how impressed he is with himself.

"That's why you're sometimes unreachable by phone or radio?" says Clay.

"No coverage down there. And we turn off the radio," says Kimmich. "Can't risk any of those bikers on the property hearing us."

"And you think drug dealers are running product through Lukas Keskinen because he . . . ?"

Kimmich raises his eyebrows. "He's in charge of the local motorcycle gang."

"And you think he's teaming up with gangs outside the area to run drugs into Riverwood?" says Clay.

Kimmich doesn't offer a verbal confirmation but more of an *if the shoe fits* kind of gesture with upturned palms.

Zoey smiles. "Do you know the name of Lukas Keskinen's motorcycle gang?"

Kimmich shakes his head.

"They're called the Shriners. Ever hear of them?" says Zoey.

"I know Keskinen's a Shriner," says Kimmich. "I see him and the boys riding mini bikes every Fourth of July parade. Wearing their little fezzes and vests. That's doesn't mean they're not dealing drugs. I've seen them out there ganged up on their Harleys."

"They're ganged up on their Harleys," says Zoey, "because people sponsor them by the mile. They ride up to Duluth or down to Iowa City. All to raise money for the children's hospital in Minneapolis."

"Andy," says Clay, "I hate to break it to you, but there's no motorcycle gang trying to run drugs into Riverwood. You and Wahlquist have been wasting your time."

Kimmich looks down, shakes his head, then looks up. "Yeah, we'll see about that."

CHAPTER 34

"The problem with turning over rocks to look for one person is that you see all sorts of things under those rocks that you wish you hadn't." Zoey sips whiskey from a glass in Clay's living room. "I now know more about Andy Kimmich than I care to. And I'd better have a talk with that girl Skye. Let her know what she's doing is against the law and she could get herself kicked out of school. Or worse. Much worse. And poor Lukas Keskinen. Kimmich and Wahlquist . . . No good deed, huh?"

"Isn't Lukas Keskinen a professor?" says Clay.

"Bioinformatics and computational biology," Zoey says with a laugh. "At the University of Minnesota campus in Rochester. And Kimmich and Wahlquist are chasing bad guys who Ash made up. This is the funniest thing that's happened in a long time." She takes another sip of whiskey and adds, "Why is this so smooth? How come it doesn't burn?"

"Aged in a sherry cask," says Clay. "Aged a long time. It was a gift from the coaching staff when I left Galway."

"Clay Hawkins," says Zoey. "You broke out the good stuff for little old me? What's a girl to think?"

They're sitting on the couch together, their drinks on the glass coffee table. Jason Isbell sings "If We Were Vampires" through the speakers. The lights are low and glow orange gold. After talking to Andy Kimmich, they discussed where they should go to discuss Andy Kimmich even though they could have remained at the station. Clay suggested his place because Braedon's spending the night at Sue and Carol's, and part of him—a big part of him—wants to feel what it's like to invite a woman over to his home, something he hasn't done since Braedon was delivered to him a dozen years ago.

Clay has not lived a life of celibacy but he has kept that part of his life private. He questions whether or not that sets a good example for Braedon. As if sex is something to be ashamed of. But keeping that part of his life out of Braedon's view also makes Braedon's life simpler. He might not have a mother, but he has a father who is one hundred percent devoted to him.

It was easy when they lived in Europe. Clay was gone half the time with whatever team he was playing for. But it's been harder since moving to Riverwood. Rochester is where Clay has done most of his dating. Braedon has slept over at Judd's several times, but Clay hasn't felt comfortable bringing a date home even then.

He's brought Zoey home because she's not a date. That's his reasoning anyway. His lie to himself. But now that he's here with her, drinking whiskey and listening to music in low light, he can't kid himself anymore. And worst of all, Clay knows that Zoey knows what's going on. He's used to being a step ahead of people, but he's not a step ahead of her. More likely he's a step behind.

There's one thing he's sure of: Whatever is happening here, the feelings, desires, and doubts are mutual. He doesn't need his extensive training in psychological profiling to read Zoey. She's just as interested in what might come of this as he is. Just as interested and just as concerned.

"Do you miss living over there?" says Zoey. "In the old country?"

"Sometimes," says Clay. "I miss everything being right outside my front door. Restaurants. Shops. Parks. Maybe I'll move back someday. Or to a bigger city in the States. But right now, I think it's more important that Braedon has the experience he's having here."

Zoey's dark eyes shine in the warm light. She sits close enough to reach out and touch Clay. There's a smile in her eyes. A smile and an invitation. And a knowledge. The way she was looking at Clay when they were questioning Kimmich—it's like she knew he wasn't just a soccer player in Europe. She knew he worked for US intelligence. Not she *knew*. She *knows*. He hasn't told her. He can't tell her. But somehow she knows. And not having to hide that from her gives him great comfort. If she flat-out asks him, he'll have to lie, but for now, he feels there's an openness between them. An honesty. Besides, if Zoey intuited that Clay never stopped working for his country, then she can intuit that it would be a mistake to ask him about it. To put him in that position.

"I . . ." starts Zoey. "I don't want to confuse police business with personal business. And I think we might be engaging in both at the moment."

Clay sets down his drink. Now he's intuiting something about Zoey. There has to be more to her story than he knows. Why did she leave northern Minnesota to police an equally small community in southeast Minnesota? Why didn't she go to a city? Or into federal law enforcement? Or private security? She's so damn smart. Other opportunities had to be available. These questions make him even more intrigued with Zoey Jensen. Like she's a puzzle he feels compelled to solve. He says, "You're right. I think we might be."

"My suggestion," says Zoey, "is that we finish discussing police business and then . . ." She looks at Clay with her big brown eyes. "Continue with personal business."

"I second that suggestion," says Clay.

"Good. Because I don't have the best feeling about your uncle Teddy. Every possibility has turned into a dead end. The boys on bicycles were up to no good, but they haven't led us any closer to Teddy. Ash was up to no good, which led us to Kimmich admitting his illegitimate daughter is pay-to-play, but all that just leaves us where we started. And back to the boys, finding Teddy's earring and other things on Miller's Bluff is just flat-out strange. Why would Teddy be on Miller's Bluff in the middle of the night? And why would he take his earring out? It makes no sense."

"Not to mention he brought a sawzall," says Clay. "Is it possible he's cultivating something on that bluff he shouldn't be? Like marijuana? Or poppies?"

"Why?" says Zoey. "Teddy and Deb live on a few acres, right?"

"Five."

"Just like Ash's imaginary friends suggested, Teddy could just grow it on private property."

"What if Deb disapproves and Teddy needed another spot?" says Clay.

"I suppose that's possible. But it's Miller's Bluff, not Humboldt County. And it's Minnesota, not California. You pretty much need a greenhouse to get a decent growing season."

"Are there any valuable plants up there?" says Clay. "Rare flowers? Mushrooms?"

"Magical pinecones to start an enchanted Christmas tree farm?" says Zoey.

They laugh for a moment, then their laughter fades. Clay inches closer to Zoey and says, "Maybe we should pick this up tomorrow. I'm kind of distracted right now."

"Am I your distractant?"

"Distractant?" says Clay.

"Something that irritates you is called an irritant," says Zoey. "Something that deodors you is called a deodorant. Someone who you consult is called a consultant. Therefore, something that distracts you is called a distractant." Zoey slides an inch toward Clay.

"Yes," says Clay.

"Yes what?"

"Yes, you are my distractant."

"Good," says Zoey. "But we have a problem."

Clay takes Zoey's hand in his. "And what's that?"

"Your pants are lighting up."

Clay looks down and sees a rectangle of light on his right thigh. "Hold on." He reaches into his pocket and removes his phone. "It's Braedon," he says. Clay answers the call. "Hey, bud. What's up?"

Braedon's crying. "I found . . ." He takes a few uneven breaths then tries again. "I found . . ."

"Slow down, Brae. Take your time. What happened?" Clay feels Zoey squeeze his hand. He returns the squeeze and gives her a concerned look.

Braedon's breathing steadies. "I found my mom."

CHAPTER 35

Clay switches the phone from one ear to the other. "What do you mean, Brae?"

"I felt bad that everyone's out looking for Teddy," says Braedon through the phone's small speaker. "Everyone except for me. So I thought maybe I could help if I did a reverse-image search for Teddy on my computer. I thought maybe he somehow got his picture posted online since he disappeared. But I didn't find any pictures of Teddy other than some Instagram posts. And then I remembered I have that picture of my mom . . ."

It hits Clay that Braedon refers to his mother as *my mom*. Not *Mom*. He's never met her. Never spoken to her or written her. Never addressed her in any way. She is a mythical creature to Braedon like *my fairy godmother* or *my guardian angel*. Clay shuts his eyes and rubs his forehead. He knows where this is going. He feels another squeeze from Zoey.

"Dad . . . Dad . . ."

"Yeah, bud?"

He's crying again. "She has another family in England. The kids are younger than me. And she has a husband. And they live in a fancy house and . . . and . . . She looks, in the pictures, she looks really happy. Like her life is perfect."

Braedon cries hard for a solid minute and during that time, Zoey slides over to Clay and presses her shoulder into his.

"Can you come pick me up?" says Braedon. "Please? I want to come home."

After Clay fills Zoey in on Braedon's call, he kisses her good night inside the house with a tenderness that hopes for more. His heart has nothing to give her at this moment but he tries to make up for it with his eyes. The two of them will have to pick up where they left off on another day. Because Clay must go to Braedon. Now.

"Get out of here," says Zoey with a smile on her lips and in her eyes. Both hands holding Clay's. "I'm going to stay here and go through your stuff."

Clay would laugh on any other night. But tonight he just pulls her into a hug and whispers, "When you get to the refrigerator, please throw out anything that smells funky."

Seven minutes later, Clay pulls in front of Sue and Carol's house and is surprised to see he's not the only one. Judd's car is in the driveway. Judd, who was going to spend the night at Mei's up in Rochester. Sue waits for Clay just inside the screen door. As Clay starts up the walk, he says, "How is he?"

"Big night for the little man," says Sue. "He'll get through it. You did."

Not the same situation, thinks Clay, but he understands what Sue's saying. She pushes open the screen door and leads Clay into the living room where Braedon sits next to Judd on the couch. Mei sits in one of the wing-backed chairs, and Carol sits in the other. Clay takes a seat on the other side of Braedon, puts an arm around him, and pulls him tight.

"How you doing?" says Clay.

Braedon shrugs, and the tears reappear.

Clay lets him cry it out for a bit, then says, "I'm sorry, buddy. It sucks. And it's brutal. And not fair. And very wrong of her. Not that she met someone else and had kids with them. That's okay. Can't blame her for that. But it's wrong that she's chosen to not be in your life, and I don't blame you for feeling hurt. I would, too."

Braedon nods through his tears.

"I told him," says Judd, "that she's only hurting herself. That she's going to regret making the choice she did. And that frankly, she can go to hell."

Clay wouldn't have used those words but at least Judd is being supportive. Clay says, "You don't have to make any decisions right now, Brae. It's okay to just sit with this for a while, see how you feel."

"What do you mean?" says Braedon. "What kind of decisions?"

Clay hesitates. He's not sure of the best way to answer that question. Sue sees his hesitation and the wanting in Braedon's eyes.

"Well," says Sue, "you can contact her if you want to. Tell her about yourself. Your life. See if she responds. She might. She might not. You could do that now or anytime in the future. Or maybe never. It's up to you."

"I don't know . . ." says Braedon. "I don't know what I want to do."

"I think talking to a therapist might be a good idea," says Mei, "before you make any big decisions."

"That's a good idea," says Carol. "Because if you contact your mom, you might not like the answer you get. Or you might not get any answer at all. And you need to be prepared for that possibility. A therapist can help with that."

Braedon lifts his head and scans the room. In his heart he knows that the love from these people is enough to make up for the rejection by his mother. He can't articulate that, not even in his thoughts, but he feels it and it gives him strength. "Yeah . . ." says Braedon. "Maybe . . . I don't know what to do about talking to a therapist either."

"You don't have to know what to think," says Clay. "Just sit with this for a while. There's no rush because now you know your mom's name. You know her husband's name. Her kids' names. If she moves or if her family gets off social media, you'll still be able to find her. You may want to wait until you're older. Or not. But I agree with Mei, you should talk to a therapist."

"What do they do?" says Braedon.

"Therapists?" says Clay. "Mostly they listen. You talk about what's going on in your life and your feelings and they help you sort through it all."

"Have you ever been to one?" says Braedon.

Clay feels Judd's eyes on him, as if an admission of seeing a therapist might show weakness. Even though Judd's girlfriend is the one who suggested the idea. Clay decides to ignore his father's opinion—what's new?—and tell Braedon the truth. At least about seeing a therapist. "Yes, Brae. Lots of times."

"Really?"

"Sue brought me to one after Grandma Pam died."

"She did?" says Judd.

"I ran it by you first," says Sue. "You said no, so I took matters into my own hands."

"I had no idea," says Judd.

"It was very helpful," says Clay.

"Really?" says Braedon.

"Yep. And when I played professional soccer, most teams wanted the players to see a sports psychologist so our brains could be as fit as our bodies."

Judd's phone rings. He gets up, walks out of the living room, through the dining room, and into the kitchen where he takes the call. "Hey, Mike. What's up?"

"I just pulled over Wags Becker. Followed him out of Knut's and he was swerving all over the place."

"Yeah?" says Judd as he lowers his voice to just above a whisper.

"First thing I do is ask if he's been drinking," says Mike. "Wags says he's had a couple. Maybe three. But he swears he's fine. So I know he's drunk as hell."

"Yep," says Judd.

"The only thing that can screw up this bust is me. So I play it by the book and ask for license and registration."

"That's the way to do it," says Judd. "Hey, Mike, can we talk about this in the morning? I'm with my grandson right now."

"I really think you'll want to hear this tonight," says Mike.

"All right. Make it as quick as you can, then."

"Will do. So I ask for license and registration and Wags says they're in the trunk. Who the hell keeps their license and registration in the trunk? No one. So I step back and ask him to get out of the car, go back there, and get them. He doesn't say a word. He just opens the car door, gets out, and walks around back to the trunk. He pops it open, and boy, oh boy, Judd, I wish you could have seen his face."

"What happened?"

"Son of a bitch was so drunk he forgot what he had back there."

Judd sighs. "Give it to me, Mike."

"He tried to shut the trunk so I told him to step back. Figured I didn't search his trunk without permission. He told me his license and registration were back there. He opened it. So I'm in the clear."

"Probably," says Judd.

"But he didn't listen. He started to close the trunk when I stepped in and stopped him. And guess what I saw."

"Don't got time for guessing now, Mike."

"Right. Sorry. It was a big box of catalytic converters. Nine of 'em by my count. But I played it cool. Like the catalytic converters were no big deal and I just wanted his license and registration. Dumb shit really did have 'em in the trunk. I don't know what the hell he was thinking. So I walked him back to the front of the car and asked him if he wanted to blow into a tube or walk the yellow line. He chose the tube. Idiot blew a .16. I cuffed him, took him back to the station, and locked him up."

"And why do I need to hear this tonight?" says Judd. "You remember I'm not the chief, right? Maybe you're blowing a .16."

"Come on, Judd," says Mike. "You know why. Teddy was stealing those converters for Wags, and Wags was selling them for the rare metals. I think Wags knows what happened to Teddy. And if he hadn't passed out on his cot, I'd know, too. But you might want to be here when he wakes up."

CHAPTER 36

Braedon's back in his own bed and having trouble sleeping after the eventful night. He checks the world clock on his phone. It's 8:30 AM in Scotland. He tries Emily.

"What are you doing up?" says Emily. She's out walking with her family in a green park but has fallen back to take Braedon's FaceTime call.

"Some big stuff happened tonight. Want to hear about it?"

Emily looks at her family, stops to let them get ahead more, then says, "Yeah, I do. Did you find Teddy?" She starts walking again.

Braedon shakes his head. "No. The police arrested someone tonight. They think he might know something about where Teddy is. My grandpa is there now talking to the guy."

"And your da?"

"No," says Braedon. "He's home to be with me. After what happened."

"Which is?"

"I found my mom."

Emily stops. "You what?"

Braedon recounts the story. With a little hindsight, and at least for the moment, he's more proud of his investigative work than he is hurt by his mother's betrayal. Maybe that's out of necessity—he doesn't want to cry in front of Emily.

"That's bloody brilliant, Braedon. I can't believe you found her on your own."

"Yeah," says Braedon. "Sue told me that's what the police do now. Search for people on the internet. She gave me the idea."

"Are you going to contact her? Your mum?"

"Don't know," says Braedon. "But . . ." Braedon hesitates.

"What?"

"Maybe when I get to visit, you and I could go see her."

"In London?"

"Yeah."

"How would we get to London?"

"Train."

"Yeah, but I mean, London's not in the EU. I don't know if we can go there without our parents."

"Oh," says Braedon. "I didn't think of that. Maybe Dad would go with us."

Emily keeps walking. Her eyes look off to the side as if she's deep in thought. Braedon expects her to say something, but she doesn't. Finally he says, "What are you thinking?" Again she doesn't answer and her eyes stay to the side. "Emily? Can you hear me?"

"Yeah . . ." says Emily.

"Why aren't you saying anything?"

"Well . . . I don't know if I should."

"What do you mean?" says Braedon.

"I guess . . ." Emily hesitates. "I mean . . ."

"What?"

"Braedon, don't you think your dad already knew?"

Braedon's head gets fuzzy. If his father knew where Braedon's mother was, he would have told him. Because to not tell him is a form of lying. And Dad's always been truthful with him. Hasn't he? "I don't think he did know," says Braedon.

"But think about it," says Emily. She has a sick look on her face. Like she doesn't want to say this but has to. "Your dad is super smart. All the teams want him to be coach. When he was a player, the commentators always said he was the smartest player on the pitch. That's what my da says, as well. I mean, it's great that you found her. It means you're super smart like your da. But he probably did it before you did. He just didn't say anything 'cause he didn't want to hurt your feelings."

Braedon considers this for a little too long.

"Hey, sorry," says Emily. "We're at the breakfast place. I have to go. But talk to you later? Like when it's morning for you?"

Braedon bites his lower lip and nods.

"Okay. See you later, then."

Braedon ends the call without speaking. He's afraid his voice will break. He's afraid if he lets his thoughts out, the tears will come, too. He puts his phone on its charger, turns out the light, lies there in the dark, and stares up at a ceiling he cannot see.

"Why are you here if you're not a cop anymore?" says Wags. He sits on the cot in his cell, his hair a mess, a plastic bottle of water at his feet and a paper cup of coffee in his right hand. "I mean, I don't have to talk to you."

"You don't have to talk to anyone," says Judd. "And I'm here because Chief Jensen asked for my assistance in the search for my brother, Teddy."

"Oh, great," says Wags. "My tax dollars at work. Paying for an old has-been cop so he can look for his fuckup brother. That's government for you."

Judd swivels in the office chair he pulled over from Kimmich's desk. He's positioned himself right outside the bars of Wags's cell. "Not in this case," says Judd. "I'm working for free. You can think of it as giving back. I know that's something that's important to you."

"Fuck you," says Wags.

"Language," says Mike, who sits on his desk, one leg on the floor and one up. "You want a lawyer, Wags? Because we can have this conversation when your lawyer's here. Maybe that'll be tomorrow. Maybe it'll be the day after tomorrow. Maybe it'll be in a week, especially if you didn't pay your legal bills last time you were in this situation. Doesn't matter to me. I'm in no rush."

"What good's a lawyer going to do me? I had nothing to do with those catalytic converters. I don't know how they got in my trunk. But I did blow a .16. You got me on that. And on that only, I plead guilty."

"That's something you do in court," says Judd. "Not here. Of course, this is a small town with a small police force. Mike and Andy and Chief Jensen, they like to keep things informal. Maybe not follow the letter of the law, if that's what's best for the community in the long run."

"Ah," says Wags. "You want to make some kind of deal. I don't know what I have to offer, but I'm willing to listen."

Judd gets up from his office chair, walks to the coffeepot, and refills his cup. He's mid-pour when he says, "Let's go back to those catalytic converters that you don't know anything about."

"I don't. Someone's trying to set me up."

Judd heads back toward his chair. "I'm sure that's true," says Judd. "Happens all the time. Just the other day, I looked into the back of my Tahoe and found a whole mess of unmounted diamonds. Someone must have just put 'em in there. Figure I'll make myself a crown."

Wags gets up off his bunk and walks to the bars of his cell. "I know you're not going to believe me," he says, "but I swear. I don't know where those catalytic converters came from. Clay was asking me about catalytic converters the other day. Said he heard I'd been stealing them. I told him it wasn't true. Then Clay went up to Robert's scrapyard and asked if they buy catalytic converters. Now I have a bunch of them in the trunk of my car, so maybe you should talk to Clay because that's where this whole thing started."

"You know I don't really give a shit about those converters," says Judd.

"No," says Wags. "I didn't know that. If you don't care about the converters, what in the hell are we talking about?"

"I want to know if Teddy tried to sell you any."

"No," says Wags. "He didn't."

"Because, let's say, you told Teddy you'd pay him X amount for each catalytic converter. And let's say, you may have told him where he could get some, then maybe he did just that. And then maybe Teddy put those converters in your trunk so you could drive them to wherever you're going to drive them. Maybe all the way up to the cities. No sense taking the risk of keeping 'em in your shop."

"Listen," says Wags. "I'm sorry Teddy is missing. I really am. Personally, I like the guy. I like him a whole hell of a lot better than I like you. If I'd seen him, I'd tell you. If I had any idea where he might be, I'd tell you. If I had even a clue of what he's been up to, I'd tell you that, too. But I don't know anything about Teddy. Other than he's a nice guy, he has that cool earring that Joe Strummer supposedly gave him, and he had his ups and downs. All stuff you already know."

Judd thinks on this for a good minute before he says, "Mike, do what you have to with him. And Wags, if I find out you're lying about seeing Teddy or knowing what he's been up to, I am going to make your life even worse than it already is."

"How are you going to do that, Judd? You're not police anymore."

"Oh, I know," says Judd. "Being a private citizen makes my options considerably more interesting."

The station's front door opens. Zoey Jensen walks in, sees Judd and Mike outside of the jail cell and Wags in it and says, "I thought something fun might be going on in here. How come no one called me?"

CHAPTER 37

At 7:30 the next morning, Clay is making coffee in his kitchen when he hears a knock on the front door. He makes his way through the living room and into the foyer where he opens the door to see Judd and Zoey standing on his front porch holding a bag of something that smells sweet.

"Figured you'd be awake," says Judd. "It's time for a catch-up and strategy session."

"Yeah, sure," says Clay. "Come on in. Just made coffee."

Zoey follows Judd into Clay's home and says, "Good morning, sir." She's wearing her uniform, tips her cap, and says, "Hey, nice place you got here."

They gather around the kitchen table with coffee, fritters, bear claws, and croissants.

"Mike sent the catalytic converters up to the lab in Rochester to see if they can find any prints or hair or DNA on the damn things," says Judd. "But the forensics lab is all backed up with a murder case. I don't expect results anytime soon."

"Is Wags still in custody?"

"Yep. My guess is he doesn't have the money for a lawyer. He'll meet with a public defender today, but with his record, they'll probably cop a plea for the drunk driving and deal with the theft charges when they come. Mike's talking to the DA later this morning. We'll know more after that."

"You should have seen the old man in action," says Zoey. "Hasn't lost a step."

"The old man?" says Judd. "I'm sitting right here. Still young enough to hear what you're saying. Maybe you should call me something else."

Judd doesn't have a smile on his face but Clay can hear a playfulness in his voice. That's not something Judd ever fakes. He likes Zoey. Probably always has. It's just been hard to tell when he's armored up in bitterness and resentment. Maybe Clay and Judd have not one woman trying to bridge their relationship but two. Mei and Zoey.

"Old pro," says Zoey. "How about that, Judd?"

"I'll take it," says Judd. "Thank you. Now. I think we need to go back over everyone we've talked to. Everyone. The Lindelof boy at Kwik-Trip who sold Teddy the gloves. The three boys who took Teddy's earring and tried to extort forty-five grand from me. Wags, who we have in custody. Deb because maybe she hasn't told us something she thinks is too trivial. Ash because Teddy owes him money and that sawzall came from his pole barn. The guys who play pool at Knut's. Because my *old pro* sense is that someone knows something they're not telling us. Or they've been lying to us."

"My money is on those three boys," says Zoey. "And/or Wags. Something's off there."

"I bet everyone lied." This from Braedon as he walks into the kitchen with one eye still half closed from sleep. He wears joggers and a Dorset-Cornwall T-shirt. He helps himself to a bear claw and says, "Because people are liars. All of 'em." He takes a bite of pastry and turns toward Clay. "Even the people who aren't supposed to lie. They're just liars and don't care about other people's feelings. Or the truth. 'Cause they're lying liars." Braedon opens the refrigerator, grabs a carton of milk, exits the kitchen, and heads down the hall that leads to his bedroom.

"What the hell was that about?" says Judd.

Now it's Judd and Zoey who stare at Clay.

"Shit," says Clay. "I have a pretty good guess. I'll go talk to him. Make yourselves comfortable. If this takes a while and you want to leave, we'll catch up later."

"Was that all the milk?" says Zoey. "You got any creamer or anything?"

Clay can't help but smile. "There's more of both in the fridge."

"Thanks. And good luck in there."

Braedon sits on his bed, arms folded, knees up. He hears a knock on his bedroom door and his father say, "Can I come in?" Braedon wants to freeze out his father but he also wants to have this conversation. Otherwise he wouldn't have said what he said in the kitchen.

"I guess," is all he can manage. He watches the doorknob turn and the door open. Clay enters the room, grabs the chair from Braedon's desk, and pulls it toward the bed. He sits, takes a breath, and says, "Did you contact her?"

Braedon stares at his feet and shakes his head.

"But you think I've known all along where she is and what she's been up to."

Braedon stares at his feet and nods his head.

"What makes you think that?"

"Because . . ." Braedon turns to look at Clay. "You're smart. If I figured it out, and I'm only twelve, than you must have figured it out a long time ago. But you didn't tell me, which is a lie by omission. Which means, you've been lying to me."

Clay interlocks his fingers and rests his hands on his lap. "Well, Brae, you're pretty smart yourself because everything you're saying is correct."

Braedon tries not to look surprised. Or happy with himself. He had no proof that his father knew where his mother is and that she has a family. It was a bluff. Emily suggested the tactic and it worked. He's in no mood to give Emily the credit right now. Right now he'll take that credit for himself. He shrugs and says, "I know."

Clay sighs. "You want to hear the truth?"

Braedon nods.

"Do you feel you're ready for it? You're old enough?"

Another head nod.

"Okay." Clay shifts in his chair and says, "When your mother showed up at my door and handed you to me, I figured she'd return any minute to take you back. When that didn't happen, I figured it would be the next day. And then the next week. And the next month . . . I was sure she would change her mind. After a few months of me being wrong, I hired a private investigator to find out more about your mother. She found out your mother's last name and where she lived. I held on to that information, still thinking she'd contact me and want to be in your life. But she didn't. When you were five, I went back to the private investigator and asked for an update. That's when I found out she's married, living in London, and has two kids.

"My heart broke for you, Brae. But I knew it wasn't about you. She didn't even know you. It was about her. Something in her life or personality, I don't know what because I only knew your mom for about eight hours, but something made it impossible for her to be your mother. Maybe she was too young. Maybe her family disapproved of me. Maybe she didn't like me. But I can tell you two things. I wanted to make it work, the three of us, being a family. I asked her to stay and give it a go. She declined.

"And the other thing I know is that giving you to me was not easy for her. I saw a profound pain in her eyes. It was like she had pulled out her own heart to give you away. I promise you, Brae, that is the absolute truth."

Braedon sniffles. "Then why did she do it?"

"I don't know. But maybe you can ask her someday." Clay reaches out and puts a hand on Braedon's shoulder. "I'm sorry I didn't tell you earlier. When I first learned the truth, you were too young to understand. You've been old enough for a while, but I was so concerned about our move to the States and how you'd handle it that I didn't want to add another hard thing for you. And then this past year, you've been doing so great, making friends already, plus you and Grandpa Judd getting along the way you do, it's really a beautiful thing to see . . . I didn't want to wreck that by telling you that your mother has another family."

"But you should have told me," says Braedon.

"Yeah," says Clay. "I should have. And I'm very sorry I did not. I made a mistake. I should have known better."

Braedon loves hearing this but he doesn't want to show it. He's learning how to become a man, and not gloating seems like part of the deal. He's not sure why but he never sees his father or his grandpa Judd gloat. Gloating is for those idiots on TV, whether they're talking on a news program or in a post-game interview. It's always better to play it cool, like you expected to win and each victory is just another ho-hum day.

Braedon keeps his arms folded and his jaw tight and says, "Anything else you want to tell me?"

Clay thought this question might be coming and he's prepared for it. "Yes," he says. "There is one more thing."

CHAPTER 38

Braedon can't hide his surprise. His facade of anger melts away and his curiosity takes over. Curiosity and astonishment that his tactic worked and gratitude for his father's forthcomingness. "What is it?"

"Can you keep a secret, Brae?" says Clay.

"Yeah," says Braedon.

"Because if I tell you this, you have to promise you won't tell anyone else. And I mean anyone. Not Daniel. Not Emily. Not Sue or Carol. Not Deb. Not Teddy. Not your mother if you get in contact with her. Not the school counselor. And when you go talk to a therapist, you can't even tell them. The only person you can talk to about it, other than me, is Grandpa Judd. And that's because he already knows. But no one else. Can you make that promise?"

Braedon nods, his eyes big and open and inquisitive.

"It's a matter of safety for you and safety for me."

"I promise, Dad. Really. I swear I won't tell anyone."

"Okay. I believe you."

Braedon smiles for the first time since Clay came into his room.

"When I was playing professional soccer in Europe and when I was a coach over there, I was also working for the United States government as an intelligence agent."

Braedon's smile fades. His eyes get even bigger and he says, "You mean you were a spy?"

"Yes," says Clay. "Not like James Bond or anything. I mostly just went out to bars and restaurants in whatever city I was playing in and listened to people talking, hoping to pick up information from diplomats and the people who make and sell weapons. Once in a while, I delivered a hand-written message. Or maybe I put it in a dead letter box."

"What's that?"

"It's a place or a thing where spies leave messages for each other. Like under a rock in a park or in the toilet tank of a bathroom."

"Cool."

"Yep," says Clay, "spies have been using them for hundreds of years. Still a good method."

"Are you still a spy?" says Braedon.

"That's a good question," says Clay. "I'm not working as a spy now—there's not a whole lot to spy on in Riverwood—but I am still in contact with my superiors in Washington. They may want me to work for them at some point in the future. But not anytime soon."

"Why not?"

"Because in Europe I was working undercover. No one knew I was a spy. Not my teammates or coaches. No one knew except for the United States government. Then my cover was blown by a double agent."

"Is that a traitor?" says Braedon.

"Yes. Someone who says they're a spy for one country but they're really spying for the other country. And once my cover was blown, I couldn't do it anymore, plus it was dangerous for me to stay in Europe. And it was dangerous for you, too. That's one of the reasons we moved back here so fast. Didn't even wait for your school year to end—just took off and begged them to let you finish the year remotely. And everyone thinks I'm doing such a nice thing, turning down offers to coach in Europe or MLS so I can give back to my high school soccer team, but it's a little more complicated than that." Clay shifts in his seat. "Questions?"

Braedon thinks for ten seconds and says, "Did you ever shoot anyone?"

"I never did," says Clay. "Not when I was in the army and not when I was working in intelligence."

"Did anyone ever try to hurt you?" says Braedon.

"Only once. When my cover was blown. I was lucky to get out of there without being seriously injured. That experience is what helped convince me it was time to get out of Europe."

"But you said we could visit."

"We can. And we will. But we can't go for at least a year or two. I need to lay low for a while."

Braedon thinks again. It's not easy. His head is spinning from Clay's admission of wrongdoing and this new information about being a spy. But he manages to formulate a question. "Are we safe now? Is there any chance they can find us?"

"We're safe, Braedon. When a spy leaves the game—that's what we call it sometimes—or the theater of espionage—they're usually left alone. The other side may or may not know I'm here in Riverwood—but they know I can't do any damage from here."

Braedon says nothing. He feels his father's hand on his shoulder, and tilts his head to rest it there.

"You and me, Brae, we have to stick together. So let's keep the communication open between us. Even if you think I won't like something, you can tell me. And I'll do the same and tell you." There's a knock on the door. Clay says, "Come in."

The door opens just a fraction and Zoey's head pops in. "Need you ASAP." There is nothing light in her tone or her expression.

Clay knows that look, and his heart sinks. He drops his head into his hand and says, "If you want to know what's going on, Brae, come out to the kitchen with me."

The color has drained from Judd's face. That's the first thing Clay notices when he enters the kitchen. Braedon notices, too, and without thinking takes a step back and leans against the refrigerator door. It feels safer a few steps away because something's wrong. Something is very wrong.

Zoey takes her seat at the kitchen table next to Judd and says, "I just got a call from Thomas Becker." She looks at Clay and then Braedon and then back to Clay. "Thomas told me he has nightmares every night. He said he thinks he's having these nightmares because when they found Teddy's things, they also found Teddy."

"What?" says Braedon, unable to prevent the word from escaping his mouth.

Clay looks back at his son and says, "Let's just listen, Braedon."

"Do you want me to leave?"

"Not unless that would make you more comfortable," says Clay. "Your choice."

Braedon knows what his father is doing. Treating him more like a grown-up after having lied by omission because he thought Braedon was too young. Braedon isn't sure if he likes his new status. "I'm okay," he manages.

Clay looks at Judd, who is focused on Zoey. Stoic. Tight-mouthed. Breathing slow and steady.

"Thomas thinks," says Zoey, "that when they found Teddy, he wasn't breathing."

Judd shakes with restraint. Like he's using both feet in the car, pressing one down on the gas and the other on the brake.

Zoey continues. "Thomas said he wants his nightmares to stop. He hopes that telling me the truth will make them go away. But I don't know what to believe because all three boys, in our separate interrogations, said Teddy wasn't there when they found his belongings." She looks at Clay. "I suggest we drop in on each house unannounced and press them on their story."

Something clicks in Clay's head. It's a vision. Nothing supernatural or clairvoyant or anything like that. It's from his imagination, the greatest gift an investigator can possess. And for the first time since Teddy disappeared, he thinks he might know what happened to his uncle. At least part of the story.

"Yeah," says Clay. "I think we should do that right away. Dad?"

Judd nods and says nothing.

CHAPTER 39

"Is Grandpa going to be okay?" Braedon rides shotgun as Clay drives.

Clay gave him a choice. Braedon could stay home by himself, go to the police station and hang out with Sue, go to the fly shop and hang out with Carol, or go to Judd's and hang out with Mei. Clay was surprised when Braedon chose Mei, but Braedon's question makes his choice less surprising.

"Grandpa will be okay," says Clay. "This is hard for him. You and me, we don't have any siblings, so we don't know what it's like. But Teddy is not only Grandpa's brother, he's not only Grandpa's twin brother, but he's the person Grandpa is closest to. We don't know if what Thomas Becker told his parents is true or not, but if it is, we'll all be okay. Doesn't mean it'll be easy, but we will be okay."

"Are you sad?"

"I'm concerned," says Clay. "If it's true that Teddy is dead, I'll be very sad. And that's okay. It should be sad. We should be sad."

They ride the remaining few minutes in silence. When Clay pulls up to Judd's house, Mei stands on the porch waiting for them.

Judd and Zoey decide that Clay should be the one who questions Thomas Becker this time. Judd spoke to him the first time, and maybe because Judd is Teddy's twin brother, Thomas was afraid to tell the truth. Or maybe it's just that Judd has resting angry face. And with Graham acting like the boys' leader, maybe Judd's hard eyes are needed to crack him. Zoey goes to Markey Franzen's house. They will conduct separate interviews in the boys' homes, and meet at the police station when they're done.

Steph doesn't answer her phone so Clay drives by the C3 beauty salon. Her car is parked in back. He parks next to her and goes in. He finds Steph washing a client's hair. He waits until Steph wraps a towel around the person's head and walks them back to the cutting station. Then he walks over and says, "Steph, sorry to interrupt. Can I have two minutes?"

Steph excuses herself, and they head to the small break room. Clay explains what's about to happen—he's going to Steph's house to question Thomas one more time. "Do you know that he's been having nightmares?" says Clay.

Steph shakes her head. She looks like she's in shock. She hasn't made eye contact with Clay since he started talking, but now she looks at him and says, "You'll be kind to Thomas, I hope."

"Of course. Does that mean I have your permission? Because I need it to talk to an unaccompanied minor. Neither you nor Wags will be with him."

Steph nods. "You have my permission. God, I hate that Thomas is mixed up with those other boys. This is not his fault." Steph reaches out and grabs Clay's forearm. "He's a good kid, Clay." The tears start. "Please tell me this won't ruin his life."

"It depends on what really happened," says Clay. "Hopefully we'll find out soon. Zoey's sending a K-9 team to Miller's Bluff."

Steph goes pale. She takes a few deep breaths to calm herself down. "Thomas is my boy. He's my baby boy."

Thomas Becker answers the door looking like he slept in his clothes. Clay had called ahead, but it appears the boy made no effort to prepare himself or the house for company. Dirty dishes litter the kitchen counters, and the place smells of burned toast and Cap'n Crunch. They sit at the kitchen table, which is round and made of oak. Thomas doesn't offer Clay anything, nor does Clay ask. He wants to get this over with.

"The nightmares must be pretty bad," says Clay.

Thomas looks down and nods.

"Do you want to change your story?"

Another nod.

"What happened?"

"Everything just like I told it before, except it wasn't just Teddy's stuff. Teddy was there, too. And he was dead."

Clay takes a breath to calm himself. "Why are you so sure Teddy was dead and not just unconscious?"

"I know what death looks like," says Thomas. "I've seen pets, two grandparents in open caskets, deer on the side of the road. Dead things look like something fake. Like the taxidermy on the wall at Knut's. Teddy wasn't breathing. His skin wasn't the right color. It was like he wasn't in there anymore."

"What did Graham say?"

"Graham said that we'd get blamed for it because that's what always happens. Whoever finds the dead person actually killed them. That's what everyone thinks."

"And you believed him?"

"I guess. I was scared shitless. Finding a dead guy. I was panicking. I'm like, we got to call the police or an ambulance or something. We have to report this. But then Graham got really mad and told us we're not saying anything. And if we did, he'd tell the police that me and Markey killed Teddy and we'd probably go to jail for murder even though we had nothing to do with it."

"Anything else you remember about Teddy lying there on the ground?"

"Like what?" says Thomas.

"Any cuts or scrapes? Bruises, maybe? Were any of his limbs at odd angles? Did anything look broken?"

Thomas shuts his eyes for a moment, then opens them and says, "He looked kind of beat up. And dirty. Like he was wrestling on the ground with someone, maybe. There were smudges of dirt on his clothes and on his face."

"Was he lying face up?"

"Yeah. It creeped me out."

"Did you roll him over? See if he had any injuries on his back?"

"No. No one touched him except for Graham when he took the earring."

Clay waits a moment before responding. He is calm. He is warm. He is kind. Any judgment he has is far from Thomas's view. "Is it possible," starts Clay, "that Graham had something to do with Teddy's death?"

"No," says Thomas. "I'm a hundred percent telling you the truth. I swear I am. We were on our bikes. I was with Graham from the entire time Markey and I swung by his house to get him. Then we all rode together and found Teddy together. Dead. I think . . . I think if Graham didn't have that stupid idea to get money out of your dad, then maybe he would have admitted to finding the body. But Graham didn't kill Teddy. I'd tell you if he did. Because shit, man, I wish he would get locked up so I don't have to deal with him after telling the truth."

"So Graham's definitely the ringleader," says Clay.

Thomas nods. "He came up with the story and made us go over it a hundred times so we'd all say the same thing. We kept it really close to the truth—everything except Teddy's body being there. Graham kept quizzing us like we had a test coming up."

"And when the six of us went there the morning after you got busted, how did you know Teddy's body wouldn't be there? Or did you purposely lead us to the wrong place?"

"When Graham came up with the plan and took the earring, we covered up the body with some branches and leaves because if someone found Teddy, then our whole kidnapping plan would be cooked. I thought we would find him that morning we went up there with you guys. Our plan was to say we didn't see him under all that stuff. But his body wasn't there. I don't know what happened to it."

Clay nods. "Did you tell Graham or Markey that you were going to tell us this?"

Thomas shakes his head. "I haven't talked to either of them since that day at the police station. We're all grounded. No phones. No video games." Thomas half laughs. "Eli brought me a stack of books to read. I can't believe it but I've actually read one already. It was really good. I've never read a book that I didn't have to. Now I like it."

"Eli Hensel? Whose dad owns the scrapyard?"

"Yeah."

"Huh," says Clay.

"Huh what?"

"Are you friends with Eli Hensel?"

"No. I just know him. Kind of."

Clay lets that sit for a while, then says, "Well, there's something positive that's come out of all this. What book did you read?"

"*James*. It was long, but what else do I have to do?"

"Good book. That was nice of Eli."

"Yeah," says Thomas. "He's a super-nice dude."

CHAPTER 40

"It's not looking good," says Judd. His voice is small and weak but steady.

They're gathered at Deb's house just after 11:00 AM. Judd, Clay, Braedon, Mei, Zoey, and Deb sit in the doublewide's small living room. The somber mood tries to hold its own against a beautiful June day. The screen door and screen windows let the summer air just about turn the doublewide inside out. A clear blue sky allows the sun to illuminate every shade of green in the trees, shrubs, and grasses. Deb's potted flowers all seem to be blooming at the same time. And the birds are so taken with all this beauty that they have to sing about it.

"We now have three eyewitnesses saying Teddy was dead," Judd adds. "Damn kids should have told us the truth from the beginning—they've put us through hell. And now I think we have to assume the worst. Still a lot of unanswered questions, like where the hell is Teddy's body?"

"I ordered a full search of the bluff and surrounding area," says Zoey. "A K-9 unit is on the way."

Judd responds with a nod. Cawing crows and wind fill the small home until Deb speaks.

"This is the worst part," says Deb. "The knowing and not knowing. If Teddy was still where they found him, then we wouldn't be in this purgatory. I mean, it sure feels like he's dead. The complete absence of contact. But we can't grieve. At least I can't. Not yet. Not until it's final."

"Nor should you," says Mei. "I see this at the hospital when a patient is clinging to life. There's very little chance of recovery, but the family cannot grieve. They can be devastated and heartbroken but part of grief is healing and that process cannot begin until after the person has died."

"I'm going to the bluff, too," says Deb. "I can't sit here any longer."

Clay sits on the couch. Braedon sits on the floor, leaning back against Clay's shins. Clay puts his hands on his son's shoulders and says, "Deb, we'll do everything we can to make this purgatory time, as you call it, as short as possible."

Zoey says, "I'm sorry things are looking the way they are."

Clay watches Deb process what she's hearing, or at least her attempt to. *Thank God it's summer,* he thinks. She can get outside and see life. And beauty. The world's afterlife following Minnesota's unforgiving winter. A small consolation, but it's something. And in situations like this, something is better than nothing.

Mei says that she and Braedon have been cooking all

morning and that they'll serve lunch. Judd doesn't want to leave Deb for a minute. As Braedon and Mei head into the kitchen, Clay asks Zoey to step outside.

"I have a hunch," says Clay. He speaks just above a whisper since every window in the doublewide is open. "About how Teddy died. Want to go for a ride before that search team is crawling all over the bluff?"

Forty-five minutes later, they stand atop Miller's Bluff. They can see the entire town of Riverwood and then some. The creeks and rivers of Fillmore County wind and merge in and out of forest and fields. Clay remembers coming up here as a kid and thinking, *My world can't be this small.* And it is small. Small but beautiful.

"I've never been to the top before," says Zoey. "Pretty."

"But there's something that's not pretty. That's why the city council voted to get rid of it."

"The power lines," says Zoey. "And the metal towers that hold them up."

Clay nods, steps over to the base of the stanchion, and says, "Call for help if I fall." He swings one leg up and begins to climb. Up he goes from brace to brace until he reaches a ladder for maintenance and repair. Clay knows he should have some sort of safety harness, but there's no wind, and he's still in excellent shape. He doesn't dare look down—he knows how that will feel. He keeps his eyes on the old power line that still runs over the bluff. The city replaced it with a buried line and hasn't gotten around to taking this one down yet.

He's ten feet from the top when he sees it. One of the thick, heavy power lines is cut halfway through. The old insulation is singed and charred around the cut mark. Clay's hunch is correct. He can't prevent his eyes from blurring with tears. But like a soldier on the battlefield who's just seen his friend fall, Clay knows mourning will have to wait. He climbs all the way to the top and carefully lets go with his right hand, grabbing the stanchion more tightly with his left. He reaches into his back pocket, removes his phone, takes a picture, and starts down.

When Clay sets his feet on the ground, Zoey's eyes reflect what he's feeling. He goes to her, falls into her embrace, and feels his shoulders heave with sobs. For Clay, the grieving process has started.

"Tell me," says Zoey.

Clay wipes away his tears, takes a breath, looks up at the power line, and says, "Teddy was trying to cut down the power line. That's why he had the sawzall. There was no current running through the lines. The city council was just taking its time hiring someone to cut it all down. That thick copper wire is worth quite a bit at the scrapyard. Tens of thousands if you cut down enough of it. My guess is Teddy tried to saw through it. That's when he lost his balance and fell. Or maybe lightning struck."

"The tower?" says Zoey.

"Possibly," says Clay. "Or it could have struck anywhere along the power line. Even miles away. That kind of power running through a line thick enough to carry it—it would have killed Teddy instantly. Either way, he probably fell onto the hard limestone. Remember, they didn't turn him over. The backside of him might have been banged up pretty bad. And if the limestone was wet, he would have slid down to the spot where the boys found him. If it rained up here, it would have washed away the blood."

"Was there a storm early Friday morning?" says Zoey. "I don't remember one."

"It must have blown through pretty quickly," says Clay. "One of those early summer storms. But it definitely rained. I know because I'd planned on going fishing Friday morning, but there was a stain on the water from the runoff. Wasn't a big storm or the river would have been chocolate milk. Completely unfishable. But there was enough brown in the water to keep me off the river."

"So what happened to the body?" says Zoey.

Clay shudders and chokes down tears. "Maybe an animal or person dragged him away. Hopefully the dogs will pick up his scent." Clay walks around the area, looking at grasses and shrubs. "Everything looks perfect," says Clay. "Which means it was probably a person who used the path."

Zoey gives Clay a moment to find a balance between investigator and grieving nephew, then says, "So not the boys? Someone else found him and decided to hide the body?"

"That doesn't make much sense, does it?" says Clay.

"No," says Zoey. "It doesn't. But who else would have known he was up here? And why would they want to hide the body?"

Clay disappears in mind and spirit. It's something that's happened to him before. Both on the pitch and as an agent. More frequently in athletics when the conscious mind yields to what feels like other forces. How are the most magnificent athletic moments achieved? Most athletes don't understand it themselves. How did they score that seemingly impossible goal? Or make that mind-boggling catch? In the post-game interviews, all they can do is give the credit to God. Of course, they always say

God was with them. They never say God wanted the other team to lose.

Clay's heard artists talk the same way. *I'm just a conduit for the universe. The universe is working through me.* Clay believes just the opposite. Everything he's ever seen, heard, smelled, experienced . . . it's all inside him. He is a product of everything he's been exposed to. He's like a hard drive full of data. Accessing it, assembling it, interpreting it is a conversation between one part of his brain and the other.

So when he has sudden realizations, he doesn't question where they come from. He doesn't give credit to an outside force. And most importantly, he doesn't doubt his realizations. When the voice in his head speaks with such clarity, it's rarely wrong.

"We need to talk to Thomas Becker again," says Clay. "And this time, I want his parents and a lawyer to be present."

"I'll have Mike and Andy bring him in," says Zoey. "And I'll bring in a second team to search Liar's Creek from the bottom of Miller's Bluff all the way down to the Mississippi River."

CHAPTER 41

"I don't know about this," whispers Judd. He stands with his back to the storage cage in the basement of the Riverwood Police Station. His voice is hoarse, his eyes are puffy, and his skin has lost its luster.

"It's our best shot at learning the whole story," says Clay.

Judd presses his back into the chain-link and says, "I suppose. Better than me speculating for the rest of my life."

"That's the idea," says Clay. "Trust me—this is the best way."

Something breaks in Judd. Breaks in a good way. Something old and rigid and unforgiving yields. "I do trust you, Clay." Judd lets his shoulder touch Clay's. Clay does not pull away. And Judd, who's not a pragmatist like his son, who doesn't believe human beings are just data collectors and data accessors and processors, silently thanks Teddy, or the spirit of Teddy, for helping raise Judd and Clay's relationship out of the muck.

Thomas Becker is bound at his wrists and ankles while sitting at a metal table. His father, Wags, has been brought down from his cell upstairs and is also bound with restraints. Thomas's mother, Steph, sits on one side of her son at the table. On the other side sits Thomas's lawyer, Caroline Roth, a septuagenarian who is officially retired but takes pro bono cases for abused women and troubled youth. She's called the Kevlar Lady because nothing gets past her.

Zoey sits across the table from Thomas. She wears her full uniform. Her hair is gathered tightly behind her head. She is all business. Officers Mike Wahlquist and Andy Kimmich are not present.

"Thomas," says Zoey. "This is your last chance to tell us what happened in the early hours of last Friday morning. You may have noticed that Officers Wahlquist and Kimmich are not present. That's because they're taking your friends, Graham and Markey, into custody and arresting them as accessories to the murder of Teddy Hawkins. They will no doubt be wanting to cut deals with the district attorney, so you can do yourself a favor by finally being forthright and honest about what happened."

"He doesn't have to say a damn word," says Caroline. "You haven't even charged him yet."

"Is this really necessary?" says Steph, squeezing one hand with the other so hard it's turned white. "I mean, he's just a kid."

"He is just a kid," says Zoey. "Which is why, Caroline, we haven't charged Thomas yet. No one likes charging and incarcerating minors—"

"Incarcerating?" says Steph. She is on the verge of tears.

"Just be quiet," says Wags. "The cops are putting on their

show. Let 'em do their little song and dance. And Thomas, listen to your lawyer. She's the best chance you got."

"All good advice," says Zoey. "We're just giving you an opportunity, Thomas, to make this as easy on yourself as possible. Murder is the most serious charge of all. And combined with your extortion plot to relieve Judd Hawkins of forty-five thousand dollars, you're in some serious shit. You're likely to be tried as an adult. And the DA and judges go a lot easier on suspects who cooperate. You help us, you could be out of jail by the time you're thirty."

"Thirty?!" says Steph. "My son didn't do anything!"

"Steph," says Clay. "Please let Chief Jensen speak. And let Caroline do her job."

"I'm his mother, Clay!" Steph's voice echoes in the cinderblock basement. "His mother. My job is to protect my son!"

"Mom," says Thomas. "You're not helping." He turns to Zoey and says, "I admit we lied about Teddy not being there when we found his stuff. And you know we tried to pretend that we kidnapped him. But we didn't kill Teddy. We found him already dead. I swear that's the truth. We had nothing to do with however he died. Nothing."

"You're sticking to that . . ." says Zoey.

"Yes! Because it's the truth."

"I believe my client is making himself quite clear," says Caroline Roth. "Which he's doing in the spirit of cooperation. If you want to browbeat a confession out of someone, I suggest trying elsewhere. But if you insist on taking the same tack, it would help if you provided evidence."

Zoey says, "We have eyewitness testimony—"

"Bullshit," says Wags. "You got nothing."

"Wait," says Thomas. "What eyewitness? Because whoever it is, is lying."

"All right," says Zoey. "This is going nowhere. Just remember, I gave you a chance to cooperate."

"He *is* cooperating," says Caroline. "He's just not confessing to a crime he didn't commit."

"I got something to say," says Judd, stepping forward off the chain-link fence. "Thomas, if you cooperate, I won't press charges for assault and I won't press charges for extortion. And Clay won't press charges for you boys stealing his truck. That will leave just the murder charge, which could knock a few years off your sentence. My advice is to come clean now, and you'll be one step closer to a clean start."

"But . . ." Thomas begins to cry. "We didn't kill him. I swear that's the truth. We went to Miller's Bluff to ride our bikes and we just found him there. Already dead. If he wasn't dead, we would have called for help." He wipes his eyes on his sleeve and adds, "Yeah, we were stupid. The kidnapping thing wasn't my idea but I went along with it. So I admit it. I'm guilty. But not of killing Teddy. We didn't do that. Why won't you believe me?"

"Good question," says Zoey. "And I'll answer it. The reason we don't believe you is that someone removed Teddy's body from the place you claim you found him. It's a nice story that you found him already dead—"

"It's not nice—it's true!" says Thomas.

"But without a body, we can only assume that you and your friends disposed of it to cover up what really happened. Because who else would have a motive to move Teddy's body?"

"You *assume* the boys moved the body?" says Caroline. "Good luck with that in a court of law."

The old wooden stairs creak as Officers Wahlquist and Kimmich descend into the basement. Zoey turns to them and says, "Do we have what we need?"

"Yes, ma'am," says Wahlquist. "Both suspects have been interrogated and are detained upstairs."

"Well, then that's that," says Zoey. She turns toward Thomas and says, "Thomas Becker, you're under arrest for the murder of Teddy Hawkins. You have the right to remain silent. Anything you say can and will be used against you in a court of law. You have a right to an attorney. If you cannot afford—"

"He didn't do it!" Steph is on her feet, red-faced and screaming. "Thomas had nothing to do with Teddy Hawkins's death or removing the body."

Clay says, "Steph—"

"Shut up, Clay! Shut up and listen! I know what I'm talking about because . . ." She points at Wags and says, "Get him out of here. Get him out of here and I'll tell you everything."

Braedon and Mei sit at Judd's kitchen table, Braedon's laptop open before him. "Do you think I should?" says Braedon.

"I do," says Mei. "But maybe not right away. You're going to talk to a therapist first, right?"

"Maybe," says Braedon. "But I keep writing to my mom in my head. I can't stop it. It's all I can think about. Even at night. I wake up, and that's what I think about. Writing a message to her. Telling her I know who she is and where she is. And that I want to see her if she wants to see me. I can't even be sad about Uncle Teddy because I'm thinking about it so much."

"Do you know who Harry Truman was?" said Mei.

Braedon nods. "He was a president, right? The one who dropped the atomic bomb."

"Yes. He did do that. He did a lot of things. And he had this habit, if he had strong feelings about something, he'd write a letter about it. Whether it was to opposing politicians or striking train workers, whatever or whoever got him worked up. He'd often write passionate page after page, and then when he was done, guess what he did with the letter?"

"Sent it?" says Braedon.

"Not usually. Usually, he didn't send it. He ripped it up and threw it in the trash."

"Was he mad after he ripped it up?" says Braedon. "Did he wish he had sent it?"

Mei shakes her head. "No and no. It was writing the letter that made him feel better. It was writing it that got all his thoughts and feelings out. He just had to write it to feel better. He didn't have to send it."

"So what you're saying is, I should just write a message to my mom but not send it."

"Yes. Write it and then see how you feel. And then see how you feel the next day. And the day after that. Maybe you wrote something you wish you hadn't, or you wished you had included something that you didn't. Then you rewrite it and see how you feel about the changes. There's no rush to send it. You can even read what you wrote to the therapist. Or to your dad or Grandpa

Judd. Read it out loud. See how that makes you feel. See if anyone has any advice."

Braedon thinks about that for a minute, then says, "That's a good idea, Mei. Thanks. I'll go write a message to her now. But I won't send it. I'll do what you said. I'll see how it makes me feel." Braedon closes his laptop and pushes back his chair.

"Before you go do that," says Mei. "I'd like to ask a favor."

"From me?"

"Yes."

"Sure," says Braedon. "Anything."

Mei smiles. "I would like your permission to marry Grandpa Judd."

"You want *my* permission?" says Braedon. "Why?"

"Because you're his closest family member."

Braedon shakes his head. "No. Dad is."

"Sadly, Braedon, that's not true. Hopefully that's changing and one day your dad and Grandpa Judd will be just as close to each other as you are to Grandpa Judd. But for now, you're Judd's closest family. That's why I'm asking you for permission."

Braedon considers Mei's request and says, "Does that mean he'd move to Rochester with you?"

"I don't think so," says Mei. "Your grandpa and I haven't discussed it because I haven't told him yet that we're getting married."

Braedon laughs. "Told him? I thought you were going to ask him."

"Let's not get hung up on semantics," says Mei. "The point is, I'd like to live in Riverwood near you and your father and Deb.

I think Judd will need you all now that Teddy's gone. And it's only a half-hour drive to Rochester."

"That's pretty far," says Braedon.

"I grew up in Los Angeles," says Mei. "A half-hour drive barely gets you around the block. I'm happy to do it until I retire. So what do you say, Braedon? May I have your grandpa Judd's hand in marriage?"

CHAPTER 42

Zoey nods at Wahlquist.

"Come on, Wags," says Wahlquist. "Let's go say hi to the boys upstairs."

Wags aims his chin at Steph. "You watch your mouth. Just watch your goddamn mouth."

Wahlquist helps Wags to his feet and then escorts him up the creaky wooden stairs. Thomas's jaw tenses and he looks away.

"Maybe it's better if Thomas goes upstairs, too," says Clay. "And Caroline."

"Happy to go with my client," says Caroline.

"Agreed," says Zoey. "Andy?"

Andy Kimmich helps Thomas to his feet and leads him away with Caroline walking a step behind. A strange calm falls over the basement room. All eyes are on Steph.

She waits until she hears Thomas's footsteps on the floor

above, then says, "Thomas had nothing to do with Teddy Hawkins's death or removing the body. I know, because it was me."

"Stop, Steph," says Zoey. "I'm sorry. I've seen this a hundred times. A parent claiming responsibility to save their kid from—"

"No," says Steph. "Listen. Please." Steph sits down, drops her face into her hands, takes a breath, then puts her hands on the table. "Wags had been threatening me because of the divorce. He threatened to hurt me and he threatened to hurt the kids. And on top of that, do you know that I'll have to pay Wags spousal maintenance? He hasn't done a damn thing to help raise the kids. He's barely contributed to supporting the family financially. He has not been faithful. And yet because I make more money than him, I'll have to pay. And it's not like he's going to chip in for the kids' college. It's on me. It's all on me."

Steph reaches over and places her hand on the back of the chair where Thomas just sat. "Someone has to provide for my kids. Someone has to keep them safe from their father. I told you, Judd, back when you were chief, that Wags threatened me and the kids. You said there was nothing you could do. Same with you, Zoey. You said until he did something, you couldn't help me. So I helped myself."

"And how'd you do that?" says Zoey.

"I tried to frame Wags for stealing catalytic converters because I wanted him to go to jail. He couldn't hurt us from jail. So I told Clay that Wags had a bunch of catalytic converters stashed away. I figured he'd tell you, Zoey, and you'd arrest him or at least bring him in for questioning. But nothing happened . . ." She eyes Clay, then looks back at Zoey. "Then I put a bunch of catalytic converters in the trunk of his car. I found an old key he thought he'd lost, and one night I drove over to his apartment and put the catalytic converters in the trunk."

"Where did you get the catalytic converters?" says Zoey.

Steph drops her eyes. "I went to Hensel's scrapyard. I wanted to buy a few of them and do it that way. Robert wasn't in, but his son Eli was. And we had a conversation."

"About catalytic converters?"

"Yes," says Steph. "At first. And then he told me about how he was working at the scrapyard to save money to move to London. He wants to write a modern-day version of *Oliver Twist*. I asked him how it was working for his father, and he said it wasn't that bad. He'd worked there in high school and also worked at a scrapyard up in the Twin Cities to put himself through college. He said for an aspiring writer, it's a good job. He can read and write when no one else is there. And the grittiness of a scrapyard makes him feel like he's not losing touch with the working class."

"How nice that he lowered himself to be among the people," says Judd.

"He's a smart, sensitive young man," says Steph. "Everything Wags is not. God, I was so stupid to marry that man. Anyway, Eli and I talked for over an hour, and then he asked if I wanted to have a drink sometime. It was very flattering. I'm twenty years older than him but I figured, what the hell? Men have been chasing women twenty years younger since the beginning of time."

"You and Eli are having an affair?" says Zoey.

Steph nods, keeping her eyes away from Clay's. "And during our time together, we came up with a plan to solve both of our problems. We would find scrap metal and recycle it for cash. But not at Hensel's. We didn't want any record of what we were doing in town. Instead, one or both of us would drive the metal up to the cities and take it to the yard where Eli had worked in college. He told me that they tended to look the other way when questionable items were brought in."

"Questionable meaning stolen?" says Zoey.

Steph nods.

"And where did you get the metals?" says Clay.

Steph's lower lip begins to tremble. She waits for it to steady. "Teddy came into the salon one day. He asked if I had any work for him. I had hired him in the past to do some handyman chores. Changing my outlets to the GFCI ones. Replacing cartridges in my faucets. Changing out the old fluorescent tubes for LCD ones . . ." She looks over at Clay and says, "I'd known Teddy since I was a kid. You would take me over to Teddy and Deb's. They'd make us dinner. We'd all watch a movie together after. Teddy's always had his issues, but I've always liked him as a person. I've trusted him. And so I brought up the idea of finding metal and bringing it to me. I told him I'd give him one-third of whatever I could get for it. No questions asked. And he'd be protected—I'd never tell anyone where it came from."

Steph swivels her head toward Zoey and says, "That was the extent of us forming a criminal conspiracy. Teddy got to work. He brought me a few catalytic converters one day. Another day he brought me several sections of copper pipe. One night he wanted me to meet him at the salon, so I did. He had a bunch of copper sheeting back there. I have no idea where it came from."

"Dorset-Cornwall," says Clay. "Teddy helped himself to some building materials."

Steph nods. "It was all going well. Teddy brought in metal.

Eli and I drove it up to the cities and drove back with cash. We split it three ways. Eli saved up for his move to London. I don't know what Teddy did with his share. And I took care of my family."

"You mean," says Clay, "you took care of your family with off-the-books income to make it look like you made less money at the salon. That way your spousal maintenance payments to Wags would be less. That's why you wouldn't let me pay for my haircut. It's why you've been remodeling the salon."

"Yes," says Steph. "And then Eli noticed that the old power lines were still up. I mentioned it to Teddy, and he said he thought he could cut down quite a bit of it."

"Did you drive Teddy early Friday morning? First to Kwik-Trip for the gloves and then to Miller's Bluff?"

Steph nods. "He didn't want anyone to spot his truck. Sometimes kids go up there at night. And those mountain bikers and hikers start early in the summer. He was going to cut down the line, hide it in the brush, and walk out of there like a hiker. He was supposed to call me for a ride home from the pay phone outside Kwik-Trip. Then Eli was going to pick up the power line the following night. But Teddy never called . . ."

"How did you communicate with Teddy?" says Judd. He says this with a soft resignation in his voice. He isn't angry at Steph. He seems more relieved now that he's getting answers.

"I have a burner," says Steph. "That I bought up in the cities. I never sent anything that could get either of us in trouble. Just times and dates. Anything specific we discussed in person. When Teddy didn't call from Kwik-Trip, I figured he found another way home. When he didn't show up to our meeting place after I texted him, I wasn't too concerned. Teddy had a lot of nice qualities, but reliability wasn't one of them. And then I overheard the boys talking in the garage. I was in the storage space above the rafters—that's where I kept the scrap metal before hauling it up to the cities. The boys didn't know I was up there."

"What did you overhear?" says Zoey.

"Everything. They found Teddy dead. They took his earring. They hoped to use it to get ransom money out of Judd. It was eight o'clock on a Friday morning. Broad daylight. I had to be at the salon in an hour and figured someone would discover the body if they hadn't done so already. As soon as the boys left the garage, I drove to Miller's Bluff, hiked up the path, and there was Teddy. Very dead. Just where the boys had said he was when I eavesdropped on them. They'd covered him up pretty well, but I added a few more leaves and left. Then I went back later that night and pulled him down to the path and into the creek." She breaks down and the tears come hard. "I'm so sorry, Judd. I was trying to cover my tracks."

"You mean your and Eli's tracks," says Clay. Steph looks at him with her sodden face. "You didn't manage to drag Teddy all the way down the path by yourself. Eli helped you."

Steph responds with a barely noticeable nod. She catches her breath and says, "Thomas and Graham and Markey had nothing to do with Teddy's death. Do not ruin their lives over something I did."

CHAPTER 43

After some conversation in Zoey's office, weighted by fatigue and sorrow, she, Judd, and Clay come to the conclusion that the boys must face some consequences for their infractions of not reporting a dead body and robbing a corpse. That's with Clay and Judd not pressing charges for extortion, assault, and auto theft. The three investigators don't regret waiting until now. They kept the boys cooperative—Thomas felt he had a safe space to reveal what he revealed.

Zoey will work something out with the DA. First thing is they want the boys to tour the Minnesota Correctional Facility in Oak Park Heights near Stillwater, a high-security penitentiary for violent offenders. In short, scare the hell out of them. And they'll ask for a sentence of one hundred hours of community service spread out over a full year. All while on probation. Nothing that will make the boys hardened criminals but instead give them some thinking time with the threat of severe punishment should they happen to color outside the lines.

Zoey released Wags from custody now that a judge has set a date for his drunk driving sentencing, but not before warning him that if he ever threatens Steph or their kids again, she will do everything in her power to make his life unlivable in southeast Minnesota.

Wahlquist and Kimmich drove Thomas back home. They had never arrested Graham or Markey. Never brought them into the station. All the talk about that in the basement was a bluff. An effective bluff coupled with the threat to arrest Thomas drew the confession out of Steph.

Now Steph is locked in a cell while one cop, one ex-cop, and one ex–intelligence officer discuss her fate.

"How would you like this to end, Judd?" says Zoey. "How should we handle Steph and Eli Hensel? They masterminded a criminal conspiracy. Teddy did the stealing, but they drove the metals up to the cities and sold it for cash off the books. We got 'em on possession and sale of stolen merchandise, evading income and sales tax. Plus failing to report a felony, aiding and abetting, disposing of a dead body. I'm sure we could come up with a few more."

"I think it might be better for Riverwood to keep Steph and Eli out of jail," says Judd. "No taxpayer-funded trial for two first offenders who would probably get off with probation anyway. And if Steph goes to jail, her salon will go under, which wouldn't be good for the town. And her kids would become orphans because

Wags isn't going to do shit as a parent. I say we nudge Steph into volunteering her stylist skills at the women's prison in Waseca. Make her feel like she has to earn getting let off the hook. We'll find something like that for Eli, too."

"That's generous of you," says Clay with admiration in his voice. "And forgiving."

"Maybe it is," says Judd. "Or maybe I'm just tired. What do you think, Zoey? It's your town."

"I'd rather build community than tear it apart," says Zoey. "Let's let Steph and Eli know how fortunate they are. That their town cares about them and their futures."

"Then that's that," says Judd. "It's over. Thank you. I need it to be over." Judd stands and heads toward the door. He reaches for the handle then stops. With his back toward Clay and Zoey, he says, "Thanks, you two. Never got to work with a couple of pros my equal before. And then some. If there was ever a case that I needed it, it was this one." He turns back to face them and adds, "Couldn't have made it through this without you."

Judd and Braedon fire up the grill. Nothing fancy. Hot dogs and brats with store-bought potato salad, coleslaw, and baked beans. All served on paper plates with cans of beer and pop.

Deb, Clay, and Mei are putting it all together in the kitchen when there's a knock on Judd's front door. The cardboard sheet still fills the space where the sidelight window used to be. Clay goes to the door and answers it. Zoey stands on the front stoop, still in uniform. Clay sees the look on her face and knows why she's come.

A team searched Liar's Creek all the way to the Root River and then some, but Teddy's body surfaced on its own near the tiny town of Houston, Minnesota. It was being driven up to Rochester where Teddy's dentist had already emailed Teddy's records. Teddy must have been caught on something near the river bottom, and spending over seventy-two hours in the water didn't make for a pretty sight. Dental records were plenty to ID the body. The Hawkins family would not be burdened with seeing Teddy's disfigured and bloated corpse—they were free to remember him as they last saw him.

There is something fitting about eating such a simple meal on paper plates with canned beverages after hearing the confirmation of Teddy's death. The meal is like Teddy, both less than it could have been but also nice the way it is. They share stories around the dinner table, including one from Zoey, whom Judd invited to stay. She pulled Teddy over once for speeding, and when she asked for his driver's license, he handed her one that had expired eight years ago. He claimed he had no idea. She let him go with a warning.

Judd told stories about their childhood. He and Teddy built a catapult that could launch a pumpkin the length of a football field. If it weren't for Judd's restraint, they could have done some real damage with that thing. Deb said for all his faults, Teddy was a loving and devoted husband. Clay brought up the early morning that he and Teddy walked down to the river and cast mouse patterns for monster brown trout, only to return to the trailer to find Judd's squad car parked out front. It was when Clay felt Teddy's hand on his shoulder that Clay understood that his mother had died.

Zoey helps clean up, then thanks Deb for including her. It's the first of her exit lines. The first and the last because Clay gives her a look that says *please stay*. She doesn't have to confirm it with words. She knows. And when she opens the plastic tortoiseshell jaws that bind her hair behind her head, she magically changes from Zoey the cop to Zoey the friend. And for Clay, perhaps more than a friend.

No one leaves until after midnight. And that's after both Clay and Judd insist that Deb spend the night at one of their houses. But Deb declines their offers. She wants to get this first night over with. The first night alone in the home she shared with Teddy while knowing he's never coming back. To experience the finality of it. The hard reality of it. Deb and Teddy had been together since high school. Now Deb, at sixty-three years old, will be on her own. It will take some getting used to. But she is sixty-three. Postponing the inevitable doesn't make much sense.

Outside, where more goodbyes are said, Clay whispers to Zoey, "My dad's taking Braedon on a fishing trip up north next week."

CHAPTER 44

"Oh, that's terrible," says Emily. "He was in the river all that time?"

"Yeah," says Braedon. "But it's better that we know. It's better we're not guessing what happened to him."

Braedon sits up in bed. He feels both sad and calm. Like a real person of the world. Not a kid growing into it.

Emily walks a beach in Scotland, the sun rising over the North Sea. "It's a good thing that lady told the truth, otherwise you might never know how it happened."

"Yeah," says Braedon. "She's not a real criminal. She just did one bad thing. Protecting her son." Braedon hears the words come out of his mouth and feels a stab of pain for not having a mother like that. A protector. He swallows hard.

Emily shrugs like it's no big deal. "I suppose anyone could do one bad thing."

Braedon blinks the sting out of his eyes and says, "Yeah, that's what Dad says. He thinks all people got some good and bad in them so he doesn't get real judgey when a normally good person does a bad thing. He says it can happen to anyone. It even happened to me when I snuck out with Daniel when I slept over at his house. That's why I didn't get in huge trouble. I just have to paint the shed out back."

"Maybe that's what happened with your mum. She did one bad thing. Do you think you'll send her a message?"

"Dunno," says Braedon. "But I did write to her. I just haven't sent it. And I might not. Mei said it helps just to write it."

"Helps what?"

"Helps a person get their thoughts and feelings out."

"Oh," says Emily. "Like when people post stuff on social media so everyone can say *hang in there* and *so sorry* and stuff like that?"

"Yeah," says Braedon. "I guess."

"What did you say?"

"Do you want me to send it to you?"

"No, silly," says Emily. "I want you to read it to me."

"Oh," says Braedon. "Okay. Hold on." Braedon flips over to the document he wrote to his mother. "Can you still see and hear me?"

"Yeah," he hears Emily say. "Looks the same."

"Okay. All right." He swallows.

"Dear Eve,

"My name is Braedon Hawkins. I am twelve years old. I live in the United States. And I am your son. I have a picture of

you. My dad, Clay Hawkins, gave it to me when I was little. It was taken at the party where you met him. And then a little while ago, I had the idea to use it to search for you, and that's how I found you.

"I don't blame you for not raising me. Maybe you were going through a hard time or couldn't for some other reason. Dad is doing a good job. And I had a nanny who helped when he was away playing football. A few months ago we moved to Minnesota and I have a grandpa and old friends of Dad's who feel like family.

"You don't have to write me back if you don't want to. I don't want to cause any problems in your life. But if you ever want to, I'll put my email address and phone number and Snapchat and Insta at the bottom.

"I just want to say hi and say I hope you're happy and living a good life. And maybe someday, if you want, we could write messages or talk or even meet in person. But only if you want. I promise I won't bug you.

"Your son . . .

"Blah, blah, blah." Braedon flips back to FaceTime and adds, "That's it. That's the whole thing."

"It's lovely, Braedon."

"Do you really think so?"

"Yeah. It kind of made me cry a little. I hope you send it. You know, someday, when you're ready."

"You really think I should?"

"Absolutely."

"Thanks," says Braedon. "Thanks for saying that."

"Not at all," says Emily. "Who knows, maybe you and I will go to London one day to visit her."

"Yeah," says Braedon. "Maybe. And oh, hey. Whatever happened to your mum and da? After they were fighting? I've been so caught up in everything here I forgot to ask. Sorry."

"Oh, that," says Emily. "It all blew over the next day. We were in a shop and Ma saw this painting for sale and fell in love with it. But it cost three thousand euros. She didn't even dream of buying it. Then later before dinner, Da said he was going out for a pint and came back with the painting all wrapped up like it was Christmas. Now they're carrying on like they just fell in love or something. It's disgusting."

"Your parents?"

"Yeah."

"Kind of embarrassing," says Braedon.

"I want to die."

The day after Teddy's funeral, Judd and Braedon head north to a fish camp on Lake of the Woods. It's a seven-hour drive from southeast Minnesota to the top of the state. They will be gone for six days. The trip coincides with Deb leaving town to visit her sister in Seattle, and Mei's week of continuing education where she'll learn how to work with a robot during valve-replacement surgery.

Clay had planned on spending this week at home fishing the Root River and its tributaries. But he changed his plan after Teddy's body surfaced in that river. Clay needs some time before wading its current again—it's too easy to imagine Teddy's body moving downstream. Too easy and too haunting.

Instead of staying put, Clay heads out for a week of fly-fishing in Wisconsin's driftless area in and around the town of Viroqua. He stays at the Hotel Fortney, an obnoxiously romantic place on a quaint-as-hell Main Street.

Zoey tells Kimmich, Wahlquist, and the rest of the department that she's vacationing up north to visit family. Only Sue suspects otherwise. But she keeps her suspicions to herself. She's on Zoey and Clay's side. It's a match she's hoped for since Clay moved back to Riverwood.

"It was too your idea I come along," says Zoey.

"I remember you inviting yourself," says Clay.

They sit up in bed drinking white Russians made with full-fat oat milk—Zoey is lactose intolerant—after spending the entire day on the river. They showered and dressed for dinner and decided they looked too good to go out. They ordered room service instead.

"No," says Zoey. "I said I'd like to learn how to fly-fish. And you said you would teach me and you were going to Viroqua for the week. And I said sounds like a plan."

"The way I remember it," says Clay, "is I said I would teach you *but* I was going to Viroqua for a week. Implying that I would teach you when I returned. And you said *sounds like a plan*. Then you showed up at my place with your stuff, and here we are."

Zoey laughs into her drink. "And then I said let's just hang out for a week in a romantic hotel in a cute town and see what happens."

"And I said"—Clay's smiling so hard it hurts—"okay, but we're getting separate rooms."

"No you didn't. You said separate beds. And then I said fine. I don't want to get kicked in the middle of the night by a professional soccer player."

"This is our third night," says Clay. "I haven't kicked you once."

"That's why I haven't slept in the other bed," says Zoey.

"And that's what led to the sex," says Clay.

"Is that what we did, have sex?"

Clay laughs hard. "I don't know. It was hard to tell. You wouldn't stop talking the entire time."

"Well, someone has to teach you what to do."

They laugh themselves into silence. A long, comfortable, sad silence. Clay feels guilty for how much he's enjoying this trip. Zoey understands. She waits patiently for Clay to get through the moment. The regret. The sadness. His missing Teddy. A minute later, he lets it go with a sigh and reaches for Zoey's hand.

CHAPTER 45

They celebrate the Fourth of July on the fifth of July. Zoey had to work on the fourth: Crowd control at the parade down Riverwood's main street. Pulling over drunk drivers on ATVs. Writing citations to exploders of illegal fireworks. But today they gather at Clay's house for a family cookout.

Sue and Carol brought over their electric smoker last night. Beef ribs have been in there since 6:00 AM. Now Braedon's in the backyard with Daniel. They're both talking to Emily on FaceTime, telling her that Braedon sent the message to his mother ten minutes ago. It's 3:00 PM in Minnesota. That's 21:00 in the UK or 9:00 PM. Braedon's mother may not see the message until tomorrow.

Sue and Carol are on the back patio taking the ribs out of the smoker. The meat has to rest for an hour before serving. Sue and Carol insist on that and tent the platter with foil.

Zoey, Deb, and Mei drove off to Value Foods. Zoey forgot to bring whipping cream for the rhubarb crumble. Mei and Deb went along for the ride.

Clay stands over the kitchen sink peeling back corn husks and removing the silk. He then replaces the corn husks and drops the cobs into a tub of water to soak so the kernels can steam-cook on the grill. Judd halves cherry tomatoes and tosses them into a big bowl of spring greens. He wears a ring of black silicone on his left ring finger. Mei wears the same in pink. They're engagement rings. Mei proposed during the fireworks last night. Got down on one knee and everything. Made it kind of hard for Judd to say no. That's the joke he's been telling all day.

Clay and Judd work in silence for a few minutes, hearing only the sound of Judd's knife on the cutting board as he halves the tomatoes and Clay's peeling of corn husks. Then Judd says, "Is it serious? Because it looks serious."

"We're only a few weeks in," says Clay. "But so far, so good."

Judd nods to himself and says, "You could do a lot worse than Zoey Jensen."

Clay smiles. "Is that a wholehearted vote of approval?"

Judd doesn't answer right away. He bisects a cherry tomato, tosses the halves into the salad, then bisects another. "Has she told you her story?"

Clay's smile fades. He's not sure if he's going to like what's coming. He says, "I know she was married before. I know she's not in contact with her ex. She doesn't have kids. Before moving to Riverwood, she lived her entire life in Granite Pines except for the four years she spent at the University of Minnesota. Is there something I'm missing?"

Sue enters the kitchen through the slider to the deck and says, "One platter's not big enough. Got another?"

"Sure do," says Clay. He opens a cabinet door under the kitchen island and takes out a white ceramic platter. "Big enough?"

"I think so," says Sue. "Thank you." She takes it and heads back outside.

Judd sips from a bottle of beer and then sets it down. "Zoey's ex is a man named Shane Welter," says Judd. "The town of Granite Pines is full of Welters. The family goes way back to before Minnesota was even a territory. And Shane, he was the chief of police in town. Zoey was his lieutenant."

"I didn't know she was married to a cop," says Clay. "I figure she'll tell me more when she's ready."

"I'm sure she will. I'm just telling you this now because I think you have a right to know."

"That she was married to a cop?"

"Shane Welter was a bad cop. Rotten. You know what I'm saying?"

"Dirty," says Clay.

"Yep," says Judd. He halves another tomato. "Zoey's the one who busted him. Sent him to Stillwater for twenty, not eligible for parole for ten. Half the town hates her for it. All those Welters and all their supporters. She had to leave for the good of the police force. And to be frank, for her own safety."

This is news to Clay. He takes a moment to think it through. It does nothing to diminish the way he feels about her. Except maybe he admires and respects her that much more. "Just like me," says Clay. "Holing up in Riverwood after things went bad."

He drops another de-silked cob into the tub of water. "What'd she bust him for?"

"Fentanyl," says Judd. "Bringing the stuff in through commercial shipping vessels that docked in Duluth and then hooked into networks that distributed all over the country. The bust made the news for half a second—that was before you came home. She was going by her married name then—Zoey Welter."

"And you're telling me this because you think I should know before I get too involved with her?"

"I'm telling you this," says Judd, "because Shane Welter and his lawyers just won their appeal two days ago. Got off on a technicality. Shane's been released from prison. I don't know why Zoey hasn't told you, but yeah, I think you should know."

Clay looks out the window and sees Braedon and Daniel speaking animatedly to the phone in Braedon's hand. Carrying on like the twelve-year-olds they are.

"Thank you for telling me," says Clay. "I'm falling pretty hard for Zoey. It doesn't change anything in that department."

"Didn't expect it would," says Judd. "Wouldn't for me either if I were you. I'm just . . ." Judd trails off. The plastic clamshell of cherry tomatoes is empty. He walks it over to the sink, rinses it out, and drops it into the recycling bin.

"You just what?" says Clay.

"Maybe you and me," says Judd, "maybe you and me can talk more. Start chipping away at all those years when I could have done better by you. Should have done better. A lot better."

They hear a car pull into the driveway, gravel crunching under its tires. Car doors open and shut.

"We were both in a lot of pain back then," says Clay. "We got through it. That's not nothing."

Judd nods. That's as close as they're going to get to anyone saying *I'm sorry* or *I forgive you*. At least for now. The front door swings open. Mei, Deb, and Zoey step into the foyer. Their voices fill the house like birdsong.

ACKNOWLEDGMENTS

Liar's Creek is my tenth published novel. In the previous nine, I have acknowledged the people who've helped me along the way, personally and professionally. I have acknowledged the people I love. I will continue to acknowledge humans in future books. But this one is for the dogs. My dogs. I have dedicated this book to them. I don't know if I could write without dogs. They cajole me out of my chair for a walk so I'm not too sedentary. They bark at rabbits and squirrels, alleviating me of property defense duties. They take long afternoon naps at my feet—hearing their dog sighs lets me know someone cares that I'm toiling away at my job that most people don't think is a real job. Or maybe I'm projecting. Only Maisy has found her way into one of my novels. She's the black and white poodle mentioned in this book. Sadly, she passed before the book published. They all have, except for Clara, who follows me around the house as if I'm a big shot. They'll never know I've dedicated this book to them. Their friends won't bark at them across the street, "Hey, saw Matt dedicated his latest book to you! I ate fifty pages of that book. It's awesome!" But I'll know, and the people I've skipped over for dedications will know. And that's what's important.

ABOUT THE AUTHOR

Leslie Parker

New York Times and *USA Today* bestselling author **Matt Goldman** is a playwright and an Emmy Award–winning television writer for *Seinfeld, Ellen,* and other shows. Goldman has been nominated for the Shamus and Nero Awards and was a Lariat Adult Fiction Reading List selection. *Liar's Creek* is his tenth novel. He lives in Minnesota with his family.